TO

KNOX

THE RETREAT

THE RETREAT

or

*The Machinations of
Henry*

by
FORREST REID

'There's tempest in the sky'
The Three Little Kittens

First published in March 1936 by Faber and Faber Limited
This edition published in April 1989 by GMP Publishers Limited
PO Box 247, London N17 9QR, England

British Cataloguing in Publication Data

Reid, Forrest, 1875-1947

The retreat
I. Title
823'.912

ISBN 0 85449 102 3

Distributed in North American by
Alyson Publications Inc.
40 Plympton Street, Boston, MA 02118, USA

Printed in the European Community
by Nørhaven A/S, Viborg, Denmark

INTRODUCTION

The Retreat is the central volume of Forrest Reid's Tom Barber trilogy. It was first published in 1936, five years after *Uncle Stephen*, and eight years before the final volume *Young Tom* (1944). The central character, Tom, is here thirteen: in *Uncle Stephen* he is fifteen, and in *Young Tom* eleven. So, also in terms of its hero's age in this "reverse of a sequel", as Reid called it, *The Retreat* has a central place.

As always, the epigraph to a Reid novel makes clear something of the author's intention. Here the fourteen-line quotation from the religious poem also called *The Retreat* by Henry Vaughan (1621-1695) gives us two famous key-phrases, "my angel-infancy" and "shadows of eternity". All Reid's writing is, in effect, something of an attempt to return or retreat to a pristine world of "angel-infancy". Later in the same poem we find the line "I by backward steps would move", which might serve as an epigraph to the whole trilogy! But it is more than just recall or reliving – Reid goes much more deeply than, for example, Ray Salisbury in our own day into the myths and mysticism of a childhood that is, essentially, late Victorian in its outlook, education, and ethos. The child in Reid is never "father of the man", but is his own independent self, in his own self-created eternity.

Reid's own childhood, inevitably, furnished the background for most of his fiction, and it is quite remarkable how consistent his "looking back – at that short space" is over a writing career lasting more than forty years. *The Garden God* (1905), his first novel to be written but the second to be published, can be seen to contain the germ of the trilogy that is Reid's masterpiece. All the elements are there: the search for an ideal companion, the constant reference to classical (especially Greek) literature and philosophy, the search for harmony with nature and, perhaps above all, the passionate belief in a dream-world:

"Given such influences – his unconventional upbringing, his ignorance of the world, his beautiful surroundings – was it a wonder that that strange faculty for dreaming with which he had been born should have been perfected – perfected until in broad daylight he would slip unconsciously from one world to the other, and gravely tell his father of marvellous happenings, fantastic adventures, which never could have taken place?"

Reid's upbringing was, however, conventional enough. Born in 1875, in Belfast, to a middle-class Presbyterian business family, he was the youngest of twelve children, of whom six survived. Brought up by a nurse, Emma Holmes, whose departure soon after the death of his father in 1881 had a lasting effect on him – movingly recounted in *Apostate*, his volume of autobiography (1926) – Reid never really left the world of provincial middle-class Belfast, or the world of those seventeen years he describes in it.

His friend and confidant E.M. Forster, who was to write a brief introduction to the 1955 American single-volume edition of the Tom Barber trilogy, once wrote to him, "your main activity is reconsideration – you are always turning over in your mind something that had happened long ago, and are hoping to find a more perfect expression of it than you have succeeded in finding." *The Retreat* is, at the same time, the most realistic and the most enigmatic part of the trilogy which was the most perfect expression of that "reconsideration".

More than in *Uncle Stephen* or *Young Tom*, *The Retreat* reveals a close personal involvement on the author's part. Where in the case of *Uncle Stephen* he could say the book was " 'lived', for I undoubtedly was Tom", *The Retreat* was the closest Reid came to his long-lost nurse, Emma – it "was really her book," he affirmed. Reid's most recent biographer Brian Taylor goes further: "the subject of *The Retreat* was recognisably Forrest Reid's own, and one is tempted to add almost was Reid himself."

Reid's affections and fictional concerns were always for "the boy before the down appears on his cheeks" – that is before the corrupting worlds of adulthood and sexuality intrude, despoil, and destroy. This was both the limitation of his art and its unique quality. As A.E. (the Irish poet and critic George William Russell) wrote of *A Garden by the Sea* (1918-19), "Mr Reid...has somehow kept his memory of boyhood so alive in himself that he writes almost with the feeling of a contemporary." Boyhood is not just seen through the hero's eyes in Reid, it is lived, felt, experienced.

Part of the successful evocation of boyhood in *The Retreat* depends, very clearly, on the amalgamation of recently lived experience with boyhood "reconsideration". Reid, with the closest of the young friends of his middle age Stephen Gilbert (later to become his executor), had holidayed at the Fort Hotel, Greencastle, in county Donegal. It and nearby Glena-givney are the setting for Tom's holiday with his companion Pascoe, and are the starting-point for three of the greatest set-pieces in all of Reid's writing: the two trips to the beach (including the encounter with the angel Gamelyn), the dream-vision of the Garden of Eden, and the climactic bonfire which all but destroys Pascoe's Aunt Rhoda's garden.

These scenes show Reid's central preoccupations at their most explicit. His boys bathe together in an almost ritual celebration of their joint nakedness in almost every single novel he wrote. But there is no erotic sub-text here: his visual counterpart is Henry Scott Tuke rather than Wilhelm von Gloeden. Reid's are watercolours rather than photographs, with details hinted at, the imagination teased rather than titillated, the spirit of place evoked in the enjoyment that being there could give, rather than any illicit or corrupting influence the place might have.

Revealingly, in chapter 14 of *The Retreat* when his friend Pascoe, after they have been bathing, hears Tom say, "I don't see why we need dress ... it's more interesting to have no clothes on, it makes you behave differently", his reply is "you always behave as if you were naked." This is part of what makes Tom a unique representation of unselfconscious innocence, the most idealised yet real of all Reid's fictional boys.

The boys' doggy companion, Chrysanthemum, is another characteristic Reid presence, a necessary component of that friendship that goes beyond the merely human:

"even the earth he would have liked to be as nearly human as possible. Though human wasn't exactly what he meant: Chrysanthemum, for instance, wasn't human. What he meant was more just having feelings and the power to communicate them – a capacity for friendship..."

This capacity, for empathy and for friendship, goes back to Greek ideals, and, in particular, to Plato, who is frequently quoted in *The Garden God*, and who is a clear, if usually hidden, presence in most of Reid's later novels. What Reid meant by "the Greek tradition" he explained when discussing Fred Walker in *Illustrators of the Sixties* (1928), published a year after *Demophon*, the novel which best demonstrates his classical terms of reference: "when I call it Greek, I mean no more than that it is founded directly upon nature, that it accepts life as it is and turns it into beauty."

"Accepts" is probably the key-word here. Tom's efforts, throughout the trilogy, are directed always towards finding the companion who will accept him as he is – his family, his friends, his schoolmates and school-teachers all leave something to be desired. His animals, notably the dogs in *Young Tom* and Henry the cat in *The Retreat*, provide a kind of semi-mystical link between the real world and the dream-world of magic companionship Tom seeks. Hence the sub-title "The Machinations of Henry" – a reference which may seem odd but which, in fact, gives us a clue to understanding the different, intermingled levels of Tom's existence.

For he, like all Reid's heroes, lives half in dreams, and moves easily between dream and reality. *The Retreat* opens with a dream, and a magician who is not too dissimilar to Uncle Stephen, and ends with another dream, almost an epiphany, inspired by the sight of cats on a graveyard wall. Henry is the link between dream and reality each time. Forster gives us a momentary glimpse of the unworldly Reid in London which directly recalls the graveyard vision in chapter 20 of *The Retreat*: "his visits to Bloomsbury were rendered tolerable by a cemetery, where cats confabulated upon some railed-in tombs."

The vision of Eden happens while Tom is on holiday, and Henry has been left at home in Ballysheen. His place is taken by the angel Gamelyn, "his naked companion", on Tom's first trip to the beach, without Pascoe. Gamelyn, the same ideal boy that Graham Iddesleigh finds in *The Garden God*, brings together the human and spiritual needs separately filled by Pascoe and Henry in the rest of the novel. He is unthreatening, a creation of Tom's natural fancy, what E.M. Forster called "that indwelling power" which gives Tom all the mental space he needs despite the restrictions placed on him by time, place, and circumstance.

All of Reid's writing about dreams leads to the stunning, and entirely convincing vision of the Garden of Eden in chapter 15 of *The Retreat*. It is convincing precisely because of Tom's down-to-earth attitude even in his moments of greatest fantasy: "alone in Eden" he would eat the apple of Knowledge out of natural curiosity, only to find it tastes "dry and bitter". And, of course, "nothing happened." When, at the request of the serpent he takes off the pyjamas he is wearing "nobody expressed admiration." An Abraham and Isaac-type vision, a few sharp barbs against Eve ("everything was so much nicer before she came", says the serpent), a magician with a black cat...and Pascoe wakes him up to go for a bathe. The real and the magically descriptive co-exist (magic realism *ante letteram*!) with that same unselfconsciousness that Tom shows in his own nakedness. The seemingly portentous – "time is an illusion", or " 'there is no invisible world', said the serpent...'there are degrees of perfection of the organs of vision – that is all' " – are balanced with the "ugly, gloomy, even sordid" impression the so-called beauty-spot of Port-a-Doris leaves, and the slightly sexual overtones in the distaste Tom feels for its crudeness and squalor.

Nowhere is the mixture of out-of-this-world dream-fantasy better blended with reality than in the great bonfire scene in chapter 17. "Rapt in enjoyment" of what should have been a simple, natural pleasure (as bonfires were for Reid himself), Tom "retreated a few paces, and then stood still, lost in a rapture that was dreamy yet exultant." But this time the retreat from reality is not the safe retreat of dreams. Other people now "were outside his world, but the fire was in his world." Things can go too far, and "something a little less

Neronic" would have been preferable to the "ravages" of the fire which, we are then told, "had been considerable."

Tom's fantasies and dreams seldom have to be brought back to earth so sharply. Very often, though, it is the dangerous invisibility of the dividing line between reality and imagination which causes him the greatest perplexity – the whirlwind in the schoolroom, the vision in the graveyard, the appearance of Gamelyn – and must make the reader too wonder which is real and which not. The simple romance between Miss Jimpson the mathematics teacher and Mr Holbrook the music teacher is a level of "plot" which, to Tom and to the reader, is almost banal. But with the music Tom sings, with the whirlwind, and with the appearance of the dog Caleb at the very end of the novel ("the dog who invariably accompanies Tobias and his Angel in old Florentine pictures") we are immediately taken back to the realm of the imagined, or the only partly real, while remaining on the simple level of the romantic sub-plot.

That there are a few small inconsistencies in the trilogy – particularly in Tom's relationship with his parents – is to be expected over so many years of writing, and with the time-scale shifting ever-further back into childhood. The process is one of continuing clarification – of a deeper and closer examination of what is inevitably lost in the move away from the naked innocence and simple-seeming realities of childhood.

Reid is neither fey nor twee, arch nor coy, although his subject-matter abounds in high-risk areas for all of these. The life of the mind of Tom is so thoroughly realised that the reader must go with Tom completely or not at all: what is outside Tom's frame of reference is not part of the Tom Barber trilogy. So, adult knowingness, laughter at childhood foibles, or awareness beyond his years are never part of Tom's story. It is this that is the hallmark of Reid's achievement, and makes his "retreat" into the world of childhood so real, so vivid, and so close to everyone's dimly recollected experience.

John McRae

THE RETREAT

Happy those early days, when I
Shined in my angel-infancy!
Before I understood this place
Appointed for my second race,
Or taught my soul to fancy aught
But a white, celestial thought;
When yet I had not walked above
A mile or two from my first Love,
And looking back—at that short space—
Could see a glimpse of his bright face;
When on some gilded cloud, or flower,
My gazing soul would dwell an hour,
And in those weaker glories spy
Some shadows of eternity....

HENRY VAUGHAN

Part One

CHAPTER I

An old man, clad from throat to silver-buckled shoes in a wide loose-sleeved black robe, stood at a window peering out into the darkness. His silken silver hair fell in one long smooth lock over a high narrow forehead; his face, minutely lined, was fine as a cameo, and his skin the colour of an ancient parchment. The ears were very slightly pointed, the nose strong and straight, the mouth small. The hand that grasped and held aside the black curtain was fine too, and though time had wrinkled it and revealed the blue veins running up into the wrist, it had not spoiled its shapeliness.

The old man looked frail and wasted, as if his body were no more than a dry transparent husk through which the flame of life shone bright but heatless. He was like one of those delicate skeleton leaves one finds in some sheltered hollow in the woods—desiccated, perfect in form, yet so fragile that when one holds it up against the sun the light shines through. His dark still eyes had a tranquillity of detached contemplation rather than of amiability, for beneath their abstraction glittered the latent energy of a cold and formidable will. "Tib—Tib——" he called. "Tibby—Tibby." But the world outside was dark and frozen, the latticed window shut, and he called so softly that it was little more than a murmur. Then he let the curtain drop back soundlessly into its heavy folds, and returned to a carved high-backed chair by the hearth....

It was late—very late—some hour between midnight and dawn—and a strange, precarious silence filled the room. On a stool, blotted in the shadow of the chimney corner, with eyes that a moment ago had been closed in slumber, but were now glinting and watchful, sat a slim boy of twelve or thirteen, also dressed in black. He had fallen asleep there, he did not quite know when, but it must have been several hours ago, and he guessed that his master either thought he was asleep still, or more likely had forgotten him.

He was a peculiar old man: the boy had begun to fear him. What was he doing now for instance, and for what or whom was he waiting? Did he sit up every night like this, in that straight-backed chair, with its green threadbare velvet cushion? It would be better for him if he were to say his prayers and go to bed, for though by no means exceptionally pious himself, the boy had been brought up in the Catholic faith, and he remembered uneasily that since he had entered the old man's service they had never once been to mass nor had a priest crossed their door. At first he had fancied that his master himself must be a kind of priest, but now he held another view. He was no priest—of the true church at any rate—nor was that mysterious sign of two interlocked triangles, drawn in gold on the white marble table, a Christian symbol. The boy comforted himself with the reflection that Tibby at least was gone, and the hope that he would never come back. . . .

He wished he had not fallen asleep, but that nearly always happened after he had been looking at the pictures in the black polished stone. He tried to remember the pictures, but he could not—he never could—and the stone itself was gone, locked up once more, he supposed, in the cabinet where his master kept it. He wished he had gone to bed, wished he could summon up energy to go now; but a kind of languor held him, mingled with curiosity and a vague expectancy, for surely his master was not sitting there in mere idleness, though what his purpose could be was hard to imagine. If it were not that no visitors ever came, the boy would have thought he was expecting a visitor now. And it *might* be that: it was just possible that the old man was not so solitary as he seemed to be. The boy slept soundly in a little room in the other wing of the house: if someone were to come in the night he would know nothing of it. Only, to crouch here forgotten was almost like hiding, almost like spying; perhaps he should make a movement, a sound. Yet he did neither. . . .

In the great bare room three of the four walls were hung with

6

moth-riddled, perishing tapestries, at present only dimly visible even to the boy's keen young eyes. The lamplight, he thought, must have grown weaker while he slept. It floated towards, but no longer quite reached, the outer edges of the room, so that the walls remained in an equivocal shadow that was neither light nor darkness. And next moment it seemed to him that the light was not so much failing as being thrust back by this shadow, which was condensing in certain places, and very slowly gaining ground. At the same time he became conscious that the temperature of the room had sunk, as if the windows had been stealthily opened to admit the icy air from outside. But he knew this could not be so—knew the windows were fast. Besides, the black velvet curtains which hung before them had never once stirred.

The old man's head had begun to nod forward on his breast, but now abruptly he sat up. None too soon, it seemed, for the flame of the lamp had begun to wink ominously. Yet it must have been the cold which had aroused him, for his eyes had been shut. As he stood up his face was angry and impatient. He went to attend to the lamp, though what he did to it the boy could not see, because the old man's back was turned to him. He could only see that his hands hovered about it and that when they lifted the flame lifted also. Then, still with his hands outstretched, he stepped forward slowly, muttering incomprehensible words, and the shadow retreated before him, and the darker cloudy patches melted away.

The boy was less surprised than he would have been some months ago, but he hurriedly drew a cross upon his breast and whispered a Latin prayer he had been taught. Once more the lamp burned brightly, and now, in the increased light, all the objects the room contained were clearly visible. They were not numerous—a few chairs, a cabinet whose tall black doors somehow suggested the wings of a sleeping bat, a tripod surmounted by an empty brazier, two tables, and some shelves of books. The floor was bare, and at one side of the immense open hearth stood what appeared to be a kind of furnace built of brick and surmounted by a cone. The larger of the tables was drawn between the windows. It was square and massive and littered with oddly

7

shaped vessels of copper and crystal. On the smaller table, the white marble table in the centre of the room, there was nothing but the burning lamp.

The old man returned to the hearth and cast on more wood. As he did so the boy could see his lips moving, though they made no sound. The wood was dry and soon broke into a flame. Golden jets of light spurted beyond the radius of the lamplight, licking up against the tapestried walls, flickering and darting, like the tongues of serpents. They had a curious effect, beautiful and fantastic, for at one moment there was only a veil of trembling shadow, and at the next a stiff and formal landscape peopled with ghostly figures leapt into view—all the more lifelike because the figures and the trees visibly moved. The boy, however, knew the origin of this movement, and that it was not of his master's making. It was natural: he had seen it happening in the daytime. Every room in this crumbling half-dilapidated house was full of draughts, and it must be only such a draught now, passing between the wall and the hangings, which caused them to ripple and to swell.

Again he began to feel drowsy, and again he closed his eyes. Suddenly he opened them to find that he was alone. At once his sleepiness vanished. The lamp was still burning, but the fire had ceased to blaze and was sunk to a hot red glow. The boy had never been alone in this room before, and he glanced nervously about him with quick yet stealthy movements of his head. It was here that his master carried on his secret labours, and always when he left the room he locked the door behind him. The boy stepped swiftly across the floor, for the thought of being shut in was not pleasant, but the key was in the lock, so his master must be coming back. With that a spirit of inquisitiveness seized him: it was his chance to examine and explore, and he might never have another. The alchemical apparatus he did not dare to touch, but might there not be simpler instruments of magic—cloaks of darkness, flying broomsticks, wishing-caps—he knew not what? He had never seen the doors of the cabinet opened for more than a moment or two, when his master had opened them to get out the shining black stone. But in those moments his quick eyes had

8

caught glimpses of the interior—of dried herbs and chafing dishes, of crystal phials and a rod of hazelwood that was perhaps a wand, of a sickle-shaped dagger and a sword. He knew the exact uses of none of these objects except the stone, but the cabinet was large and deep, its interior dusky enough to hide many secrets, there must be other things, and perhaps the purposes of some of them could be grasped. He resolved at any rate to take a peep, for this key too was in the lock. Nevertheless, when he tried the door, it would not open.

And all at once the boy was afraid. Why had he been left alone like this? Was it a trap? A minute ago he had felt bold, excited, adventurous; now he was abruptly transformed into a coward. He had heard no sound, nothing appeared to have happened, nothing was changed except himself. He still stood by the door of the cabinet, but he no longer thought of opening it. An icy presentiment of horror gripped coldly and woefully at his heart, his blood chilled, his breath stopped, for he knew with every nerve of his body that the visitor his master was expecting had arrived— had at that very moment entered the house. Only what visitor? He had no name, no identity, and he had given no warning of his approach. The boy stood paralyzed, listening intently. He listened, and presently it was as if every part of him had become merely one wide quivering ear. He heard now many faint sounds—sounds in remote closed rooms—sounds, in this room, that had hitherto been inaudible—the frost drawing patterns on the window pane, a spider weaving his web. . . .

And then he heard a louder sound—clear though still distant —knock—knock—knock—in the lower part of the house. Knock —knock—knock—it was drawing nearer, it was mounting the stairs, it was at the end of the passage. The boy's wide eyes were fixed in terror on the door. He might still have time to lock himself in, only he knew this would be useless: when the knocking reached it, the door would open slowly and inevitably, as to the Hand of Glory.

That last dreadful summons on the door itself would be worst of all. Better to avert it, better to go to meet it, and he sprang across the room and flung the door wide.

9

Instantly his fear was gone. He half laughed, half cried, in the sudden wonderful uprush of relief, as there stepped across the threshold no hideous phantom, but the loveliest little creature he had ever beheld. It was a deer—still far too young to have horns—with dark soft eyes and smooth dappled coat. And those four small delicate hoofs it must have been that had made the knocking which had so frightened him. It had sought him out, was actually in the room, bringing with it a kind of wild fragrance of the woods. It had come to look for him, this little messenger without a message, for as he put his arm round it and began to stroke it, it turned and they walked together down the dark passage and the darker stairs, and along another passage leading to a side door which stood ajar.

The boy pushed open the door; but the winter and the night were gone. Gone like a dream—gone and, almost before he had taken two steps, forgotten. The old man was forgotten, the room forgotten, the house forgotten. There was nothing—nothing but a world of gleaming sunshine—a world of cool green leaves and running water. . . .

Tom opened his eyes in the darkness. His heart was still thumping, but he had a feeling of gladness. It must be the middle of the night, he realized, or very early morning, for the tree whose leaves were brushing softly against the window pane was hardly distinguishable. As usual before getting into bed he had pulled up the blinds, always carefully drawn down by Mary, and now as he grew wider awake he stared out through the dim square of glass into a penumbral world. Not a sound could he hear except when the branches stooped to stroke the window. And then, soft and far, a rounded melodious note was repeated twice. It was the old grandfather's clock in the hall conscientiously striking the hour, but Tom liked to fancy that it was calling to him, for it was a nice old clock, and he had persuaded himself that there was, if not an actual friendship, at least a sort of secret understanding between them. . . .

He had been dreaming, and he perfectly remembered his dream; but the strange thing was that though it had been plea-

10

sant and happy it seemed to have left a shadow on his mind. Had there been an earlier dream which he could not recall? He remembered trees, and sunlight dancing on a stream, and a deer. He had been in a kind of narrow valley with a stream flowing through it; and it was spring. But what had happened earlier? Or had anything happened? If not, why was he in a perspiration, and why had he kicked off his bedclothes as if he had been struggling against a nightmare? There had been *something*—something frightening—though it seemed silly to say so when it had left not a trace behind it. Unless this in itself were a trace! For there had been a series of similar awakenings—three at least he could remember in the past fortnight—and always that feeling of having escaped only just in time. But escaped from what? The merest hint, Tom thought, and the entire thing would come back to him; but that hint was withheld. When he tried to break through the intervening blank he could not, and the struggle was even physically painful, as though a band were being pressed tighter and tighter round his brain. It was as if he were pushing against a void, and the strain grew so acute that he felt as if a spring in his mind were on the point of snapping. The instant he relaxed his efforts he had a feeling of relief. He would not try to remember, and to dismiss the whole thing still further from his mind he sat up in bed and sang in imagination the tune of "Who is Sylvia?"

When he lay down again he still felt a little shaken and exhausted, but he turned on his side and shut his eyes. This was the right treatment, for very soon he felt comfortable and drowsy. Perhaps some day an instrument would be invented for recording people's dreams. It did not seem to Tom at all impossible, nor even much more wonderful than when Mr. Holbrook put a black shining disk into a wooden box and presently Caruso, who was actually dead, began to sing to you. That, again, wasn't very different from the *Arabian Nights* story of the fisherman who unsealed the stopper of a brass jar and released a genie who had been shut up in the jar ages ago by King Solomon. . . .

Tom must by now have been very drowsy indeed, for through his closed eyelids he saw a great dark camera, shrouded with

11

mysterious black curtains or doors that were somehow like the wings of a sleeping bat, set there beside his pillow, waiting to photograph his dreams. He was just wondering if bats really could see dreams, and in that case if owls and cats could, when he heard a light scratching on the panel of the door. He knew what *that* was in a moment, and after waiting till it came again slid out of bed. He opened the door and stopped on the threshold to tie the cord of his pyjamas, while faint little mews, scattered like grace notes through a rich purring, rose out of the darkness, and the black plump body of Henry rubbed and pressed against his legs.

Henry must have come to watch his dreams; but since he wouldn't be able to talk about them afterwards, that wasn't much use. It would have to be a person—a person with second sight, Tom decided, though he didn't quite know what it was you actually saw when you had second sight. He knew that there *was* such a thing, however, because Mother's grandfather had been "gifted" with it. It had always run in the Collet family, Mother said, and she ought to know, because she was a Collet herself. In fact, though when she had married Daddy she had been obliged to take his name and become a Barber, she still seemed to prefer being a Collet. Tom made these reflections standing spellbound like Apollonius of Tyana, though for a less protracted period; then, the meditation completed, he shut the door and hopped back into bed.

Next moment Henry was on the bed too, plucking with his front paws at the counterpane, and continuing to purr.

"Stop!" said Tom, for he knew Henry was pulling out threads —indeed he could hear him doing it—giving little picks that made a noise nearly as loud as raindrops. He was the most frightfully destructive cat, and had ruined Daddy's leather arm-chair by stropping his claws on the back of it.

Henry stopped picking, but he continued to move about the bed until he had found a hollow that suited him. Then he curled himself up and began to purr again, but now much more softly. Tom lay listening to him. It was a queer sound, he thought, and Henry must make it somewhere at the back of his nose. Tom puckered up his own nose and tried, but it wasn't very good. He

12

could make a noise, but not that kind of warm, broken, comfortable noise. It was easier to mew, and indeed he could mew quite well, though Henry pretended not to recognize it. He mewed now, while from the garden outside came the first chirps and twitterings of early birds. The early worms, Tom supposed, would now be burrowing in all haste back into the tennis lawn. He mewed again, and there was no twittering. "I've frightened them," he said for Henry's benefit, but Henry did not reply.

CHAPTER II

When Tom next opened his eyes it was broad daylight and the sun was shining. But after listening for a minute or two he knew it must still be pretty early, for he could hear none of the domestic sounds which usually began about seven. He rather liked those early-morning sounds— Phemie's violent assault upon the kitchen range—which always seemed to be resisting tooth and nail—and Mary's more circumspect movements in the dining-room and study. Phemie, Mary, and William composed the indoor and outdoor staff, and Phemie and Mary were sisters though you never would have guessed this to look at them. Phemie—whose full name was Euphemia—was several years older than Mary, and bossed her like anything. Both were Roman Catholics, while William was a Protestant and an Orangeman, and walked with an orange-and-purple sash over his shoulder on the twelfth of July. Phemie had been crossed in love many years ago, and now hated men though she didn't mind boys. She had a loud voice, muscles of iron, and a temper which Mother said all cooks inherited from the cook in *Alice in Wonderland*. Nevertheless, Tom preferred her to Mary, though he preferred Mary to William, who was the gardener, and lived with his wife and family in a cottage not far from the old Ballysheen graveyard, about a mile away.

All this district was Ballysheen, and Doctor Macrory said there had once been a church near the graveyard, though nothing was left of it at present except a few stones. And even the loose stones had nearly all been carted away at one time and another to build walls and byres and cottages. For that matter, Doctor Macrory said there must long ago have been another house—a big house —where Tom's own house now stood. It had disappeared completely, and was not mentioned in any local history, but the builders had discovered traces of it when they were laying the foundations, and Doctor Macrory himself had poked about while the digging was going on. Doctor Macrory was very much interested in things of that sort. By profession he was a physician, but his hobby was archæology, and he had written several pamphlets on the subject. Tom hadn't read the pamphlets, but he had seen them, Daddy possessed them, and they were bound in green paper, with Celtic designs.

All Daddy's friends were scientific, which, according to Mother, accounted for the narrowness of their views, their lack of imagination, and the irritating way in which they pooh-poohed anything they couldn't understand. It was queer that Tom's friend Pascoe should be scientific too, because Tom, Mother said, took after *her* family, and was a Collet.

On the other hand, she had one day told him that he got his brains from Daddy, though they were a different kind of brains. This seemed a little complicated, and became still more so when in answer to his question as to *how* they were different, she discovered that the person he really took after must be Uncle Stephen, of whose existence Tom had not till that moment heard. So sometimes he was a Collet and sometimes he wasn't; it depended a good deal on the humour Mother happened to be in, and whether she was pleased with him or not.

In one particular, however, she rarely varied her opinion, and this was that neither he nor Daddy possessed as much practical sense as a child of six. Six was Mother's favourite age; it was always a child of six who would have known better than to say or do whatever it was that Tom or Daddy might have said or done; and when Tom pointed out that you can't remain six for ever,

14

she laughed, and replied that if he and Daddy hadn't it was only because they were five. This appeared to worry her more about Tom than about Daddy, though there were occasions when it had the contrary effect, and then she would kiss him. But Tom himself knew that he was different from Daddy, who was never in a hurry to do things, and never got heated or excited no matter what happened, whereas both Tom and Mother did. He wondered if Uncle Stephen did: it was natural to wonder about a person you resembled and who was so mysterious as Uncle Stephen. He couldn't make out what Mother thought of him. He didn't believe she *knew* much about him. Yet he hovered there somehow in the background, a distinctly romantic figure. Once, ages ago, he had asked her if she would rather have Uncle Stephen than Daddy, which had annoyed her a little, though afterwards she had repeated it as a joke. . . .

Henry some time during the night must have moved down to the foot of the bed, where he now lay asleep, curled up in a black circle. Tom felt a lazy inclination to pet him, and called "Puss, puss", but it produced no effect. So he raised his feet under the bedclothes, making an uncomfortable hill. Still Henry did not budge; only he gave Tom a long secret look out of green slits of eyes before closing them again. That was like him: he never did anything unless he wanted to do it himself. It had been a most peculiar look too, Tom presently thought; just as if Henry knew something about him—something faintly discreditable. Tom believed he did know things. Only why had he looked like that? It wasn't on the whole a friendly look—rather the reverse— though it certainly suggested that there was some kind of understanding between them. The more Tom considered it the less he liked it. There wasn't *any* understanding between them. Henry knew nothing about him except what everybody else knew, so he had no right to pretend that he did. Tom raised his feet again, this time higher, lifting Henry up in a kind of loose, sprawling crescent, so that he looked as if he had either no bones or else were dead. Yet even then he wouldn't move. He merely opened his mouth, showing a tiny scrap of pink, and emitted a

15

faintly irritated mew. He had suddenly become an ordinary cat again.

He had no business to keep changing about like this. Ordinary cats didn't. Therefore, by the rules of logic, Henry couldn't be an ordinary cat, whatever he might pretend. Pascoe had produced electric sparks from him, though of course that didn't prove much, except that he was crammed with electricity. But Henry did things on his own account—queer, very nearly magical things—when he and Tom were alone together in the house. Before the others, even before Pascoe, he put on an innocent expression, as if he had never done anything more thrilling than to lap up a saucer of milk. But when only Tom was there it was a different story. Then he no longer troubled to look innocent. It seemed to be Henry's opinion that Tom didn't matter, and just to show this he would start off by making the whole house queer. He had done it yesterday evening when they were alone and Tom was at his lessons. Henry had walked to the study door and scratched on it—his usual sign that he wanted to be let out. Then, when the door was opened, he had strolled slowly on down the passage as if he were going to the kitchen, while Tom, pondering, had stood watching him as far as the corner. Yet when he had turned back into the study again and shut the door, there Henry was—on the hearthrug, washing his face, just as if he had never left the room at all. Meanwhile, the things in the study had changed their places: Tom's *Latin Grammar*, which he had left open on the sofa, was now on the floor, closed, and the frame with his photograph in it had been moved forward from the other photographs—he was sure that if it had been like that before he must have noticed it. It was strange—very strange. And if it came to that, who *was* Henry, and where had he come from? Nobody knew. He had simply walked through the open back door into the kitchen one afternoon about a month ago, and Phemie had immediately decided that he had come to bring her luck and mustn't be turned away. That was all nonsense, of course, as even Phemie soon knew. The very next day she had upset a pot of boiling water and scalded her foot. But *why* had Henry come? He was a full-grown cat, sleek and lithe, with a coat like black

16

satin: anybody could see he had never been hungry or homeless in his life.

And certainly he hadn't troubled himself to bring much luck to poor Phemie! She had broken a teapot and a vegetable dish on the day after the scalding, and Henry had ceased to be a kitchen cat. His next move had been to wile himself into the good graces of Daddy. This had been accomplished easily—merely by following Daddy about the garden and jumping up on the arm of his chair. Daddy tried not to look flattered, and said nothing; but every time Mother said—and she said it about five times a day— "Henry's *devoted* to Daddy!" it was easy to see he was as pleased as Punch.

Tom knew better. The devotion was mere policy. He could prove it. Henry wasn't in the least interested in games with string, for example. They bored him. Tom had tried him again and again, and he had simply yawned or turned his back. Yet if Daddy dangled a piece of string or waved his handkerchief, Henry immediately crouched and quivered and pounced.

That wasn't how he behaved with Tom. Once, when he was sitting alone in the drawing-room at dusk, tired of reading and too lazy to get up and turn on the light, Henry had actually begun to play the piano to him. Only a note or two—very, very softly, and really rather beautifully—for it had sounded more as if the piano were singing in its sleep than being played. Tom had liked it, and so most surely had Henry; but did ordinary cats play the piano?

Then there was the matter of the tennis balls, more mysterious still, because this time Henry hadn't been there. And mind you, Tom himself had put the tennis balls away in their cardboard box, and put the box on the oak chest which stood beside the cloakroom door. Yet he had hardly been in the cloakroom a minute before he heard a bouncing noise in the hall, and, running out, found the tennis balls, all six of them, rolling over the carpet in different directions, with nobody to roll them, nobody near them.

When things like this happened, you couldn't help beginning to wonder why. And they had happened pretty often of late, usually in the evening. They didn't frighten you, perhaps—in fact they were rather exciting—but they did give you a queer feeling of uncertainty, as if nothing was quite what it seemed, and things like tennis balls, or photograph frames, or pianos for that matter, were a good deal more alive than they had any right to be. It was Henry's doing, of course, and he knew that Tom knew it was. He knew and didn't care—which was probably the meaning of the strange look he had given him just now. What Henry's green eyes had said was: "*I* know, and *you* know, that there's something most unusual going on in this house; but the others don't know, and if you tell them they won't believe you. That's why it doesn't matter about you, and why it wouldn't matter if you did tell. They'd only make fun of you—especially that daddy of yours, who thinks you're queer enough as it is."

"He doesn't think me queer," Tom contradicted, but without much conviction; and Henry didn't even bother to open his eyes. This annoyed Tom, so he continued with more spirit: "Anyway, you'll get down off the bed." And he jumped out himself and pushed Henry on to the floor.

It was a poor argument, and he felt a little ashamed, so he picked Henry up again and set him once more where he had been. "You needn't start purring," he told him. "I only did that because I don't approve of bullying: I still think you're pretty awful."

Saying which, he took off his pyjamas, and stood in a patch of sunlight, letting the sun stroke his naked body with its warm breath. He liked it, and liked the feeling of the carpet under his bare feet. Henry, seeing him up, jumped down from the bed and began scratching at the door, but Tom watched him unsympathetically. "Why don't you go?" he asked in a cold voice. "It's too much trouble to do a magic, I suppose. Go on—vanish! *I* won't be surprised."

In spite of this sarcasm, Henry merely lifted his voice in a very unmagical mew, so Tom had to open the door for him. Then he went to the window and looked out into the garden. The garden was bright with its first dewy freshness, and as usual there was a squabble going on among the birds. Of all the quarrelsome creatures! And they were supposed to be so angelic. Probably it was the row they were kicking up which had attracted Henry, who, as Tom was well aware, could get out by jumping from the bathroom window-sill to the roof of the coalhouse. Yes, there he was, gliding between the bushes like a black panther. But the birds saw him also, and with a sudden whirr of wings rose in a cloud. The birds detested Henry, and had every reason to do so, for he hunted them from morning till night. Often he got one too; an absent-minded bird had no chance whatever with Henry: Tom could quite understand their feelings. . . .

A flat lawn with a sagging tennis net in the middle of it stretched in front of the house. All round this lawn were flower-beds and trellises festooned with rambler roses. On the left was a line of trees, and on the right a border of flowering shrubs—syringas, azaleas, rhododendrons—just now a splash of brilliant colour. Tom could smell the perfumes that drifted from them, and he could smell the roses and the grass. Suddenly he wanted to be out there.

He put on a shirt, a pair of grey flannel shorts, stockings, slippers, a jacket. He knew he should have taken a bath, or at least washed properly, but all he did was to pour a little water into a basin and give a perfunctory dab or two at his face with a sponge. He was on the point of leaving the room when he remembered his prayers and knelt down by the bed. He had two prayers —one in prose and one in verse. The poetry prayer he always said last. Both were short, but they included, Mother told him, everything he really needed. They left out of account, none the less, a lot of things he really *wanted*—a bulldog, a donkey, long trousers, hairs on his legs, a bicycle, not to miss catches at cricket, and not to be called "Skinny". Sometimes Tom added these items, sometimes he omitted them. In spite of past failures he put them all in to-day, like a Christmas or a birthday list, where one leaves the final choice to the giver.

He ran downstairs, put on his shoes in the kitchen, emptied the biscuit jar in the dining-room (it was nearly empty, anyway), and went out through the side door into the garden.

It was a fairly large garden, walled all round to the height of

19

some five feet, but not too large to be looked after by one man. Tom thought at first of marking the tennis court, the lines of which were rather faint, till he remembered that it was William's day for cutting the grass. That altered matters. If William found the court freshly marked he would make this an excuse for leaving it alone—"not liking to interfere with Master Tom's work." William was splendid at excuses, and, like Henry, so plausible, that though actually the most frightful slacker, he was regarded by everybody as a model of industry. "Slow but sure," Daddy would say of him; or "Hurried work's usually scamped"— things like that, when it ought to have been: "William does as little as he can, and never anything you ask him." Only it wasn't easy to tell exactly *how* slow William was, because through long association with the garden he had acquired a kind of protective colouring and his movements were veiled. If you merely glanced at him as he stood with a hoe or a spade in his hand between two bean-rows or stooping over the cabbages, he produced an illusion of activity, but if you watched him closely, as Tom had done, this illusion vanished, and a curious affinity between William and the sundial emerged. Not that Tom would have cared, if he hadn't been such a grumbler. But he bemoaned his lot every time you spoke to him, so that you'd have thought he was a slave driven by Egyptian taskmasters. He wouldn't, for instance, be in the least grateful if Tom were to cut the grass for him now: he'd just accept it as a matter of course and point out how it might have been done better.

Tom had reached this point in his summing-up of William when the hall-door opened and Mary appeared, carrying a long-handled brush with which she began to sweep out the porch. The instant she caught sight of the figure on the lawn she stopped. "What are you doing there, Master Tom?" she asked in a tone of suspicion and disapproval.

Tom was amused. "Admiring the view," he replied; at which Mary gave a sniff—inaudible, but perfectly perceptible even from that distance. She took no further notice of him, however, from which he deduced that she regarded his remark as cheek.

As a matter of fact the old house *did* look rather nice, he thought. There was honeysuckle climbing up one side of the porch, and clematis climbing up the other, while ampelopsis spread over the walls. Also he liked the oriel windows and red-tiled roof and irregular chimney stacks. Not that the house was really old, having been built by the people from whom Daddy had bought it; but it had been designed from the beginning to have an old-fashioned appearance—warm, comfortable, and homely—and it really *had* been that kind of house until Henry had begun to play tricks with it.

Still, Tom couldn't stare at it for ever, even to impress the suspicious Mary, so he took a path through the shrubbery, which terminated in a small green postern door set in the angle where the south and west walls met. This door was locked at night, but the key was always left in the lock, and next moment Tom was outside the garden, on the high bank of a glen thickly carpeted with long green spiky bluebell leaves, and overgrown with larch, hazel, and birch trees. The glen was long and very narrow, as if at some remote volcanic period the earth had split asunder here. A stream ran through it, which never dried up even in the hottest summer, and Tom scrambled down to it, because the walking was easier there. He saw a squirrel and stopped to look at him; he disturbed a hare who had come down from the meadows and at Tom's approach fled up to them again. He followed the stream, jumping from side to side of it, and as he proceeded the steep banks of the glen gradually grew shallower, till at last the ground was level, and only a field of meadow grass bright with buttercups lay between him and the river. In wet weather the ground was soft and boggy here, so that cows sometimes sank up above their knees and had to be hauled out by ropes, but just now it was firm enough. Anyhow, Tom knew every inch of it, and passing lightly between two beds of yellow irises, and scrambling through a hedge, reached the towpath.

"Shall I bathe or not?" he was asking himself, and the question was difficult to answer, for though he wanted to be able to remark at breakfast that he had had a bathe in the river he wasn't really fond of cold water, nor even sure that it agreed with him. "I'm afraid a lot of things don't agree with me," Tom

21

mused. "I'm quite easily made ill." And he particularly wished not to be ill just before the exams, because he was rather a dab at exams, though not such a dab as Pascoe. But he really knew far more than Pascoe did, only the kinds of things he knew weren't so useful. Besides, he was hopeless at mathematics.

He stood with his greyish, greenish eyes fixed doubtfully on the water, while the wind made little whisperings and songs as it swept over the rushes. Then he knelt down to try the temperature with his hand. This experiment elicited a sigh; nevertheless, after the briefest hesitation, he divested himself of his clothes and stepped cautiously into the shallow water at the edge. Why was it, he wondered, that he should think of leeches and eels at such a moment, instead of darting silver fish? But he did think of them, and dreaded at every step lest he should put his foot on something soft and fat and slimy which would move. He took only three or four steps and then stood still, not much more than knee-deep, among a patch of dark broad glossy leaves. He splashed a little water over himself, wetting his dim brown hair, and this was the bathe.

Buzz! A large bumble-bee, after some preliminary fussing, alighted on Tom's shoulder and began to walk down his body, which looked very white among the dark leaves, though his hands and neck and freckled blunt-featured face were sunburned. The bee tickled him, but not unpleasantly. He was a very handsome bee, with an air of importance, and his black and orange velvet coat was rich and splendid. He looked so important, indeed, that Tom fancied he must be a Mayor or an Alderman at the very least. People like Daddy (who was a professor), and Doctor Macrory (who was an archæologist), and Mr. Holbrook (who taught music), hadn't at all such an important air. This was the kind of affluent, pompous bee who would be a Member of Parliament, or a City Councillor, and whose wife would open Sales of Work.

Tom poured more water over his head—to make sure that it would look sufficiently wet at breakfast—and while he was doing this an old grey horse came plodding along round the bend of the river. A rope was attached to the horse, a barge to the rope, and there was a man walking by the horse's head, and another man standing at the helm of the barge, steering it. The man who was walking was on the farther side of the horse, so that he did not notice Tom, but the steersman spied him at once and bawled out at the top of his voice: "Hi, Joe, here's a water-lily!" This caused Joe to lean a beery stubbly face over the horse's back, and it also drew a laugh from him. They were really very rude! Tom thought.

But there was not much time for thinking and he would have done better to have acted. "Look out for that bloody rope!" he heard the steersman shout. "What the——"

Tom heard no more, for just then the rope reached him and he was swept off his feet—splash!—on the flat of his back. He emerged spluttering, spitting, choking, and very angry. The horse had already passed him as he floundered to the bank and scrambled out. It was lucky, Tom thought, that he had been so close to the bank, or the barge might have gone over him. Much they would have cared even if he *had* been drowned! He would have liked to tell them his opinion of them, but it was the bargemen who shouted remarks. These were derisive and indecent— eked out by much raucous laughter. The man who was leading the horse was not even funny: the steersman was—a little. The old grey horse, unaware of the accident, was the only respectable member of the trio.

Tom dried himself, partly with his pocket handkerchief, and partly with his trousers. But he never remained cross for long, and before the barge had disappeared round the next bend he had ceased to be either angry or shocked. After all, it had been his own fault. With a little presence of mind he could easily have avoided the rope, and the bargemen couldn't possibly have stopped the barge. So he finished dressing and trotted happily back to the house.

23

CHAPTER III

The bell had rung and Daddy and Mother were already at the breakfast-table when Tom appeared. He kissed them both and sat down.

"What have you been doing to your hair?" was Mother's expected question.

"It's only water," Tom replied. "I had a bathe."

Mother rose beautifully to this. "A bathe!" she repeated incredulously.

"Yes," said Tom, "in the river."

"But why?" Mother, after all, was less impressed than he had hoped. In fact she was looking at him in quite the wrong way. "Is this some new fad?" she went on, though Tom had no fads at all. "I've told you before that I don't think it's safe for you to bathe in the river—particularly by yourself. You might easily step into a hole that was out of your depth. It's just the sort of thing you *would* do."

Tom's light and airy manner had to be abandoned. "I want to learn to swim," he protested. "And I can't learn on dry land."

"You can't learn without somebody to teach you," Mother said, "and there's nobody now James-Arthur's gone. Besides, you'll have plenty of opportunities in the holidays, and it's much easier to learn in the sea than in fresh water. Everybody knows that rivers are dangerous."

They were far more dangerous than she imagined, Tom reflected, but he kept this to himself. "It isn't dangerous if I stay close to the bank," he argued. "Lots of boys bathe in the river."

"Not alone," Mother answered, "and not boys like you. There are just as likely to be holes near the bank as anywhere else. The bed of a river isn't like the seashore: one minute you may be in three feet of water and the next in ten."

"I doubt if he was in three feet of water," Daddy here interposed. He had been glancing at the newspaper, but he now gazed over the top of it at his son. "I should put it at eighteen inches in spite of those dripping locks."

This guess was so very nearly accurate that Tom blushed. It

was like Daddy to take that tone, he thought, and he had half a mind to tell him how nearly drowned he *had* been!

For that matter Mother did not seem too pleased at the interruption either. "You surely don't approve of his bathing by himself!" she said to Daddy. "Suppose he got caught in the weeds. In some places the river's thick with them, and even if he could swim, you know what Tom's like!"

"Yes," said Daddy playfully, "I know what he's like. Probably it was a naiad or an undine who enticed him in. I can't imagine anything less attractive overcoming his natural distaste for cold water."

Tom smiled, but only from a sense of duty. He knew that Daddy was alluding to an adventure he had had when he was smaller, and had then been foolish enough to talk about. He wouldn't be so foolish now, nor was he going to be drawn into the trap.

"*Was* it a water-nymph, Tom?" Daddy went on teasingly. But Tom merely smiled again and remained discreetly silent.

Mother, to the surprise of both of them, suddenly came to his rescue. "It's rather strange that you should want to encourage him, Edgar, considering the attitude you take up at other times about such things!"

Daddy looked taken aback—indeed quite startled. "How am I encouraging him?" he asked. "And what attitude do you mean?"

"Your usual attitude," Mother returned. "I understood that you disapproved of fairy tales and thought they did a lot of harm. I've certainly heard you say so."

"Only when people believe in them," Daddy answered mildly; "and Tom, we know, has long since passed that stage."

"Still," Mother persisted, "if he told you that he *had* seen a water-nymph you'd be annoyed with him."

Daddy did not reply, but he looked at Tom for sympathy, which the latter withheld. It served him jolly well right, Tom thought: perhaps he wouldn't be in such a hurry to butt in another time; and he met Daddy's gaze with serene and slightly derisive eyes.

25

This had the effect of making him come to his own assistance. "I don't quite grasp, my dear, the precise object of this attack. It can hardly be that you yourself have seen a water-sprite. At least, if you have, you've kept remarkably silent about it."

"Yes, that's what I mean," Mother said quietly. "It must be so comfortable to be able to feel like that."

"Like what?" Daddy asked, not looking too comfortable.

"To be so sure about everything that you can afford to be indulgent and ironical."

"But——" Daddy protested, half laughing.

"I don't mean about water-nymphs especially," Mother went on, "though they'll do as an example. They can't exist, we know, because their existence isn't recorded in scientific books and you yourself have neither photographed nor dissected one."

"Who's being ironical now?" Daddy asked meekly. "The scientist is as open to conviction as most people, I expect; and if he demands a little more evidence than some it's because it's his job not to take things on trust."

"It may be his job," Mother returned, "but if nothing was taken on trust life would be a very poor affair."

"Very," Daddy agreed. "I'm only suggesting that trustfulness may be combined with common sense—and that all witnesses aren't equally reliable."

The last words were intended for him, Tom supposed, and Mother perhaps thought so too, for she asked after the briefest pause: "What exactly do you mean by that?"

Daddy glanced up quickly. "But surely, my dear——!" he exclaimed in a tone of deprecation. Then, as Mother only waited, he gave a little shrug. "Let us put it this way then, for the sake of argument. If Doctor Macrory were to tell you that a water-nymph haunted the river, it would be a rather different thing, wouldn't it, than if the news came from Tom?"

"No, it wouldn't," answered Mother without hesitation; and since Daddy merely opened and closed his mouth soundlessly, while his eyes expressed a kind of wonder: "Why should I believe Doctor Macrory rather than Tom?" she asked sharply.

Daddy sighed. "That's not the point," he murmured. "It's not a question of veracity or inveracity. We'll suppose that neither of them would deliberately tell a lie. Still, there would remain several reasons for attaching more weight to Doctor Macrory's evidence than to Tom's. A: he has a trained mind and a trained eye, which Tom hasn't. B: neither his friends nor his enemies could describe him as imaginative. C: he's a shrewd and far from impressionable man, whereas Tom is only a small boy, and one, moreover, with a distinct taste for the marvellous."

"Yet Tom has very good sight," Mother interrupted before Daddy could get on to D, E, and F; "much better, I should think, than Doctor Macrory, who has to wear glasses. And we were talking about seeing things."

"Yes, yes," Daddy assented, at the same time taking up the newspaper in token of surrender. "Fortunately he hasn't seen anything in the present instance," he added, "so we may dismiss the argument as hypothetical."

Clearly this was funking it, and Tom guessed from Mother's face that she thought so too. At any rate she wasn't going to dismiss the argument, nor abandon her advantage. "You'll admit, I suppose, that William Blake was a genius?" she said; and Tom could see, though he didn't know why, that if Daddy answered "Yes", he was going to place himself in a corner.

Yet he made the admission: he seemed to have reached a stage when he would admit nearly anything; and immediately afterwards he put a question of his own. "Much as we might like to regard Tom as a genius, we haven't up to the present found any particular grounds for doing so, have we?"

He said it quite pleasantly, and even with a conciliatory smile which included not only Mother but Tom. Nevertheless, it was an error in judgement, and he might have known that. Tom knew it at all events; for whether Mother believed he was a genius or not, she certainly wasn't going to allow other people to deny that he was. "I'm not talking about Tom," she said, but in a way which plainly showed she was thinking about him. "I'm talking of somebody whom you admit to be a man of genius, yet whose every statement both you and Doctor Macrory would dis-

27

miss as absurd—too absurd even to be worth a moment's consideration.''

This was odd, and Tom couldn't help popping in with "Who was William Blake?" though directly afterwards he remembered, for they had learned one of his poems at school last term—*Tyger Tyger burning bright*. And straightway he ceased to pay attention to Daddy and Mother, and began instead to say the poem softly over to himself.

> " *Tyger Tyger burning bright*
> *In the forests of the night,*
> *What immortal hand or eye*
> *Could frame thy fearful symmetry?*''

He liked it better than any other poem he knew. . . . Except perhaps *Ulalume*—and he repeated what he knew of that also, but as he had never learned it he could only remember little bits here and there. . . .

When he once more listened to what Daddy and Mother were saying, it was to find that the conversation had lapsed into trivial remarks about roses and William, so he brought it round again to the other William by a variation on his original question. "What was William Blake like?" he asked.

He was really curious to know, or at least to hear some of the statements which Daddy and Doctor Macrory would have dismissed as absurd. He had an inkling that perhaps *he* wouldn't find them absurd; Mother evidently didn't; though it was never so easy to tell what Mother thought as it was to tell what Daddy thought—or at least to be sure that in the meantime she wouldn't have thought something else.

It was Daddy who answered him, with just the slightest lifting of one eyebrow. "He was very like your mother in his opinion of scientists," Daddy said cautiously. "In other respects a good deal of light is thrown by the only recorded remark of Mrs. Blake: 'You know, dear, the first time you saw God was when you were four years old, and he put his head to the window and set you a-screaming.'''

There was a mewing at the window at that moment, and Tom

28

turned round quickly. But it was only Henry, and he got up to let him in. He opened the window, and of course Henry entered as slowly as possible, just to keep him standing there. It was easy to see that he was doing it on purpose, for he paused when he was half-way through, and made no further movement.

"Come on, hurry up!" cried Tom impatiently, giving him a push.

Henry at this actually uttered a word which shocked Tom, even though he didn't quite catch it. At the same time he alighted on the floor with an extraordinary thud.

"Good gracious!" Mother exclaimed. "You'd think he was a ton weight!"

"It's his sins," said Tom darkly. "It's a wonder he can jump at all."

He came back to the table and for a minute or two sat wrapped in thought. "Daddy!" he said abruptly, and then paused to think again. But Daddy was staring at him, so he completed his sentence. "Did God really look in at the Blakes' window?"

"Never you mind about——" Mother began, but abruptly checked herself. And just as well, too! for he was sure she had nearly said "Never you mind about God." She changed it, however, to "Never you mind about the Blakes. You're slow enough as it is."

Tom glanced round at the clock on the chimney-piece, for it was his music morning; but there was loads of time, so he made a secret sign to Daddy to answer his question. But Daddy wouldn't: he might argue with Mother, but he would never go against her in practice. For this reason it was much more useful to have Mother on your side than Daddy; in fact it was no use having Daddy at all unless you had Mother too, though if you had Mother without Daddy you very soon got him also.

Tom pondered over this, and also over the Blake family, while he pursued an intermittent course with his breakfast. His progress was slow; he was invariably the last to finish. And this wasn't because he had a large appetite. It was because he couldn't help stopping to think. With the consequence, Mother said, that meals, which for other persons were intervals of relaxation, for her were the most arduous tasks of the day. Instead of enjoying them she had to spend her whole time in waking Tom up and goading him into swallowing each mouthful: he had been less trouble in the days when he was fed with a spoon.

This of course was an exaggeration. Mother was very prone to that. Really she exaggerated most frightfully, though she objected when Tom did. And what was the use of asking him why he couldn't be like Daddy and talk and eat at the same time? She knew it was Uncle Stephen he was like, not Daddy. Anyhow, the way she put it made it sound as if Daddy talked with his mouth full.

He thought of the barge and wondered how far up the river it had got by now. He thought of his accident, and the narrow escape he had had. It grew narrower and narrower the more he considered it, until at last it seemed to him that only by a miracle had he been plucked from the closing jaws of Death. He felt a strong desire to describe the miracle, but on the other hand he was sure that it would make Mother more nervous than ever about his bathing in the river—might make her definitely forbid him to bathe there again, which at present she had forgotten to do. . . .

"Tom!" Mother cried so suddenly that he jumped. Hastily he swallowed a mouthful of toast, with the result that he choked and then had a fit of coughing. But instead of being sorry for what she had done, Mother only said: "Well, I haven't time to sit here all morning!" and got up from the table. Daddy followed her, which left Tom all alone; so he got up too, though he hadn't really finished, and very likely would feel faint and ill through starvation long before lunch time. But it was their fault: he wasn't going to sit on eating by himself. He collected his school books from the study, got his cap from the cloakroom, and went out.

The sun was much hotter now than it had been before breakfast, and the shadows were deeper. The wind, too, had died, and the dew had been sucked up from the grass. Henry had come out, and with his back turned to Tom was sitting on the path under the study window, playing.

Or at least he seemed to be playing—a quiet and absorbing game—so absorbing that he did not look round or stop at the sound of footsteps. What was this game? Tom felt bound to investigate. It *looked* harmless enough, though of course you never could tell. Henry was playing it with his right paw only— giving little taps and scratches at the gravel. Suddenly Tom became intensely interested, for he saw that each of these seemingly careless scratches left a mark on the path. Henry wasn't playing: he was drawing!

Tom stood perfectly still, while Henry continued to draw, though he must have known he was being watched. Perhaps, however, he knew who was watching him, for he had ears so sharp that he could hear a leaf falling or a butterfly passing behind him, and might easily have recognized Tom's tread. He gave a final touch, and, still without looking up, slowly rose and pretended to yawn.

But Tom took no notice of him; he was too intent on something else; and this something was a figure traced there on the black gravel path. Just a few simple lines, yet certainly a diagram; and Tom stared down at it. Not that there was any need to stare, for it could not have been more clear to him if it had been drawn in thin lines of flame. There flashed across his mind the recollection of a description Daddy had once read to him of certain horses who had been trained to solve arithmetical problems by tapping out the answers with their hoofs. They were German horses, and Daddy had said there was probably some trickery behind the experiments, though the most careful observation had failed to detect any. But Henry hadn't been trained: this was his own work. One thing was sure; he must get Daddy and Mother to look at this marvel immediately. And then, as if he had spoken aloud, and just as he was on the point of rushing back to the house, the figure was suddenly broken and scattered into a shower of gravel, while Henry's powerful hind feet scored it across and across, sending the small grains flying.

Tom was raging with him. He had destroyed the whole thing and now nobody would believe in it. "Bad cat!" he said angrily, but Henry began to rub against his legs, arching and lowering his

31

back. He pressed his sleek flattened head into the hollows above Tom's rather meagre calves, where the skin was bare above his stockings; he curled his elastic body half round them, and from the suddenness and lavishness of these caresses Tom immediately felt sure that a third person must have appeared upon the scene. He was right, for there was Mother, leaning out of her bedroom window, and of course she wanted to know what he was doing.

He wasn't doing anything, Tom replied; adding that Henry had just made a drawing on the path. Yet for some reason this answer did not satisfy Mother, nor did she show the least interest in the drawing. On the contrary, she told him that he was a very naughty boy, and that if he didn't start for school at once she wouldn't allow him to go out in the afternoon. Also she said that she was going to tell Daddy. As if that mattered! Besides, she never did tell—at least not things of that sort, things that might get him into a row. And anyhow he was going to tell Daddy about the drawing himself.

But here was William, and Tom realized that he must be later than he had thought. He would have to run, and even then he wouldn't be in time. He couldn't possibly be. Yet it wasn't his fault, for if he had had a bicycle he could have done it easily. Practically everybody else in the school had a bicycle: boys who were far younger than he was. Pascoe had had one for nearly two years, and Brown was allowed to drive his father's car. At least he said he was, and even though, coming from Brown, this was almost certain to be untrue, still it proved——

CHAPTER IV

I t proved nothing at all, Tom knew, though he had used it as an argument when trying to make Daddy see how far less indulgent he was than the average parent. The argument had failed, because Daddy seemed to have no wish to resemble the average parent, though he had often expressed a desire for an average son. And Mother was nearly as bad. Tom had pointed out to her how much less freedom he had than other boys; Pascoe, for example, who was allowed to do all sorts of things; Pascoe's father had complete confidence in him. But it appeared that Mother had complete confidence in Pascoe also: *he* didn't go about dreaming; he was practical and reliable; the kind of boy who was bound to get on in the world. . . .

Tom jogged along the dusty road, growing hotter and hotter, till at the end of half a mile, just when he should have been getting his second wind, he found himself with no wind left at all, and relapsed into a walk.

On most mornings he got a seat in the car and was deposited at the school gates, but on Tuesdays and Thursdays he had a music lesson with Mr. Holbrook at nine o'clock, which was too early for Daddy, so he had to make the journey on foot. He could do it comfortably if he left the house at twenty past eight, but something nearly always cropped up to delay him. And Mr. Holbrook, though he usually was late himself, now and then was punctual, on which occasions he expected Tom to be punctual too. This was unreasonable, perhaps, but Mr. Holbrook wasn't a reasonable person—quite the opposite. On the other hand he was a very pleasant person—particularly if he happened to like you—for he had favourites, and you precious soon found out whether you were one of them or not. Tom saw nothing wrong in this; he was sure that in Mr. Holbrook's position he would have had favourites himself: indeed, what was the use of liking people if you didn't show them that you liked them. Besides, it made everything more lively and interesting. You never knew beforehand what kind of lesson you were going to get. That is, if you happened to *be* a favourite: the others, he supposed, knew well enough. In Tom's case it meant that he was allowed to choose his own songs—except when he chose something too difficult—and also that quite often after school he was invited to Mr. Holbrook's house to listen to the gramophone. Mr. Holbrook would put on records and tell him about singers and operas (he went abroad every year to listen to operas; that was how he spent his holidays), and he would describe them, and play little bits on the piano, and it was all highly enjoyable. Tom had never heard a real opera—in fact he had only once been inside a theatre, when Mother had taken him to see *Peter Pan*—but through these fugitive glimpses, in which Mr. Holbrook supplied the scenery and the story and piano impressions of the orchestra, while famous tenors, sopranos, and baritones sang the principal airs, he had acquired a remarkable erudition, and an enthusiasm which nearly equalled Mr. Holbrook's own.

A most agreeable feature of it, too, was that being Mr. Holbrook's "star artist" aroused jealousy in nobody. *Nor* antagonism. Tom had felt very doubtful before the last Christmas concert, for instance, of the prudence of standing up to sing "Voi che sapete" in Italian. It had seemed to him that it would be wiser to sing it in English. But when he had revealed these timidities to Mr. Holbrook, the latter had grown so impatient that argument became impossible. And as it surprisingly turned out, he need not have been afraid; nobody—not even Brown—had accused him of putting on side. On the contrary, for the two nights of the concert—which was always repeated and always crowded with parents and visitors—he had found himself, if not exactly popular, at least an important person; and though by the beginning of the next term everybody else had forgotten this, it had been very pleasant while it lasted. Since then, having heard them first on the gramophone, he had learned two other Italian airs—Tosti's "Serenata", and the "Spirto gentil" from *La Favorita*. Daddy, who didn't really care for music at all, wondered why Mr. Holbrook couldn't teach him sensible songs, and even Mother, who used to sing herself but had lately given it up, thought the last choice a little odd. Fortunately it had the advantage of an easy accompaniment, she discovered; for at home Mother played his accompaniments, though Tom could sing better when Mr. Holbrook played.

These meditations were interrupted rudely by a sudden shout behind him. "Hi! Skinny!"

Tom, who would have liked to take no notice, wheeled round at the offensive name.

34

A boy on a bicycle had ridden out on to the road through a garden gate—a large and burly boy with red cheeks, smiling mouth, dark hair and dark eyes. At least he seemed to Tom large and burly, though actually he was only thirteen. But Brown was an out-sized thirteen and much the biggest boy in the school. Mother thought him handsome, she was always praising his looks: Tom thought that if he had been differently dressed and carrying a flat basket he would have looked exactly like a butcher's boy. He was not only big, but he was as strong as a bull, had legs as thick as columns, and was forever wanting you to feel his muscles. "Hello, Brown!" he replied.

Brown zig-zagged slowly on for a few yards and then hopped off his bicycle. "Done your algebra?" he asked.

"Yes," said Tom. "Have you?"

Brown walked beside him, still smiling. "Well, as a matter of fact I haven't," he said ingratiatingly. "And the worst of it is, I've promised to play cricket. So I wonder if you'd let me copy yours? Do you mind?"

Tom hesitated, while his face grew distinctly glum. His algebra was invariably wrong, and he knew from past experience that identical mistakes in two separate copies of work were apt to lead to further investigation—particularly when one of the copies happened to be Brown's. But Brown, though perfectly aware of the reluctance, was not an easy person to discourage. "No," said Tom at last, in a tone of resignation, "I don't mind."

Brown ignored the resignation. "Thanks awfully, Skinny," he said. "I'll give you yours back in plenty of time. You're going to Holbrook, aren't you?"

"Yes," said Tom.

"Well, I'll give you a lift as far as the cricket field if you get up behind."

Tom still hung back, however; not that a lift wouldn't be most useful, but because he felt he had been weak in the matter of the algebra. "I say, Brown," he began uncomfortably.

"Yes," said Brown, waiting.

"Nothing," Tom muttered.

Slowly he unfastened his schoolbag and produced an exercise

35

book. Brown, with much more expedition, seized it and stuffed it into his jacket pocket. "Thanks," he said again—this time rather carelessly—and immediately remounted his bicycle. "Jump up," he cried, and Tom got on to the backstep.

Brown to impress him began pedalling like mad. The road was uphill, and though the hill was gradual it was long. Tom could see Brown's face getting redder and redder; he could hear him breathing, and he could even feel the heat exuding through his thick body. "Silly ass!" he reflected, yet not without appreciation of Brown's powers. It couldn't be easy to carry a double load up that hill.

When they reached the playing-fields he got down and Brown too dismounted, trying hard not to appear puffed. Together they walked over the beech-shadowed grass, Brown wheeling his bicycle and Tom thinking of the algebra. Thanks to the lift, however, he was now in no hurry; indeed he had several minutes to spare. This reminded him of his grievance against Daddy. Besides, if he had had a bicycle he wouldn't have met Brown.

He wished he could get his exercise book back again. There was nothing to hinder Brown from doing the sums himself, except that he wanted to play cricket. "I say," he once more began dubiously. "Are you going to write them out in ink?"

Since Miss Jimpson insisted upon ink—as a precaution against last-minute copying—Brown merely gave him a half-compassionate look.

"Because," Tom went on more firmly, "if you are, I hope you'll be careful. You know the row she kicks up about blots, and the paper's so thin you can't scrape them out. It's as thin as gauze is."

"As thin as blazes, you mean," Brown rejoined light-heartedly; but he didn't promise to take any precautions.

That was like him, once he'd got the thing, and Tom's annoyance increased. "Did you bring me those stamps?" he asked suddenly, for Brown had turned aside and was proceeding towards the bicycle shed. "What stamps?" he inquired, disappearing into the shed.

He knew very well what stamps; Tom had reminded him

about them every day that week. He followed him now, though without much hope. "The stamps you owe me," he said, "the two Mauritius stamps."

Brown looked surprised. "Mauritius stamps?" he repeated, as if he had never heard of Mauritius stamps before. Then he added calmly: "I don't know what you're talking about." And having fixed his bicycle, he emerged from the shed, still followed by Tom.

"You do!" Tom exclaimed indignantly. "I gave you three Cape of Good Hopes, and one of them was unused."

"That's because it was a forgery," Brown returned quickly. "You can be sent to jail for passing forged stamps; it's just the same as passing forged banknotes."

"You can't," said Tom. "And it isn't a forgery. If you think it is why won't you give it back to me?"

"Because I don't want to get you into trouble," Brown answered kindly.

Tom's face darkened. Pascoe had warned him to have no dealings with Brown, but Pascoe was always warning you about something, and always so sure he was right that it only made you more determined not to take his advice. "You promised me two Mauritius stamps," he repeated gloomily. "You promised to bring them the next day."

"That was before I knew you had committed a crime," Brown explained. "Anyway, I haven't got any Mauritius stamps."

"Then you told a lie," said Tom.

"I didn't. I said I'd bring you two Mauritius stamps—perhaps."

Brown was looking him straight in the eyes with the utmost candour, and Tom knew he could do nothing. "You didn't say 'perhaps'," he muttered.

"I did. You mayn't have heard me, but that's because you weren't listening. I said it like this." And Brown repeated the sentence, yet even now, though he strained his ears, Tom could not catch the last word.

"It was the same as a lie," he declared. "And you're the same as a thief."

Brown suddenly grabbed him by the wrist. "Look here, Skinny," he observed softly, while at the same time he screwed Tom's arm round till he was completely helpless, "all this sounds to me uncommonly like cheek."

"You're a cad," Tom gasped, twisting his body sideways to ease the strain on his arm. "You attacked me when I wasn't expecting it."

Instantly Brown released him. "Expect it now," he said, "because I'm going to attack you again."

Tom hastily retreated—an instinctive precaution which Brown's immobility made all the more ignominious. He simply stood there smiling. "I'm not going to attack you, Skinny," he said; "you're beneath it. And besides, you were quite obliging about the algebra. See you later."

With that he strolled off, whistling, while Tom gazed after him. He would never get his stamps, he knew, and he never would be able to retaliate. Words meant nothing to Brown, and physical force was out of the question. He couldn't stand up to Brown for two minutes, and even if he had the courage to attempt it there wouldn't really be a fight: Brown would merely twist his arm again, or sit on him till he surrendered. It was queer that Brown should be so invulnerable, and in most ways successful, because actually he was a stupid person. He had never been able to get beyond the third form and he was always at the bottom of that. But he was cunning, and you couldn't exactly say he knew nothing, since he knew everything that you weren't supposed to know. Really he was as stupid out of school as he was in it, yet for some reason he was successful—and popular—more popular than Tom, and infinitely more than Pascoe. It was hard to understand why.

Suddenly he remembered that the school clock had struck while Brown was twisting his arm. This was annoying, for it meant that though he had arrived in tons of time he was none the less going to be late. There was precisely the same rush and fuss as if he had only arrived that moment. He tore on to the school, clattered up the stairs, and hurried down a passage. He could hear the piano thundering and crashing, which meant that

Mr. Holbrook must have been waiting a good while. He opened a door at the extreme end of the passage, and entered.

"Late, of course," Mr. Holbrook remarked without ceasing to play. "Out of breath, of course. Too hot to do anything for the next quarter of an hour. Wasting my time, wasting your own time, wasting your father's money. If you have any excuses don't make them. Take off your jacket; sit down in that chair; and don't move or speak till you can do so without panting."

These words came in a kind of sing-song through the music, so that Tom immediately knew it was all right. He followed Mr. Holbrook's instructions to the letter, except that he said he was sorry.

He didn't know what Mr. Holbrook was playing, but he liked it. Moreover, it was very pleasant in the music-room, which seemed particularly cool and shadowy after the bright sunshine outside. And Mr. Holbrook wasn't in the least like Brown. The windows were wide open, and Tom sat quiet as a mouse.

Mr. Holbrook played for perhaps five minutes, but at last he got up, lit a cigarette, and motioned to Tom, who perched himself on the edge of the music-stool and plodded through a few scales and exercises. He was really no good at the piano, because the drudgery of practising bored him, and he shirked it whenever he could. Mr. Holbrook knew this as well as he did: in fact Tom at the piano bored them both. He wondered if Mr. Holbrook was supposed to smoke cigarettes while he was teaching: he didn't believe he was, though he always did it. Tom's hands looked very brown on the black and white keyboard, and in spite of the cooling process his fingers stuck to the notes. After a very unsatisfactory performance Mr. Holbrook sighed, pushed him off the music-stool without a word, reseated himself, and played three or four chords. "Sing," he said, and Tom, standing beside him, began to sing.

This was the part of the lesson he enjoyed. He even enjoyed singing scales and exercises nearly as much as songs; and he sang up the scale now, while Mr. Holbrook thrummed chords in unison. The treble voice sounded through the room, filling it, clear and fresh as a blackbird's. It gave Tom pleasure; it gave

Mr. Holbrook pleasure—you could tell that from his face, and also from the way he played the accompaniment. This indeed was why Tom loved singing to him. He liked singing to other people too, but not in the same way; and there were a few people, such as Daddy, whom he couldn't sing to at all unless he forgot they were listening. Nearly without a break Mr. Holbrook's chords and arpeggios dissolved into the opening bars of a melody, his eyes slid round for a moment towards the singer, while he gave a little backward jerk of his head, the customary signal.

Spirto gentil, ne' sogni miei brillasti un dì,
ma ti perdei, fuggi dal cor, mentita speme,
larve d'amor, larve d'amor, fuggite insieme, larve d'amor!

It was a curious, and probably to Mr. Holbrook quaint, example of unconscious mimicry, for every shade and accent, every rise and fall, every lingering glissando, even the plaintive twang on the "ahimè—ahimè!" before the repetition of the tune, was a faithful echo of the Caruso record. The emotion, the tone, the expression, were in fact to Tom simply a *part* of the tune, as were the words, of whose meaning he had only a loose and general impression derived from Mr. Holbrook's free paraphrase. It was not Donizetti's "Spirto gentil" he sang, but Caruso's interpretation of it, and he would have found it more difficult to alter that interpretation than to learn an entirely new air.

Nevertheless, the emotion remained, etherealized, rarefied, translated out of actuality into terms of pure music. "Bravo!" cried Mr. Holbrook, smiling, and then repressing the smile. He played a few more notes, softly and low down in the bass, before he added to himself: "It's a pity."

40

But Tom had heard him, and Mr. Holbrook, divining that he had heard, wheeled round on the music-stool. "I only mean that it's a pity there isn't more of you," he said: a remark to which Tom made no reply.

Mr. Holbrook smiled at him again, and the smile seemed to come mostly from his round horn-rimmed and very expressive spectacles. He continued to gaze at Tom, and then with a kind of impatient gesture he ran his hands through a thick shock of reddish hair, making it stick straight up till it resembled a field of corn at sunset. "I see you don't understand me," he went on. "It's not your height I'm referring to: it's your shape, your build, the skeleton inside you. That won't alter, and it's what is so important. Do you know what you ought to look like? A small prize-fighter. And you don't, do you?"

"No," Tom replied.

"Well then," returned Mr. Holbrook half-petulantly, "we needn't talk about it."

But it was he who had begun the talking, and he oughtn't to leave it just like that. "Why?" Tom ventured after a pause. "I mean, why do you want me to look like a prize-fighter?" He tried not to show it, nevertheless he couldn't help feeling discouraged and disappointed. He supposed Brown would have been more to Mr. Holbrook's taste.

Mr. Holbrook said: "You've got it all wrong. I'm only thinking of your voice—the voice that is going to come when your present voice breaks. There should be lots of room for it—the more room the better."

"Perhaps I'll get bigger," Tom suggested more hopefully.

"Of course you'll get bigger," Mr. Holbrook declared. "You're quite big enough," he added inconsequently.

"I'm not," said Tom. "I've only grown an inch in the last year."

"An inch is plenty," said Mr. Holbrook, "though two might be better—particularly if they were in the right direction." He described a circle in the air, indicating the direction he meant. Then he laughed. "I don't believe you do understand me. This is what I mean. You've got a voice, and a sense of rhythm, and

41

what is very much rarer, a sense of pitch. That's why you don't sing your notes on either the upper or the lower edge of them, but bang in the middle. And certainly you've got the temperament. All that's lacking is the chest measurement, lungs of leather, and vocal chords of I don't know what, but apparently something only to be found in Italy. It doesn't matter now, but unfortunately a boy's voice is only at its best for about a year or eighteen months, and yours was at its best six months ago. With any luck you'll be all right for the concert next Christmas, but I'm afraid that must be your last appearance. I'm not going to let you force your voice and ruin it. At the first sign of strain you stop singing. . . . And now——"

The lesson continued: certainly there was no sign of strain at present. In the midst of it, and unexpectedly as usual, the bell clanged out its tiresome summons. Mr. Holbrook took no notice of it except to twitch his nose. Tom, for his part, was quite willing to stay on: Pemby might grumble, as had often happened before, but he couldn't do anything. Still, when they came to a pause, he thought he'd better mention that the bell had gone.

"I know—I know," said Mr. Holbrook impatiently. "You don't imagine I'm deaf! We ought really to change our hour, only I suppose you like to be free in the afternoons. We can't discuss it now at any rate. Run along, and if Mr. Pemberton says anything unreasonable tell him that I kept you."

CHAPTER V

When he entered the classroom, Pemby, who was Mr. Pemberton the headmaster, had finished calling the roll. He glanced up, said "Barber—music-lesson", and put a tick opposite Tom's name. Tom sat down beside Pascoe, in the back row, near the door.

It was an English lesson: they were doing Elizabeth's reign; and Mr. Pemberton, embarking on a favourite subject, proceeded to give an account of the Elizabethan theatre. He spoke of Marlowe and of Shakespeare; of the strange fashion dramatists had in those days of working on a play anonymously and in collaboration; of Stratford-on-Avon, and of boy-actors. He seemed quite keen about it all, and though his enthusiasm was not nearly so personal and catching as was Mr. Holbrook's about operas, Tom was interested.

But presently there came a push from Pascoe's knee, accompanied by a whispered: "Did you bring him?"

Pascoe was a sturdily built, intelligent-looking boy, with tow-coloured hair, an unusually wide space between his blue eyes, a small prim mouth, and an expression of innocent severity. Tom, still listening to Mr. Pemberton, merely shook his head.

"Why?" Pascoe whispered. At the same time he drew from his pocket a small cardboard box with a perforated lid, and opened it under the desk.

Tom took no notice. Anyway he knew what was in the box without looking.

Next moment he got a much more violent nudge, this time in the ribs and from Pascoe's elbow. "Shut up," he muttered, moving farther off.

But he couldn't help giving just one glance through the tail of his eye. On the desk in front of Pascoe was a large smooth green caterpillar, obviously an athlete, and in the pink of condition. Tom felt the sting of temptation. The caterpillar raised his head to have a look round, and Pascoe hissed: "I bet he beats your champion."

The caterpillar stared Tom straight in the face, as much as to say: "There now!" but still he would not yield. Only he watched, which was perhaps much the same thing.

The caterpillar, with undulating back, proceeded to explore his new surroundings, and Tom couldn't deny that he was a very fine specimen. Secretly, too, he had begun to feel doubts about the champion, who yesterday had seemed distinctly out of form. Maybe it was only that he was overtrained, though Pascoe had

43

hinted that he was approaching his chrysalis days. Tom's hand stole to his pocket.

The opportunity was golden—at any rate as golden as you could expect in the middle of class. For Mr. Pemberton, blind as a bat always, was at present gazing out of the window, lost in the tragic fate of Kit Marlowe. His pupils, respecting his reverie, had begun to busy themselves with such soundless occupations as noughts-and-crosses and the folding of paper darts. Tom opened his cardboard box and tumbled the champion, a black "Hairy Willie" of the name of Charles, out on to the desk.

Immediately Charles curled himself into a tight ring and pretended to be dead. Pascoe sniffed contemptuously. "He's a funk," he whispered. "Anyway, he's done: I knew he couldn't last."

"He's not done," Tom whispered back. "He's resting. It's because it's so hot, and he's handicapped with all that fur. Yours is naked."

The green caterpillar, having now reached a sunken china inkpot at the top of the desk, was bending down over its dark and mysterious well. Tom was instantly reminded of the story of Narcissus, but Pascoe said: "Gracious, he's drinking the ink!" and hurriedly removed him to a place of safety. He drew a chalk line on the desk opposite Tom, and another one opposite himself. This was the racecourse, and the distance between the lines was about two feet.

"What's your's name?" Tom whispered.

"James," whispered Pascoe.

Tom was impressed. "That's queer," he said, but Pascoe, who was sometimes rather slow at seeing things, did not grasp the significance.

"It means that they're both of royal blood," Tom whispered. "Stuarts." He lifted Charles Stuart and set him on his chalk mark. Pascoe's James was already on the other chalk mark, held back, straining on the leash as it were. For the races were always now cross races: that is to say, Charles's starting point was James's winning post, and vice versa. This had been found to be the best plan, and the competitors might be guided on a straight path by their owners. Pencils were used for the purpose, though pushing was strictly barred. Otherwise, as experience had proved, the race in moments of excitement was apt to degenerate into a kind of table-hockey—particularly towards the finish.

"You're not to push," Tom warned.

"*You're* not to push," Pascoe retorted sharply.

Then both breathed a simultaneous "Go!" and their eyes grew round with suppressed eagerness.

Charles and James, probably filled with despair, started off at top speed. After proceeding for some inches, however, in this reckless fashion, it apparently dawned on them that their lives were not in danger. Their pace slackened; they sniffed the air; presently they paused to consider what all the fuss was about. Where were they? Charles and James raised questing heads— James, no doubt, seeking the green cold smoothness of cabbage leaves; Charles the darker aromatic shade of nasturtiums. But there were no cabbages, no nasturtiums, only a deeply scored and ink-splashed wooden desk. Charles and James were temporarily discouraged. Still, beyond this there *must* be cabbages and nasturtiums—soft damp brown earth and a green twilight where one could rest and eat and sleep in peace. Meanwhile there was an arid desert to be crossed—yellow, dry, unknown—possibly dangerous, and certainly unpleasant. Nor could they proceed with their customary freedom. Ever and anon, when they attempted to strike out a more promising trail, a bar of wood descended out of the sky and pushed them back. To Charles the experience was not new, though he had never been able to explain it. Still, he had traversed this desert before—whether in reality or in a nightmare was uncertain. To James the adventure was entirely novel, and the first time the pole barred his progress he attempted to climb it. But only to be shaken off, while Tom whispered indignantly: "You jerked him four inches at least," and hastily drew a new winning post for James.

"I didn't," Pascoe glared, but there was no time to argue, for just then James and Charles met.

This was bad management perhaps, though who could have thought it would have mattered! And James indeed would have

45

passed by had not Charles prevented him. Charles hesitated, reared up, blocked the path, and finally, yielding to a delirious and unsportsmanlike impulse, embraced James. So, at least, Tom said: Pascoe said he attacked him. Whatever the motive, the effect was disastrous, for James immediately turned round and hurried back as fast as he could to his starting place. A fierce altercation ensued—recriminations, denials, threats—in the midst of which Mr. Pemberton awoke out of historical reverie to the fact that something illicit was going on at the back of the room. So did everybody else, and craned round to have a look; but Mr. Pemberton breathed "S—sh!" and raised a hand for silence. In the hush that followed he advanced a few steps on tip-toe, peering shortsightedly at the offenders, who instantly, by some mysterious telepathic warning, became aware of what was happening. They were far too cunning, however, to make a movement, for they knew much better than Pemby did the range of his vision, and that from his present distance he couldn't possibly see James and Charles. But they looked up in innocent surprise when, after continuing to peer vainly, he suddenly stretched out a long forefinger of accusation. "Pascoe and Barber; Barber and Pascoe. Always the same pair: gabbling away like two old market-women—distracting the attention of the other boys—turning the hours of fruitful study into hours of unprofitable gossip. Pascoe and Barber will each bring me to-morrow morning the first part of *The Rime of the Ancient Mariner* written out neatly in ink."

So that was that—eighty-two lines, as Tom despondently noted after a stealthy reference to his poetry book.

And the morning dragged on, growing ever more close and sultry, till by twelve o'clock it had become positively breathless. Everybody felt it: all the windows were opened wide; but the air that drifted in might have been coming from a furnace. Three more classes to go; then two; then at last only one. . . .

It was in this final session that Tom—that shining light of scholarship—was obliged to make an ignominious descent from the first form to the third. He hated this—hated being shoved

46

among a lot of kids—and wished he could leave out maths altogether. What was the use of wasting time over subjects in which he never made the least progress!

Over the third form Miss Jimpson presided, and with the exception of Brown it consisted of boys younger than Tom—several of them two years younger. But Brown was a permanent adornment, and he never would have been promoted even as high as the third if it hadn't been that at the age of thirteen he couldn't very well be left among infants of eight or nine. Tom knew that Miss Jimpson longed to get rid of Brown, and looked forward to next term, when he would have to leave because he would then be fourteen. His placidity, his imperviousness to either reproaches or sarcasm, and more particularly his habit of lounging back in his seat with his hands in his pockets, got on her nerves and had an effect upon the whole class. More than once she had lost her temper and referred openly to the shamefulness of Brown's position. But. Brown had only smiled pleasantly, and now she ignored him as much as possible. Brown indeed was perfectly content with his position, which he knew would be reversed the moment the bell rang. He was neither ashamed, nor did he bear malice when Miss Jimpson ticked him off: but then, even when he was bullying smaller boys or fighting bigger ones, Tom had never seen Brown looking anything but good-natured. His mouth curled naturally into smiles, and he actually had dimples.

To-day Tom saw at once that Miss Jimpson was in no mood for nonsense. Both her appearance and her voice suggested that she found the temperature trying. She went straight to the blackboard, chalked up a geometrical figure, and instead of legitimate A's and B's and C's, proceeded to decorate it with K's and L's and M's, always a bad sign. To Tom, whose one hope was in his memory, the substitution of these different letters would, he knew, be fatal. Fortunately Miss Jimpson, instead of calling anybody up to the platform to do the proposition, gave it to the whole class to write out in their scribblers. So Tom put the A's and B's and C's back in their proper places and set to work.

But he had begun to feel very tired and drowsy. Perhaps it was the result of getting up so early after a pretty restless night, or perhaps it was just the effect of the day—not so much the heat really as the lack of air. Anyhow, he could hardly keep awake, let alone concentrate on geometry. Sleepy far-off sounds reached him through the open windows, and he couldn't help trying to disentangle them. The motionless shadow of a tree, silhouetted on the pale lemon-coloured wall beside him, made him think of trees. Slowly and unresistingly, as if drawn by an invisible thread, his spirit floated out through the window and over the tops of elms and beeches. Only the avenue did not come to an end at the school gates as it ought to have done, but stretched on and on till at last it reached the river. And from the river it reached the garden, where William was pottering about in his shirt-sleeves, and Henry was blinking in the sun. Tom saw Henry quite distinctly. He was sitting on the path, and presently he stretched out his right paw. Idly Tom drew with his pencil on the white sheet of paper before him what Henry was drawing on the black cinder path. Then his pencil seemed to stop of itself, and he saw that he had completed a figure. This was strange. It was very like the figure Henry himself had scratched that morning on the gravel, and not in the least like the figure on the blackboard. Yet he supposed it too could be made to prove something by the addition of A's and B's and C's.

Suddenly he jerked himself straight: he must actually have dozed off, for Miss Jimpson had her eyes fixed on him, and he knew that next moment she would call him up and discover that he had written only the first line of the proposition, and even that with the wrong letters. And how dark it had grown! Through a yellowish twilight he gazed at Miss Jimpson as some fascinated thrush might have gazed into the green eyes of an approaching Henry. Not that Miss Jimpson usually was alarming: indeed, Tom had always liked her—in spite of the fact that she taught mathematics. Yet now for some reason he had an acute feeling of suspense. It was as if Miss Jimpson had suddenly acquired talons and a ravening hunger, with a power to leap the whole length of the room and strike surely. Tom felt a kind of squeal rising in his throat, though he made no sound. And then—without remembering, without knowing, without thinking—he spoke the word. . . .

Instantly it happened. There was a sudden rushing noise, a blinding glare, and an explosion that shook the whole building. In the brief pandemonium that followed it was somebody else who screamed, not Tom. The wind whirled through the room, scattering papers, circling in a kind of vortex, as if trying madly to force an outlet through the ceiling. Crash! That was the blackboard—either the wind or Miss Jimpson had knocked it over. Tom sprang to his feet in an ecstasy of excitement. It seemed to him that the darkness was thickening at the centre, concentrating in a spiral twirling column, through which there blazed down two white eyes of fire. He called out something—or a voice called out near to him. Everybody had jumped up: the room was in a tumult. And next minute the whole thing was over, passing as abruptly as it had begun. But the behaviour of Brown was most astonishing of all. He was actually standing on the form, clapping his arms, like wings, against his sides, and making the most extraordinary bird cries.

"Brown!" called Miss Jimpson hysterically, and Brown himself seemed suddenly to awaken to realities. He hopped down from the form, looking for once, Tom thought, rather disconcerted. One of the smaller boys had begun to weep.

"Don't be silly, Donnelly!" snapped Miss Jimpson with a touch of temper. She had made a rapid recovery and now proceeded to control the situation. "It's all over," she declared, "whatever it was. A most unusual thing to happen—in this climate at any rate—but due of course to some atmospheric disturbance. A kind of small cyclone, I suppose, such as they often have in the tropics. I must say I've been half expecting something of the sort all morning. . . . And now, will the end boy in each row kindly gather up the papers on the floor. The others keep their seats."

Since Tom was not at the end of a row, he remained seated. Nevertheless, what had happened was so remarkable that Miss Jimpson did not insist on an immediate resumption of the lesson.

"Was it a cloudburst?" Saunderson asked, and Miss Jimpson

temporized. She glanced out of the window and saw only one heavy patch of cloud in a vividly blue sky.

"Well," she hesitated, "something of that sort, no doubt; though I don't suppose there can be a cloudburst without rain. But some kind of electrical disturbance at all events, which will probably clear the air. As I say, in tropical climates such sudden storms are quite common, and nobody thinks anything of them."

Miss Jimpson spoke in her most confident and businesslike tone, yet her explanation was not entirely successful, for little Donnelly piped up in a voice still broken by woe: "It was in the room. I saw it. It came right in through the window, and there was a man in it."

"A man in it?" Miss Jimpson repeated briskly. She hadn't the least notion what the child was talking about, but in the circumstances felt it better to reassure him. "What do you mean, Donnelly?" she went on, smiling, yet kind. "As I tell you, the whole disturbance was caused by the meeting of two opposed electric currents in the air. Surely you can understand that! Just like a railway collision. It was the collision which produced the flash, the thunder, and a sort of air storm. In fact it was just the same as an ordinary thunderstorm except that there was no rain. . . . And of course it happened more suddenly and was over more quickly."

"But I saw him," said Donnelly unhappily.

Miss Jimpson's voice grew a shade firmer. "You mustn't talk nonsense, Donnelly," she said. "There was no 'him', as you call it, to see. You were startled —as indeed we all were—and when one's frightened it's very easy to imagine things."

"I saw him," Donnelly repeated obstinately.

Miss Jimpson paused, and seemed on the point of losing patience, but laughed instead. "What was he like, Donnelly?" she asked. "I suppose you can describe him since you saw him so clearly. You'd better tell us, because none of the rest of us saw anything."

"Yes, I *can* describe him," Donnelly replied unexpectedly and rather defiantly. "He was all hunched up, with a cloud round him, and he had a dark cross face and white eyes."

50

"I saw him too," Tom felt tempted to put in; only everybody had begun to laugh at Donnelly, and Donnelly himself had turned as red as a poppy. Tom didn't want to be laughed at, and above all he didn't want to be questioned.

"I saw him too," he suddenly said.

Miss Jimpson looked at him coldly for about half a minute. Then she remarked: "In that case, Barber, you'd better write out for me fifty times: 'I must not try to make myself interesting by telling fibs.'"

"But I did," Tom persisted.

"A hundred times," said Miss Jimpson.

She was awful, Tom thought, and for two ticks he'd bring the whole thing back again.

Only, *had* he done it? There was the figure drawn on his scribbler; he looked down at it; but he had *said* something, too. It had been only a single word, and now it was gone: he couldn't remember anything except that it had begun with an A and that the next letter was Z. At least, he was almost sure it was. Az— Az—what? He mumbled over imaginary words beginning with "az", but knew they weren't right, and indeed nothing happened. *Could* it have been only his imagination? But in that case how had young Donnelly seen it? And he had seen more than Tom had!

Meanwhile, though he tried to avoid looking at her, he kept on catching Miss Jimpson's eye, and Miss Jimpson's eye was witheringly sceptical. She had no right to look at him like that, Tom felt, or to accuse him of telling lies; though somehow it was really her remark about trying to make himself interesting which rankled most. He never tried to make himself interesting—at least very seldom—and certainly he hadn't tried then, he hadn't wanted to speak at all. There she was again! Why couldn't she look at Donnelly? Just because Donnelly had said it first she didn't bother about him. Maybe, however, it was because she had repented and was filled with remorse. Only she didn't a bit look as if she was filled with remorse, though you never could tell, and Tom resolved to wait on after school to give her a chance of apologizing. Also of cancelling his imposition. He had now a

51

couple of impositions to do, and all because of Pascoe and Donnelly. Yes, he would wait.

On the other hand, he wanted very much to question Donnelly as to what exactly he *had* seen. Perhaps Donnelly would wait too—outside. He scribbled a brief note, folded it, wrote Donnelly's name on it, and passed it to the boy in front of him. Anxiously he watched the surreptitious progress of the note from hand to hand until finally it reached its destination. He watched Donnelly opening it and reading it. For a minute or so nothing happened. Then, to his intense surprise and indignation, Donnelly, instead of writing a reply, simply turned round and made a face at him. Tom was furious. That miserable little squirt, who blubbed every time he missed a question, and in winter came to school wrapped up in so many mufflers that he had practically to be unpacked! He felt a violent uprush of the most Brown-like impulses. He contorted his face into an expression of frightful pugnacity, but Donnelly seemed merely to find it funny and screwed up his face too. Then he nudged the boy next him, who turned round and grinned. Tom had only partly recovered from these insults when the bell rang.

With the first note of the clapper Miss Jimpson's head disappeared behind the raised lid of her desk, and it was not till the scuffling and noise of escaping pupils had died into silence that it emerged again. Then she gazed across the empty room in surprise. "What are you waiting for, Barber?" she asked.

It wasn't a very easy question to answer, and Tom's mumble failed to enlighten Miss Jimpson, who, moreover, betrayed no sign at all of wishing to apologize. "Come closer," she said. "I can't hear what you say."

So Tom got up, and in some confusion advanced to within a foot of the raised platform upon which were Miss Jimpson, her desk, and the blackboard.

"Come up here," Miss Jimpson said, "and don't look so scared —I shan't eat you."

Tom climbed the three steps and stood beside her. Still he did not speak, and Miss Jimpson, who was tying exercise books into a bundle, suddenly smiled at him. "Well," she asked, "what is it?"

Tom swallowed hastily. "I wasn't telling lies," he answered. "I did think I saw something."

Miss Jimpson looked at him calmly, and whether it was because school was over or not, she seemed much more approachable than before. Also, Tom thought, she looked rather pale and fagged, and a wisp of dark hair had come loose and fallen down over her left ear. "We all saw something," she presently observed. "We saw that it got quite dark for a few minutes, and we saw a flash of lightning."

"It was a part of the darkness," Tom told her.

Miss Jimpson unexpectedly placed her two hands on his shoulders, and her eyes were now bright and friendly. "Tell me this, Tom Barber," she said. "If Donnelly hadn't been scared out of his wits and imagined all that nonsense, would *you* have said a word?"

Tom was obliged to confess that he wouldn't.

"Well then?" pursued Miss Jimpson.

"All the same I did see it—think I saw it, I mean. . . . Smoky —with two eyes."

Miss Jimpson looked very hard into Tom's own two eyes before she answered. "This is very absurd. And especially coming from a comparatively big boy like you."

Tom did not deny its absurdity, and Miss Jimpson herself, after a brief reflection, appeared to recognize that that was hardly the point. "You really *weren't* telling fibs?" she resumed.

"No," said Tom.

Miss Jimpson once more pondered, and she looked rather nice while she was doing so: she was really quite pretty, Tom decided. "In that case, what do you suggest ought to be done about it?" she asked. "By me, I mean?"

Tom told her what he thought should be done. "I don't think I ought to get an imposition," he said.

"I don't think so either," Miss Jimpson agreed. "So we'll wipe that out."

53

"Thank you, Miss Jimpson," Tom replied. "Thank you very much."

Miss Jimpson laughed. She had finished tying up her bundle. "Let us hope there will be no more thunderstorms," she declared. "They seem to affect our nerves. We were all of us a little upset."

"Especially Brown," Tom couldn't help reminding her.

"Yes, Brown," Miss Jimpson echoed, frowning a little. She glanced at him questioningly, as if struck by a sudden suspicion. "I don't quite know *what* came over Brown," she murmured doubtfully.

But Tom's candour was apparent. "Neither did he," was all he answered.

Miss Jimpson looked relieved. "I thought at the time he didn't," she said; "otherwise I should have had to take more notice of it."

"Do you think——" Tom began, and then stopped. "They were bird screams he was making," he went on after a pause. "Like a macaw."

"A macaw!" Miss Jimpson repeated wonderingly.

"Yes—a kind of parrot."

But Miss Jimpson, for some unknown reason, now appeared to be less interested in Brown than in Tom himself, and it was upon him that her gaze was fixed in reflective scrutiny. "You're a very strange boy, Tom Barber," she murmured. "And I believe even much stranger than you allow anybody to suspect. Is that right?"

"I don't know," said Tom.

"What do they think about you at home?" Miss Jimpson continued. "Not that it matters much, because it's sure to be wrong."

"Why?" asked Tom, gravely.

"Oh, I don't know—except that it usually is. At any rate," she added, "I feel that a cup of tea is what we both need to restore us to perfect sanity. If you were to invite me I know I'd accept."

This frankness put Tom in a distinctly awkward position, and he blushed. "I'd like very much to invite you," he stammered.

54

"But you see I—I'm afraid I couldn't pay for you—nor even for myself."

"That *is* a difficulty," Miss Jimpson admitted. "Wait for me in the porch all the same. . . . I've only to put on a hat and won't keep you more than three minutes. But I simply *must* have a cup of tea, and I hate sitting in a teashop by myself."

CHAPTER VI

So five minutes later Tom and Miss Jimpson were walking down the road together under the lime trees. Miss Jimpson looked even nicer in her hat than she did without it: Tom felt quite pleased to be walking with her. Then he remembered that he ought to be on the outside of the pavement, and changed his position.

"Where are we going?" he inquired.

"I suppose to Nicholson's," Miss Jimpson thought. "It's the nearest place and probably at this hour we'll have it all to ourselves. The room upstairs is rather nice if you can get a table at the window; but I expect you've been there before."

"Only once," said Tom. "With Mr. Holbrook. . . . We had ices."

What a thing to say! He could have kicked himself. And he had said it in such a clear voice too—like somebody announcing a hymn. Miss Jimpson would think he was awful! Anybody would, for that matter! And covered with confusion, he determined that he wouldn't accept an ice even if she offered him one.

"We'll have ices," Miss Jimpson said. "That's a splendid idea, but I must have tea too."

It wasn't a splendid idea; it was the very reverse; yet if he told her now that he didn't care for ices it would be a lie. The whole thing had been spoiled just by that one unfortunate speech. "I didn't mean——" he protested.

"Here we are," Miss Jimpson said, not listening to him, but passing under the striped red-and-white awning into the shop, so that he could only follow her as she walked straight on through it and up the stairs at the back.

The stairs led to a bright sunny room on the first floor, containing half a dozen small white-clothed tables; and, to add to his embarrassment, the very first thing he saw was Brown seated at one of these. He was indeed the only person there, and Miss Jimpson nodded to him and smiled, while Brown smiled back and stared at them, though without ceasing to absorb refreshment. It was like him to come here and gorge himself in solitude. Tom could see from the two empty dishes that it was his third ice he was finishing. He had always more money than anybody else, and he spent practically the whole of it on grub. Miss Jimpson passed on to a table placed in the bow-window, and as Tom was following her, Brown stuck out a treacherous foot over which he came to grief.

"Sorry, Skinny!" Brown whispered, abstracting the last remains of his ice with a red and flexible tongue; but Tom, whose face was now the colour of Brown's tongue, ignored the apology and hurried after Miss Jimpson.

He sat down opposite her and refrained from glancing round, though he could hardly help doing so when he heard Brown pushing back his chair. He listened to his footsteps crossing the room, and a moment later clattering down the stairs.

Well, Brown was gone—that was one comfort—and he breathed more freely. All the same, he wished Brown hadn't been there at all, for he knew the sort of story he would make of it. He would accuse Tom of being Miss Jimpson's pet and of sucking up to her: it would be all over the school to-morrow, with additions and embellishments of the kind that Brown thought funny. If he did try to be funny, Tom determined that he would jolly well remind him of the ass he had made of himself, standing up on the form flapping his wings. You would have thought after such an exhibition he might have kept quiet for a bit, but he seemed to have forgotten about it already. Other people wouldn't have forgotten, though; no fear of that: and it was the first time within Tom's memory that Brown had placed himself in a position when he could be ragged. . . .

Only there was nobody to rag him. Tom's brief elation sank as he remembered Brown's powers of retaliation. He knew very well that even if he had the courage to attempt it, it wouldn't come off. You can't rag people like Brown. For one thing, they don't care, and for another, Brown would rather like it, because it would give him an excuse to resort to physical measures, which he would pursue happily until Tom apologized.

Still, he was glad that Henry had tried to turn Brown into a bird. He hadn't succeeded, but he had at least made him look a fool. Henry almost deserved a saucer of cream for that. Unless Brown *really* had done it on purpose; and somehow, in spite of Miss Jimpson's doubts, it now seemed to Tom that this was more likely to be the truth. Anyhow it was what he would say and what the others would 'think. Besides, Miss Jimpson secretly, Tom thought, had let it pass because she didn't much care about tackling Brown, and after all, everybody had been making a row. To connect it with Henry was nonsense. *That* part, he knew, he was just pretending, in order to make it more exciting and mysterious. And he felt a sudden inclination to talk to Miss Jimpson about Henry. It was rotten that he couldn't. But she would think he was either mad or else silly. That was the worst of it. He wished he knew somebody like the Blakes to whom you could talk about such things. The only possible person Tom had was Pascoe, who wasn't really possible except in the sense that he never repeated what you told him. As for believing, or half believing, or even *pretending* to believe (which was really all that was necessary), Pascoe was no good at all. He was too literal, too matter-of-fact, too like the celebrated child of six.

The temptation to experiment on Miss Jimpson was strong, and Tom very nearly yielded to it. Was there the slightest chance that she was less commonsensical than she looked? Spoon in hand, he gazed at her over his strawberry ice. Should he throw out just one cautious hint and see what happened? But he knew what

57

would happen, what invariably happened, and since she had already said that she thought him strange, there didn't seem to be much use in making her think him stranger. In his uncertainty he kept on glancing at her until suddenly he perceived that she had noticed this and was evidently puzzled by it. So he looked out of the window instead, watching the people passing on the opposite side of the road.

"If I weren't practically sure that I know them already," was Miss Jimpson's not very original remark, "I might be inclined to risk a penny."

Tom turned round from the window. How could she possibly know them? She didn't, of course, but he had better make certain. "What was I thinking?" he demanded.

"That I ought to have passed the age for ices," said Miss Jimpson. "Nothing but disapproval can explain that frowning brow." Then, rather curiously, she asked the point-blank question: "How old do you think I *am*, Barber? Or Tom; for I'm going to call you Tom now that we're alone."

Tom hesitated—not because he couldn't give a pretty good guess at Miss Jimpson's age, but because he knew most people preferred to be thought younger than they were.

Miss Jimpson smiled at the hesitation. "Come on," she insisted gaily, so he told her the truth. "Thirty," was Tom's estimate.

Miss Jimpson laughed. "Well, precious near it," she confessed, "though it wasn't what I hoped you'd say. . . . But age is a variable thing, don't you think? I mean so far as one's private feelings about it are concerned. There are days when one feels eighteen and days when one feels eighty."

"I've never felt as old as *that*," Tom replied. "It must be very queer."

"Queer isn't the word for it!" declared Miss Jimpson. "But tell me this, Tom: how many brothers and sisters have you?"

"I haven't any," Tom answered in surprise.

"I thought not; and that partly explains it."

"Explains what?" Tom questioned her, for he thought that Miss Jimpson was talking a little wildly.

"Explains you," said Miss Jimpson. "It means that all your home life must be different: different from that of boys like Brown, I mean. If nothing else, the family conversation is sure to be different. In your house I expect it's real conversation."

"Isn't there real conversation in the Brown family?" Tom wondered.

Miss Jimpson pushed a plate of cakes towards him. "I think it's most unlikely that they all sit dumb," she replied. "But by real conversation I meant an exchange of ideas."

Tom pondered this in silence. He didn't know the Brown family except by sight, but he knew that Brown had three sisters and two brothers, and that Brown himself came somewhere in the middle, and that they all looked very much alike. "Daddy and Mother exchange ideas," he suddenly decided. "They were exchanging them about the Blakes this morning."

Miss Jimpson looked mystified. "The Blakes!" she repeated. "What Blakes?"

"The William Blakes," said Tom. "About God looking in at the window. Daddy doesn't believe he did, but Mother does."

Miss Jimpson recognized the William Blakes. "That's just what I mean," she said. "The Browns would be talking about the Smiths or the Atkinsons."

Tom didn't see why they shouldn't be talking about the Smiths and Atkinsons, but he asked: "Is this a real conversation we're having now?"

Miss Jimpson considered. "Yes, I think so," she replied. "At any rate, it's the beginnings of one: it's not just gossip. Have another ice."

"No, thank you," said Tom.

"Then you'll have a cup of tea," and she poured it out, leaving him to add the milk and sugar himself. "What do you and Mr. Holbrook talk about?" she asked.

"Usually about music," said Tom. "I don't think we exchange ideas."

"Such nonsense!" cried Miss Jimpson. "I'm sure you do. Does talking about music interest you?"

"Yes," Tom answered. "You see," he explained, "when I go

59

to his house we play the gramophone, or he plays the piano—and it's only in between that we talk."

Miss Jimpson saw, and she looked out of the window for a minute or two without speaking. "He told me you were fond of music," she then said.

Tom was surprised. Somehow it always surprised him to find that he had been talked about in his absence. It gave him a slightly ghostly feeling too—as if he had been there and not there at the same time. Yet he hadn't this feeling when it was he himself who talked. He had been talking about Mr. Holbrook and Mother and Daddy and Brown, and it hadn't seemed at all ghostly, which was strange, because really it ought to have been just the same.

"I'm afraid I'm *not* very fond of music," Miss Jimpson was saying, and Tom thought her face had clouded a little. Not clouded exactly, for she didn't look cross or anything like that; in fact she was smiling. But something was different—or perhaps it was just that she was thinking.

"I've tried to pretend I am," Miss Jimpson went on, "but it was simply because I hate missing things, and naturally that is no good. When I was in Milan last year I sat through two operas at the Scala and was bored stiff the entire time."

"Gracious!" cried Tom, but hastily added: "Perhaps they weren't good operas."

"They were," said Miss Jimpson grimly. "They were even supposed to be specially good—with Toscanini conducting. Mr. Holbrook was disgusted with me."

"I don't see why he should be," Tom declared gallantly.

"Neither do I," Miss Jimpson agreed. "Particularly since I went, if not entirely, at any rate very largely, on his account. But men are like that—most men, Tom; not you, as you've just shown."

"I shouldn't worry," Tom told her kindly. Then: "Who was singing?" he naturally inquired, but Miss Jimpson immediately sat up and gazed at him.

"Don't!" she exclaimed. "I thought you were different, but I see you really aren't!"

60

Tom was surprised. "Why?" he asked.

"I treasured up the programmes for Mr. Holbrook," Miss Jimpson continued, ignoring the interruption, "so that he could read the names of the singers for himself—and, incidentally, to prove that I'd been there at all. You'd have imagined that would be sufficient,. wouldn't you? But merely because I couldn't *remember* the names when he asked me, he was more irritated than if I hadn't gone."

Tom's private opinion was that it *had* been pretty slack of her, though he only said: "Yes, he wouldn't like that; he'd think it showed that you weren't really interested. Surely you can remember now."

"I can't," Miss Jimpson snapped. "And I don't want to. Why should I remember the names of people who annoyed me. And that's all they did—the principals even more than the others, because they made more noise. And it was all so perfectly idiotic! Imagine a priestess of the Druids, dressed in what looked to me like a white ball-dress, standing under an oak tree——"

"That was Rosa Ponselle," Tom put in immediately, "and the opera was *Norma*, and she was singing 'Casta Diva'."

"Heavens!" cried Miss Jimpson.

"Well, it *was*," said Tom, a little impatiently. "I know, because Mr. Holbrook told me about the oak tree, and that nobody else sings that part. He's got a record of her singing 'Casta Diva', and I've heard it; it's lovely."

"I'm not doubting you," Miss Jimpson said meekly. "I was only thinking what an apt pupil he'd got. It's not much wonder he thinks such a lot of you."

Tom wasn't sure whether she meant this or not, but he thought she did, and blushed.

"I'm going to slip in one morning and hear *you* sing," she told him. "Do you think Mr. Holbrook would mind?"

Tom wasn't certain about Mr. Holbrook, but he knew he would mind himself. If Miss Jimpson felt that way about a person like Rosa Ponselle, she must be as bad as Daddy, and he didn't want to sing to her. Nor could he see why she should want to listen. "I think you'd better not," he said after a pause.

But Miss Jimpson didn't pause for a second. "Why?" she demanded. "Do you mean he *would* be annoyed?"

"He might be," Tom answered guardedly. "It's better not to risk it." And he looked more guarded still.

"I'm perfectly prepared to risk it," Miss Jimpson returned rather sharply. "And at any rate you could find out, couldn't you?"

"Yes," Tom murmured, though it was not a promise. But he felt that the ground was tricky, and that they'd better get off it as soon as possible; so, with a sleek, black, green-eyed phantom in his mind's eye, he asked her if she were fond of cats.

Miss Jimpson was dubious. "I like them better than canaries or white mice," she compromised, "and I haven't to get up and go out of the room if a cat happens to come into it. But no, on the whole: dogs every time for me."

"I used to have three dogs," Tom said sadly. "At least, they weren't mine exactly. I mean, they didn't really belong to us; they had their own homes; but they went about with me everywhere."

"And what happened to them?" Miss Jimpson asked.

"Roger was poisoned. He must have picked poison up somewhere in the fields, and when he got home, though we did everything we could think of, it was too late, and he died before the vet arrived. . . . Barker is dead too. He was getting very old and blind and a motor-lorry ran over him. . . . Pincher I expect is all right: he was a young dog. But he belonged to the Sabines, and when Mr. Sabine got another church, and they went away, they took Pincher with them."

"That's the worst of having pets," Miss Jimpson said. "You get fond of them, and then something happens. Or even if it doesn't, their lives are so short, so much shorter than ours. I had a dog once myself, and when he died I was so upset I made up my mind never to get another one."

"You could get a pet tortoise," Tom said doubtfully. "They live for ages and ages."

"I dare say, but what good would that be? It wouldn't care a straw about you: you might as well have a pet cabbage."

Tom sighed. "We've only got a cat," he said, "and I don't think he cares much either. . . . I've wanted to have a bulldog ever since I can remember, only Daddy won't let me."

He looked up to find Miss Jimpson regarding him closely. "What other things do you want?" she asked, and the suddenness and unexpected aptness of her question caused him to gaze at her in consternation.

He did not attempt to answer, but he couldn't help thinking, and he was profoundly thankful that Miss Jimpson couldn't read his thoughts. Just imagine if he had been obliged to give her the list of wants he had gone through that very morning! Especially the hairs on his legs! He looked so embarrassed that Miss Jimpson must have guessed something was amiss, for she hastily put another question: "What kind of cat is it—a Persian?"

"No, just an ordinary cat," Tom answered with relief; though truthfulness compelled him to add: "At least, he's not quite ordinary. He's a black cat and his name is Henry."

"Does he do tricks?" asked Miss Jimpson innocently. "But of course cats don't: they're too aloof and superior for that."

"They *do*," Tom couldn't help replying, in a tone both dark and emphatic. "Only they don't do dogs' tricks, and they do them to please themselves, not because they've been taught."

He saw, however, that Miss Jimpson wasn't really attending, she was doing something to her hat. "Well, you must tell me about Henry's tricks another day," she said. "What I want you to tell me now is whether I've got a smut on my nose or not. I feel that I have, though I can't see it. . . . And then we must go."

Tom inspected her carefully. "You haven't," he said.

"In that case——" And Miss Jimpson rose from her chair.

They both got up. "Thanks awfully," Tom was beginning, but Miss Jimpson pushed him along by his shoulders and they descended to the shop, where she paused at the cash-box, while Tom went on to the door, where he stood waiting. Then, out in the street, they said good-bye, and Miss Jimpson went one way and he the other.

CHAPTER VII

Tom walked home through the afternoon sunshine. He was a rather pottering walker, given to standing and gazing at anything that happened to catch his attention, whether it were a dog, a street musician, a furniture van being unloaded, or merely somebody clipping a garden hedge. This was not because he was an idler, but because so many things interested him. His mind was as easily stirred as the river sedges, and when it was deeply stirred his bodily activities were sometimes temporarily suspended.

As a rule this did not matter, but there had been disastrous exceptions. Yesterday afternoon, for instance, when having gone in to bat at the tail end of a practice game supervised by Mr. Poland, suddenly he had been so much struck by the appearance of the bowler that he had made no attempt to defend his wicket. In a dream he had stood there—and the awakening had been rude. One couldn't have believed that people would be so nasty about what was really nothing—or at any rate very little. Tom had never been called so many names in his life. Even the opposite side had joined in, though they ought to have been pleased, since it was to their advantage; while Driscoll, the bowler in question, had been angriest of all, seeing in the subsequent explanation (dragged out by Mr. Poland) a reflection on his personal appearance, whereas Tom had actually been thinking how nice he looked.

But of course he couldn't tell them that: it would only have made matters worse: and now, as he pursued his way homeward, it was Miss Jimpson who occupied his thoughts—chiefly because of the remarks she had made about wanting to hear him sing. Tom couldn't quite believe in this desire, or at least that it had not behind it a motive which had nothing to do with music. Miss Jimpson didn't care for music: she had said so: she had said that she had only gone to those operas to please Mr. Holbrook. Wasn't it very likely, then, that her new plan had been made with the same object? A sudden suspicion dawned upon Tom. Why should Miss Jimpson be so keen on pleasing Mr. Holbrook

unless she was fond of him? A romance it was. And this hypo-
thesis was no sooner born than he saw that it explained everything and must be true. At the same time it struck him as pretty
thick! That is to say, the excuse of the singing lesson struck him
as pretty thin! And mightn't it have had something to do even
with the tea and ices at Nicholson's? This illumination of Miss
Jimpson's secret designs gave Tom a shock. Clearly she wanted
him to help, and, though he felt a certain sympathy with her, he
wasn't sure that he could go quite as far as that. He would first
have to decide whether she was worthy of Mr. Holbrook, and
next find out what were Mr. Holbrook's private feelings in the
matter. Indeed the whole thing must be considered carefully—
possibly discussed with Mother—before he took any active
step.

Tom turned in at his own gate feeling important and influ-
ential—as was only natural, with Miss Jimpson's happiness hanging on his decision. He saw nobody in the garden nor in the
house, though he could hear Phemie whistling in the kitchen, a
sure sign that Mother was out. He flung his books down on the
study table and went back to the garden.

There was nothing to do unless Pascoe happened to turn up,
which he hardly expected, for they had made no arrangement.
Still, Pascoe often rode over: it took him only about ten minutes
on his bicycle, whereas for Tom to go to *his* house meant at least
half an hour's walk. He chose a suitable spot and stretched himself comfortably in the shade. . . .

Once Brown had come—uninvited, and of course simply out of
curiosity. He had stayed most of the afternoon, all the same,
though he had never repeated his visit. For that matter, Tom
didn't want him to repeat it. Pascoe was different: Pascoe would
come up into the loft where the railway was laid down, but the
only games Brown cared for were games you played with a bat
and a ball, and he was far too good at them—or Tom too bad—
for it to be much fun playing with him. He wished Pascoe *would*
come, because he wanted to talk to him and find out how the
electric storm had affected the rest of the school. Besides, they
could dam the stream—an engineering feat planned severa **days**

ago, but planned by Pascoe, so that Tom daren't attempt it without him.

Pascoe was a queer chap, he reflected. For one thing, he hardly ever laughed. It wasn't that he was gloomy or melancholy or bored, but merely that jokes didn't amuse him. He disliked, too, even the mildest form of ragging. He went about everything with a kind of intense concentration of purpose, just the way ants do. Nevertheless, it was rotten having nobody. . . .

Tom lay on his back and looked up into a cloudless blue sky. He could hear the leaves rustling on the apple trees behind him when a breath of wind passed, and presently a pigeon flew out of the weeping-ash near the summer house. A couple of swallows were wheeling over the lawn, flying very low, which was supposed to be a sign of approaching rain, but Tom didn't believe it was going to rain.

Where had William gone to? He must either have concealed himself somewhere in the shrubbery or else have gone in to the kitchen to have tea. Tom considered whether it would be worth while going to the kitchen, but he had already had tea with Miss Jimpson, so instead he got up and strolled round the house to a cobbled yard at the back. Here were what had once been stables, though at present they were used partly as a garage, and partly as a kind of tool-shed, containing a carpenter's bench, the lawn mower, and all William's gardening implements. Above was a loft, to which you could climb by a board with foot-holes in it. This loft in former days had been a hayloft, but hay being no longer required, it had been cleaned out, whitewashed, and given over to Tom for a playroom.

He had used it a lot at one time, and he still used it when Pascoe came. Its attractiveness, however, had waned of late, and it was only because he had nothing else to do that he climbed up there now.

It was quite light in the loft, for there was not only a skylight, but also a large window facing the yard. The room was long and low, with a sloping roof which left plenty of space in the middle, but at the sides slanted down to within three feet of the floor. The only furniture consisted of a couple of kitchen chairs, and a

66

solid deal table littered with papers, chalks, a box of paints, a pair of scissors, and other odds and ends. From the rafters hung crinkled Chinese lanterns, and on the floor were the railway lines, with their stations, signal boxes, and tunnels. A toy yacht fully rigged, and a Meccano erection which Pascoe had built weeks ago, stood near the wall.

A broad band of sunlight, filled with myriads of tiny floating specks, streamed in through the dusty glass. On the whitewashed wall hung a burglar's black cloth mask with eyeholes cut in it, a coloured portrait of Abraham Lincoln and his young son, a scabbard without a sword, and a cracked and tarnished mirror. Also a map of the garden and the immediately surrounding country—chiefly Pascoe's work—and two charcoal silhouettes, one of Pascoe and one of Tom, traced over their actual shadows.

All these familiar details Tom took in with a rather bored glance. He pulled the window up, stretched himself on his stomach on the dusty floor, and supporting his chin between his hands, stared out into the sunshine.

After some ten minutes of this, during which his mind had become very nearly a blank, he heard the sound of the wheel-barrow and leaned farther out. From where he lay he could see William, but William could not see him unless he chanced to glance up. Tom therefore had a view of William as William was when he believed himself to be alone, and at once he became interested. William wiped his forehead with a spotted and very dirty pocket handkerchief and muttered some remarks to the wheelbarrow. Tom strained his ears to catch what he was saying, but failed. A very one-sided conversation this, as William himself appeared to realize, for he sighed loudly, sat down on the barrow, and took out his pipe. Tom had never seen William fill that pipe, and he didn't fill it now; he merely struck a match and held it between his hands over the bowl: nevertheless he lit the pipe, and puffed a cloud of dark blue smoke into the air. This proved that the pipe was a magic one, always filled with tobacco, and, since William was certainly not a magician, it must have been given to him by an ancient crone in return for some service —carrying her bundle perhaps, or giving her a share of his lunch.

It followed therefore that William had two older brothers who had been less obliging, and the question was what *they* had received from the crone. Nothing very nice, of course, but possibly amusing. Tom leaned as low down as he could, and shouted "William!" at the top of his voice.

The effect was remarkable. William, seated on the wheelbarrow immediately below the window, jumped several inches. And he was very angry indeed. "What's ailin' you?" he snarled. "You might have more manners than to be yellin' in people's ears. It's time you were learnin' somethin' instead of behavin' like the young street-boys that knows no better."

Tom apologized. "Sorry!" he said. "I was only going to ask what happened to your brothers."

"Brothers!" William growled, stuffing his pipe back into his pocket as he got up.

"Yes, brothers," said Tom. " *Your* brothers. Are they dead?"

"No, they're not dead," returned William sourly. "Because they never was born." And he grasped the shafts of the barrow and moved away, still muttering under his breath about manners and education.

It was like being at the theatre, for William was no sooner gone than Henry appeared on the scene—silently, discreetly—stopping every few steps with one black paw lifted in the air. If ever anybody looked bursting with plots and secrets, it was Henry at that moment, and Tom watched him from his hiding place, careful not to make a sound. It was quite good sport, this. It was moreover a kind of proof that life actually did go on when you weren't taking part in it—a truth sometimes hard to realize. Should he startle Henry the way he had startled William, or should he continue to watch him? While he hesitated Henry himself reached a decision, and instead of proceeding further sat down where he was, stuck one hind leg up in the air like a post, and began to perform a complicated toilet. Somehow this had the effect of breaking a spell. . . .

Tom turned his head quickly at a sound in the room behind him. It had been made by a mouse, he was sure, and he didn't want mice up here: they would run over everything, leaving tracks and nibbling holes. He rose from the floor and walked on tiptoe to the table whence the sound had come. Such a litter of stuff! He'd have to clear it all up one of these days and burn most of it. He stood contemplating the jumble. Right on top were several large sheets of white cartridge paper. He remembered bringing them up the last day Pascoe had been here, along with the scissors and *The Boys' Own Toymaker*. Pascoe was good at making things—very neat and clever with his fingers—and the *Toymaker* gave heaps of models. You drew the outline on paper, leaving dotted lines in certain places. Then you cut out the pattern and folded it at the dotted lines and it was a house, or a windmill, or a cart, or an arm-chair, and would stand up on the table —or at least it would if Pascoe were the designer. For more complicated models you had to cut out several pieces and use gum, but this was a bother.

The scissors attracted him, being a large and special pair which Mother used for cutting out, and he was surprised that she hadn't missed them. For Mother was as clever at making things as Pascoe, and that very summer had made Tom two pairs of white linen trousers which were just as good as if they had been bought in a shop. Now he came to think of it, it was quite possible that she *had* missed the scissors, for he'd borrowed them when she wasn't there. He'd better take them down with him when he was going.

Meanwhile, they looked very sharp and efficient: in fact, in conjunction with the cartridge paper, they invited immediate use. Only he didn't want to make toys: he'd cut out a portrait. He knew what Pascoe, who had gone shares in buying the paper, would say—that it had been bought for a special purpose and was jolly expensive and oughtn't to be wasted. Still, Pascoe had used a sheet of it himself to make their map, so Tom felt entitled to one, and slipped a brown thumb and two fingers through the large bright rings. He had no clear image in his mind to start with, beyond a human silhouette, but if this happened to suggest a likeness to anyone he knew, it would be easy afterwards to make the necessary trimmings and alterations. It reminded him of the days when he had been quite small and had spent hours in

69

cutting out, though then he had only been allowed to use newspapers. This was much better, for the paper didn't bend or crumple, and the blades cut through it with a crisp sharp sound. They worked very smoothly, Tom found—almost of their own accord—and cutting out must be either a great deal easier than drawing or else he was much better at it, for something far more satisfactory than any of his pencilled efforts was emerging. It was a man, Tom already saw—an old man, he fancied—just the head and shoulders—life-size. The clear profile was really quite striking even if the rest was a bit dicky. Tom at all events was pleased with it, and resolved to keep it to show to Pascoe. He rose, placed the portrait standing against the back of the chair, and retreated a few steps to admire it.

And with that—though bafflingly, because no name suggested itself—he felt that it did remind him of someone—someone he had seen either in actual life or in a picture. But he could get no further than this, though several fugitive impressions passed through his mind. . . .

Suddenly he heard the mouse again, and this time it was actually in one of his railway tunnels. That wouldn't do: there was probably a whole family of them, and he must set a trap. He crossed the room and clambered down the footboard with the idea of borrowing a trap from Phemie. But as he passed through the stable door into the sunlit yard, he spied exactly what he needed, in the person of Henry.

The problem was how to get Henry up into the loft. He was still seated in the middle of the yard, but he had now finished washing, and, with his back turned, appeared to be contemplating the chimney-stacks. It was going to be jolly difficult to get him up, Tom reflected, for Henry had a distrustful nature and would be deaf to coaxing. It could never be managed by the footboard. Henry would struggle like mad even if he didn't actually use his claws. A ladder was the thing, because Tom could climb a ladder and keep at the same time a firm grip on Henry, whereas, for the footboard, he required to use both his hands. There were a couple of ladders in the shed, and the small one would do. He dragged it out and propped it up against the open window, which

70

he could shut once he got Henry safely inside. True, there was always the other way out, and no trap-door covering it; but he didn't think Henry could get down by the footboard.

Meanwhile, attracted by the noise, Henry had turned round and was watching him. His interest was very languid, however; nor did Tom's "Puss, puss—poor puss!" perceptibly deepen it. It was this air of complete indifference, habitual with Henry unless he himself wanted something, which Tom found so irritating. It annoyed him to be treated as if he were an inanimate object, and it removed any scruples he might have had against the employment of force. Slowly he approached Henry, and it was not till he had actually passed that he suddenly swooped down and grabbed him.

Instantly Henry was in action. His hind legs kicked against Tom's body like powerful steel springs, his front claws dug into the sleeves of his jacket; but after one mew he struggled in silence and in vain. Up the ladder they went, Henry squeezed nearly flat under Tom's arm, and Tom's fingers tightly grasping the scruff of his neck. In at the window he was thrust, and the sash quickly pulled down, leaving him a prisoner till morning.

At least that was the plan when Tom slid down the ladder and stood listening. Not a sound. This seemed odd, unless Henry had fainted. "Perhaps I'll bring you some milk later," Tom called up, but there was no reply.

Tom still stood listening. He wished he didn't suffer such frightful pangs of conscience every time he committed an assault on Henry, for he knew he hadn't hurt him a bit, except possibly his feelings. All the same, this silence was surprising, for Henry had a powerful voice and it wasn't in the least like him to submit without a protest. He could hardly have found his way down by the footboard so soon, either, though perhaps it would be better to make sure. So Tom looked inside the stable. Henry was not there. Indeed, unless he jumped it, Tom didn't see how he was going to get down that way, and the height was about ten feet.

But perhaps Henry was keeping quiet because he had already smelt the mouse or heard it, though somehow this seemed improbable too. It would be far more in keeping with Henry's

71

character to allow the mouse to escape, since he hated doing things under compulsion. Tom waited a few minutes longer in the hot sunshine, and then the desire to know what Henry really was up to became irresistible. Stealthily he re-climbed the ladder, and stealthily he raised his head till he could peep in.

Henry was there—yes; but what on earth was he doing? Not bothering about mice, that was clear. Actually he was walking in a sort of semicircle backwards and forwards in front of one of the chairs, and every time he brushed against it he arched his back and his tail rose stiffly in the air. Through the shut window Tom naturally heard no sound, nevertheless he could have sworn that Henry was purring. It was in fact exactly as if he were playing a kind of ceremonial game, the point of which was to pretend that somebody he liked very much was sitting in the chair. Yet the only thing in the chair was Tom's paper man, who had fallen down, and was now lying flat on the seat.

More and more solemn and amazed Tom's face grew, as he stared at this performance with round unblinking eyes. And then abruptly it ceased; Henry walked away from the chair and straight up to the mirror, before which he began to posture. And somehow, with this, Tom's curiosity was satisfied; he felt he had seen enough; and without waiting for further developments scrambled down the ladder so rapidly that he was within an ace of falling.

Once safely on earth, he felt a little foolish. Suppose Pascoe had been there to witness that hasty descent! But of course if Pascoe had been there nothing would have happened. His mere presence would have prevented it. Pascoe had an effect on his surroundings very like that of a powerful arc-lamp: at the sight of him cocks crew and phantoms vanished in despair. If the worst came to the worst, Tom could always threaten Henry that he would give him to Pascoe. That would teach him! That would put an end to his magic!

Yet the rational explanation was that Henry simply had been amusing himself—with the mirror! "Mirror, mirror, on the wall"—the wicked queen questioning her mirror in the story of Snow White—it might have *looked* like that, but it wasn't really.

72

On the other hand he rather regretted having ever begun to pretend things about Henry. It had been silly, or at least it would be silly to go on pretending. In the beginning it *had* been a make-up, and it just showed you that Daddy really was right about such things. Now of course he was sensible again, but even now it would have been a comfort to have known Henry as a kitten, or at least to have known somebody who had known him. In that case his advent wouldn't have so closely resembled the arrival of the Raven—from the Night's Plutonian shore. As it was, there seemed to Tom to be a marked resemblance, though Henry hadn't come tapping at a window, but merely mewing to Phemie.

In the midst of these uneasy cogitations he heard the sound of the car, and next moment it came into view, with Daddy driving. Tom ran to the doors of the garage and pulled them open, while Daddy drove cautiously in, for he was not in any way a very dashing person.

"Well, what have you been up to?" Daddy asked, when the car was safely parked and he had got out of it. "And what's the ladder doing there?" he continued, stopping to look at it.

"I put it there," Tom said. "I put Henry up in the loft because I heard a mouse."

Daddy gazed dubiously at the window. "Are you going to keep him there?" he inquired. "He won't like that."

"No; I think I ought to let him out," Tom agreed. "I think if I open the window he'll be able to get down if he wants to. Would you mind waiting just a minute, Daddy, till I do open it?"

"Waiting!" Daddy repeated. "Why?"

You'd have thought he might have done what he was asked without questions, but he didn't, it wasn't his way, and Tom gave him a reproachful, not to say an indignant, glance. "I just want you to wait, that's all," he answered. "I nearly fell down the ladder the last time."

Daddy seemed about to speak, and his expression was slightly puzzled, but in the end he said nothing. However, he waited— which was the main thing—while Tom climbed up and opened

73

the window. Henry was there, meek as milk of course, and even allowed himself to be carried down perched on Tom's shoulder.

As they crossed the yard in this fashion, Tom opened a conversation. "We had a cloudburst at school to-day," he told Daddy. "Did you have one?"

"I saw a flash of lightning," Daddy said, "and I heard a peal of thunder. But that was all."

"And Brown stood up on the form and flapped his arms and called out like a bird," Tom continued. "He did it because of the electric currents."

"The electric currents?" Daddy murmured, apparently not grasping the connection. "You mean he gave himself an electric shock?"

"No—the electric currents in the air," Tom explained. "Miss Jimpson said it was that."

"I see," said Daddy, but Tom was quite sure he didn't see and wasn't even trying to see.

"I had tea with Miss Jimpson at Nicholson's," he went on.

"That was nice," Daddy said. "And very kind of her. Had you managed by any chance to get a sum right, do you suppose?"

"No," Tom replied; "she just asked me—socially."

"Oh, socially!" Daddy echoed. "Well, I want to speak to William before he goes, and I think you'd better clean yourself up a bit. You look as if you'd been rolling in the dust."

CHAPTER VIII

Daddy was writing a letter; Mother was darning socks; Tom sat at the other side of the table over his lessons. In spite of the array of books, he was not doing very much, she noticed. He was not even looking at them, but was sitting with his head slightly on one side, which showed that he was thinking. Mother paused in her work to watch him. He looked pale; he looked tired; she was glad that the holidays were so near. A plain little boy, she supposed most people would call him—at any rate stupid people. Perhaps he *was* plain, with his freckles, his blunt features, his dull leaf-brown hair that needed cutting. And in his eyes was a listening expression, not unhappy exactly, yet extraordinarily sad.

She had seen it before, only somehow never before had it so struck her. Why should he look like that? He wasn't unhappy. He was different, she knew, from the ordinary run of small boys —perhaps even more different than she thought—but she knew he was happy, he had everything to make him happy, and that expression didn't mean what it seemed to mean. Suddenly she told him: "I think you'd much better put away your lesson books and go to bed."

Tom did not answer. He didn't want to go to bed, though he was very tired, and his eyes were heavy, and he didn't feel very well. He tried to persuade himself that he didn't feel ill either— just vaguely uncomfortable and headachey—symptoms which had become much more marked after dinner, but which had been hovering in the background all day. He braced himself to look more lively, and Mother repeated her words.

"It's only half-past eight," Tom mumbled, turning a page. He knew this didn't deceive her, but he hated admitting that he wasn't well. It seemed so silly, besides leading to all kinds of fuss and questions, and he'd be all right in the morning.

"You hardly touched your dinner," Mother continued. "And you know you're not really working now. I expect it's the heat, or Miss Jimpson's ices, that have upset you."

Daddy, who in the ordinary way would have noticed nothing, of course at this began to gaze at him too. "Do you hear what your mother says?" he asked.

The question annoyed Tom, for naturally he had heard what Mother had said; he wasn't deaf. But this irritability was only another symptom, and he swallowed it down and answered in a subdued voice: "The exams begin in a day or two."

75

"There won't be any exams if you're ill," Mother remarked quietly.

That was nonsense, he could have pointed out. Still, he knew what she meant, and his mind, refusing the effort of concentration on his work, sought relief in pondering over the difficulty of saying anything which was not at the same time both true and untrue. Mother's statement was untrue, because there certainly would be exams whether he took part in them or not; yet in another way it was true, because there would be no exams for him if he were in bed. Similarly Henry, now lying curled up asleep on the sofa, would be speaking the truth if he said that mice were delicious; yet if Daddy were to say "Mice are delicious", they would all not only disbelieve him but get a most frightful shock into the bargain. No sooner had this example arisen in Tom's mind than it passed from the abstract to the concrete, and an unpleasant picture was conjured up of Daddy crouching over mouseholes, quivering and silent, with eyes floating and shining with greed. . . . He sighed and pushed away his book. "It's because it's so hot and stuffy," he said petulantly. "I wish I could sleep out in the garden in the summerhouse."

"I don't think you'd find *that* very enjoyable," Mother replied; "and if you leave your door open you'll get plenty of air. Think how nice it will be next month at the seashore."

"Yes," Tom sighed again, for next month seemed very far away.

"And it's not nearly so hot as it was," Mother went on. "At least, not so oppressive." But she was still watching him doubtfully, and presently she said: "I hope you haven't got a temperature!"

So did Tom, for temperatures were the bane of his existence. He was pretty sure he *had* one, too, or was going to have one. It was so stupid being like that! Anything in the least out of the ordinary upset him. Not that there *had* been anything out of the ordinary. A hot day—what was that! Nothing at all events to make you ill.

"If you like," Mother said, "we'll go out for a little walk in the garden—for half an hour. That is, if you'll promise to go straight to bed without dawdling the moment we come in.''

Tom promised, and Mother put away her work. He followed her into the hall, where she wound a sort of scarf thing round her shoulders, so light that it couldn't really make the least difference. Then they went into the garden.

The walk didn't amount to much, for they merely sauntered along the paths and up and down the lawn, while Mother stopped every now and again to smell flowers. She was very fond of smelling flowers, and she could even smell things that to Tom were quite unsmellable, such as stones, and water, and the sun baking the bricks of the house.

A greenish translucent glow still lit up the sky, and against this a few small birds were wheeling in delicate noiseless curves and patterns, as they chased the moths. Tom's first impression was of something extremely graceful and pleasing, till all at once it struck him as horrible. "They're catching them!" he exclaimed in a shocked voice. "They're eating them!" And he began to clap his hands to frighten the birds away.

"Insects are their natural food," Mother observed calmly. "They're not being cruel."

"But it's awful!" Tom cried in anguish. "They're swallowing them alive!"

Mother put her hand on his shoulder and gave it a little squeeze. "You mustn't think of things in that way," she said. "You're far too sensitive, and you must try to get over it. That isn't the way to look at things. I don't suppose the moths even know that it's happening."

"It's our fault," Tom went on, unconsoled by Mother's philosophy. "We oughtn't to put nets over the fruit. Then they wouldn't want moths."

Mother at this gave him a shake, almost as if she were trying to wake him up. "Now you're getting into one of your silly moods," she declared.

But Tom refused to be shaken into comfort. "I'm not," he said. "And it isn't silly."

"It's silly if you allow it to worry you," Mother told him.

77

"Because you can't alter it. It's the way the world's arranged, and if you don't accept it you'll never be happy. Besides, it's necessary, or there'd be a plague of insects."

"It isn't necessary for *us*," Tom argued gloomily. "We could live very well on vegetables and things."

"Not so well as you imagine," Mother replied. "As a matter of fact it would be extremely troublesome—especially in winter, when there are very few vegetables."

This might be true, yet it did not satisfy Tom. Nor merely because it was true did that seem to him to make it good, and he said so. "In the Garden of Eden," he went on, "everybody must have lived on vegetables. I mean all the animals—even animals like lions and tigers."

"Probably there weren't any lions and tigers," Mother thought. "The savage creatures, I expect, lived outside the Garden."

"The snakes didn't," Tom reminded her.

"Snakes were different then," Mother said. "They must have been quite different, because we're told that the serpent was more subtle than any beast of the field. So no doubt they were tame and gentle too, and only afterwards became what they are now."

Tom thought this a prejudiced view—prejudiced in favour of humanity. "I don't see that they're any worse now than we are," he said. "If it comes to killing things, I don't expect they're as bad." But Mother's words had called up a picture in his mind which temporarily distracted his thoughts from the callous terrestrial plan. "What happened to the Garden of Eden, do you think?" he asked.

"You know what happened," Mother answered. "It's all explained in the first chapters of Genesis."

"There's very *little* about it in the first chapters of Genesis," Tom replied. "You're told practically nothing, except that the Garden was there, and that, after Adam and Eve were driven out, it was guarded by angels. So unless something happened to it later, it must be there still."

"The place where it was of course is there still," Mother

78

agreed, "but not the Garden itself: that disappeared long ago."

"Why?" Tom demanded. "How do you know? It may still be there—hidden by magic."

But Mother did not find this a profitable subject to pursue; she thought more was to be gained by thinking and talking about the New Testament.

Tom wanted to talk about the Old. "It's true, isn't it?" he said, knowing that this would place her in a difficulty.

"Yes," Mother answered, "all the Bible is true."

"Well then, I think the Old Testament is more interesting," Tom declared.

But he could see that Mother didn't approve of this opinion, though she didn't actually say so. "The New Testament is more important," she distinguished carefully. "I mean to people living at the present time, because it contains the actual words of Christ. The other is important too, but its importance is more or less only an historical importance. It describes things that happened a long time ago, and naturally such things haven't a great deal to do with *us*."

"All the same, they were interesting things," Tom persisted. "The Flood, and Jacob's ladder, and the Witch of Endor, and Lot's wife, and Balaam's ass, and Jonah in the whale, and Moses turning his rod into a serpent—they're just like the *Arabian Nights*."

"They're not in the least like the *Arabian Nights*," Mother contradicted, "and it's very wrong to talk in that way."

"Wrong!" exclaimed Tom in astonishment. "Do you mean wicked?"

"Yes," Mother said. "You know the *Arabian Nights* stories are fairy tales, and that the Bible is God's word."

"But I only said it was *like* them," Tom protested.

"And I say it isn't like them," Mother answered. "Nor is that the proper way to read the Bible—picking out bits here and there —especially the bits you seem to have picked out—just because they happen to contain marvels."

"How ought I to read it?" Tom asked.

"The Bible was written to teach us how to live properly," Mother continued, "and to reveal the truth. It isn't like any other book."

"But I didn't really pick out those bits," Tom said, after a brief pause. "They just happen to be the bits I remember."

"Yes, and that shows they were the bits you liked. Otherwise you wouldn't have said that the Garden of Eden might be hidden by magic. You said that because you *wanted* to think so. There is very little in the Bible about magic, and when it is mentioned at all, it is condemned as wicked. If the Garden of Eden had been hidden, it would have been hidden by God."

"Yes, that's what I meant," Tom hastened to assure her.

"It isn't what you said, then," Mother told him. "God isn't a magician."

"N——o," Tom hesitated. He couldn't quite grasp the point, however, nor in what consisted the apparently so great difference between miracles and magic. But he was willing to leave this unchallenged, for his interest really was in the Garden itself. "You see," he went on, reverting to his original thought, "the flood would only flood it: it would still be there when the water drained away. . . . Do you mind if I tell you what I think really may have happened?"

Mother for a moment looked as if she did mind, but suddenly she smiled and said, "No."

"I'm not cross," she added; "it's only that these things aren't the same as fairy tales: they're true, and I want you to realize that."

Tom was relieved, and told her that he did realize it. "I think," he went on quickly, "that just before the flood came the Garden sank down into the earth, and then, after the rain had dried up, it rose again. You see, it would have been a pity to spoil a place like that. And I think all the animals who were in it—— No, I don't—what I really think is that the flood wasn't allowed to touch it at all. A magic wall—I mean a barrier suddenly rose up all round it, with watch-towers on which the guarding angels stood, waving their swords. . . . Square watch-towers," he added, his eyes narrowing till they were nearly shut. "Then Noah, if he looked out from the Ark across the water at night, would see the moving lights of the swords, but he wouldn't know what they were. It would be all dark, all black water, except for the red moving flames on the towers—the swords of the Cherubims. Even if a little bit of the Cherubims was lit up by the swords, they would still only be like shadows, standing with their faces hidden in the clouds."

"Well," said Mother, abandoning theological discussion and pressing her cool hand against his cheek, "it's time we were going in and time you were going to bed."

But Tom didn't want this at all: he wanted to talk; and the hour and the place were somehow just right, if only Mother would be right too. "Don't let's go in yet," he pleaded. "It's far nicer out here and I feel better already. Besides, there's the moon."

"What has the moon got to do with it?" Mother asked. "You're a little humbug. And anyhow I must go in, because I'm being eaten alive by midges."

She did not insist on his accompanying her, however, and he sat down on a bench outside the study window. The midges did not trouble him, and a light wind had sprung up and was whispering its plaintive sighings in his ears. Daddy, who was always too busy to sit in the dark, or even in the twilight, had turned on the light in the study, and it streamed out through the uncurtained windows. It had a quite different effect, Tom noticed, from daylight. The shrubs in its immediate radius were vividly and metallically green, but they suggested the brightness of a painted scene in a theatre, and behind this the trees assumed dark listening shapes, and the bushes were like crouching Sphinxes and Chimeras. Where the light fell, it created a superficial illusion, a glittering enchantment; but beyond was the great world of nature—profound, real, and living.

Then, in the study, Mother drew the curtains, and the enchantment vanished. The trees drew closer, while the great white moon, like a pale floating water-lily, rose higher above them. Tom had an impression of drifting up to meet it, of drifting above the tree-tops. And looking downward thence he could see the shadowy garden and the house, and a small human figure with a white face sitting on a bench. Higher still, so that now he could see the silent coils of the river and the foaming whiteness where it rushed over the weir, and the dark tangle of woodland on the farther bank. The sense of actual levitation was much more real, much less dreamlike, than it had been that morning when he had sat half asleep in school. Now he could see the grey fields, intersected by dark lines that were the hawthorn hedges. It was the country Pascoe had mapped, but soon Tom left it behind him. On and on he voyaged, over hills and lighted towns and open country, until at last below him he saw a wide dark stretch of water and knew that he had reached the sea. A white line marked the breaking of the waves against black cliffs; and where it curved in a long slender bow he knew there was a beach.

Miles and miles away he was, and yet a step on the gravel, and Daddy's voice, reached him across all that distance, and brought him at terrific speed back into the waiting empty body on the bench. "You're to come in, young man," Daddy announced. "Your supper is ready; and after that, bed."

Tom got up at once, for the moment Daddy spoke he realized that his feet and lower limbs were cold. His body was not much warmer, yet his head felt very hot. He did not mention these symptoms, though they struck him as remarkable and most likely dangerous. For if his blood was circulating properly, how could there be all these different temperatures? Meanwhile Daddy's hand, placed beneath Tom's armpit, impelled him firmly towards the house.

CHAPTER IX

Tom opened his eyes with a feeling that somebody had called his name. It was uncommonly dark, and without raising his head from the pillow he could see two tiny green lamps outside the window. The lamps appeared to be suspended in mid-air some eight inches above the sill, and shone with a bright steady glow. It was quite half a minute before he understood what they were: then he knew that Henry was watching him. . . .

Why? Henry must have clambered up somehow by the creeper, yet evidently not with the intention of coming in, for both windows were open. He must have climbed up for some other purpose, though what that might be Tom could not imagine, and he softly called: "Puss—puss!" Instantly the green lights disappeared, and he heard a rustle of leaves, followed by silence. . . .

Tom was perplexed. Not that he objected to Henry being on the window-sill; it was only his secretiveness that seemed strange. He didn't believe Henry had had any purpose at all beyond that of making himself mysterious, and with this he dismissed him from his thoughts and tried to go to sleep again.

He shut his eyes, but it was no use. His pillow was hot and uncomfortable, and he also was hot and uncomfortable, though only a sheet and a counterpane covered him. There were peculiar little noises, too, going on all round him, and they were very like voices. They came from everywhere—from under the bed, from the ceiling, from the windows, from the pictures, from the wardrobe, from the washstand—and they grew every moment more eager and confused, as if a discussion were being carried on and everybody were talking at once. In such a babel how could he go to sleep? Yet the voices didn't really say anything, were only sounds, little cries and chirps and squeaks, not human at all.

And with that, quite distinctly, he heard three words: "Follow the light."

Queerer still, he was neither startled nor particularly surprised, though he sat up and listened. It had been a very small voice certainly, and the moment he sat up it stopped speaking, in fact there was a general silence. Tom could be quiet too, however, and presently, as if reassured by his stillness, the same small voice spoke again, evidently from somewhere behind the washstand. "Follow the light," it said; and this time there could be no mistake; for a ray of light, not much thicker than a whipcord, actually darted across the room about three feet above the carpet, so that the end of it passed straight through the keyhole.

Tom did not hesitate an instant, but sprang out of bed and opened his door. He was just in time to see the ray of light gliding forward like a thread of elastic pulled by an invisible hand: next moment it had stretched round the corner at the end of the passage, and he hurried after it, passing the open door of Daddy's and Mother's room and reaching the wide landing above the staircase. Down into the hall the thread of light went, and down into the hall Tom pursued it. Then, just as he reached the last stair, the grandfather's clock began to clear its throat, and the sound brought him up abruptly.

For it was not the same sound as the clock ordinarily made, or else Tom's sense of hearing was not the same. It seemed to him now that the wheezing noise was trying to make words, trying to tell him something, trying to attract his attention. He stood still, and "Don't go! Don't go!" the old clock choked and gasped, but the words were indistinct and he could not be sure that he had heard them aright. If the warning had been repeated, or if he had been quite certain that it had *been* a warning, he might have heeded it, but there was a sudden break in the sound, and a brief silence, followed immediately by two slow clear notes striking the hour. The deep mellow chime floated out and died away, and with this the clock's power of speech died too. It appeared to Tom that for just a few seconds the tall wooden figure quivered slightly, but when he touched it, half expecting to find in it some lingering vibration of life, it had stiffened once more into immobility, and its round placid old face was sunk in its customary repose.

But the silver thread remained, and it passed through the keyhole of the hall-door, showing that the track it marked led outside the house. The door was a heavy mahogany one, locked and chained, nevertheless Tom had no difficulty in unchaining it and in turning the big iron key. He slipped back the latch and swung the door wide; and maybe the door too tried to warn him, but its voice had been drowned in oil, and it could make no sound, only turn on its hinges and let him out into the night. Tom followed the guiding thread. It led him through the soft darkness, and the cool air was pleasant, though his feet were naked and his pyjamas thin. The flowers were shut in sleep, but the garden was filled with sweetness strengthened by a heavy dew that lay on everything, deep as a shower of rain. And the night already was more a veil than a curtain; not really night, but only a shadow which would be lifted in another hour.

The light passed round the house, and Tom, turning the corner after it, saw at once whither it was leading him. Merely to his play-loft, and he crossed the yard on the cobblestones, while out of the shadow a black shape emerged, purring and rubbing dew-soaked fur against his legs. The thread of light ran up the wall like a silver vein of mushroom spawn: it passed through the window of the loft, but more than that Tom could not see.

The ladder was still there, however, propped up against the wall, and he put a bare foot on the lowest rung. And then once more something checked him, this time something within himself, a faint and vague premonition of danger. Yet he climbed up —mounting more and more slowly—and now he saw that there was a dim light in the loft, pale and phosphorescent, hardly so powerful as the light of a candle. And in fact no candle was burning, the light had no visible source—unless it issued from that fantastic figure seated in a chair beside the table.

The head and shoulders of this figure were distinct: the rest was barely a suggestion. Yet, while Tom looked, the faint diffused light trembled and drew in, giving a more realistic appearance to the whole shape, and brightening as it contracted. It had less substance than a vapour, but it was very slowly assuming the nebulous outlines of a human form, through the upper portions of which the flat paper portrait he had cut out that afternoon was still visible. And the materialization took place so gradually, and the process was so strange, that Tom, watching it, was more curious than alarmed. Besides, it was only paper after all, and one quick tear across, he felt, would be sufficient to destroy it. There was at any rate nothing to fear: that phantom had no sensible reality. It was too feeble to produce a sound or a touch: it was no more formidable than a breath on frosty air, or a reflection of moonlight in water. And already, as if exhausted, it was dimming again, and far more rapidly than it had brightened. Then Tom suddenly felt himself grasped from behind, and next instant he was lifted down and set upon the ground, while the hands that had seized him still held him, and Daddy's voice kept repeating firmly but gently: "It's all right: don't be frightened: I'm here with you and we're out in the yard; but now, I think, we'll go back to the house."

Tom said nothing at all, and he did not move. He was not frightened, he merely felt confused and somehow half asleep, conscious of very little more than that Daddy was speaking to him.

"It's quite simple," Daddy was saying. "You were dreaming, you see, and in the middle of your dream you got up and came out here. We heard you—or at least Mother heard you—unchaining the hall-door. So she woke me up and I came down to look for you."

Tom still listened without seeming to hear; but he was perfectly docile, and allowed Daddy to lead him back across the yard. Then suddenly he asked a quite pertinent question—"Did she think it was burglars?"—and Daddy answered: "No, she thought it was you; and *I* thought it was her imagination until I found the hall-door open. The rest didn't take very long."

After this neither of them spoke again until they came round to the front of the house, which was at present all lit up. Then Daddy called out: "I've got him—safe and sound;"—and Mother was there in the porch, in her dressing-gown, and with a warning "S—sh!" upon her lips.

"Don't make a noise," she whispered, drawing Tom into the hall. "We don't want to wake Phemie and Mary. . . . Where did you find him?"

"In the yard," replied Daddy cheerfully. "Half-way up a ladder. The ladder was one he had put there himself this afternoon. I had to lift him down and that's what wakened him. But it's all right, and he's wide awake now—or very nearly."

Tom said nothing, and Mother stooped and kissed him. She kissed him twice, and smiled, but rather anxiously. "He's only half awake," she murmured. . . . "I thought he had outgrown it. It must be more than a year since it happened last."

"Since what happened last?" Tom questioned dreamily; for everything now seemed to him strange and unreal, and this conversation as strange as all the rest.

"Since you came marching down into the study with your eyes wide open," Mother said, "and—— However, this isn't the time to discuss it," she went on. "You must get back to bed as quickly as possible. It's a blessing it's such a warm night. Perhaps you won't catch cold after all."

"It's far more likely that I will," Daddy observed, but Mother took no notice. She hurried Tom upstairs, packed him into bed after drying his feet with a rough towel, and put an eiderdown quilt on top of him.

All this Tom submitted to in silence: only the quilt drew a protest from him. "I can't," he remonstrated plaintively. "I'm burning!"

Mother put her hand on his forehead and then reluctantly removed the quilt. She sat down beside the bed. "Now go to sleep," she told him. "It's all my fault; I should never have allowed you to sit out in the garden with the dew falling."

"But I've sat out hundreds of times," Tom expostulated.

"Not when you weren't feeling well," Mother said. "I should have had more sense."

Nevertheless she seemed a good deal less anxious now that she had got him safely into bed, and it was Tom himself who began to feel a little worried by what had happened. He still wasn't at all clear about it, and the few words Mother had spoken in the hall, before she had suddenly checked herself, seemed particularly mysterious, referring, as they evidently did, to something that had occurred in the past—something which both she and Daddy knew about but had never before mentioned. "Why shouldn't my eyes have been open?" he began. "I mean that time when you say I came down into the study."

Mother, he thought at first, wasn't going to answer: however, in the end she changed her mind. "Because you were sound asleep," she said. "Just the way you were to-night. Only then we hadn't gone to bed."

87

Tom was less satisfied than ever. It was the first time he had heard of this sleep-walking, and that in itself was peculiar. He hated half-explanations. Besides, if he *had* been asleep to-night when he came downstairs, then he must have been asleep before that; which meant that the voices, the thread of light, the figure in the loft, even Henry on the window-sill, had all been nothing but a dream. Yet in that case how was he ever really to be sure when he was dreaming and when he wasn't? "How often did I come down to the study?" he asked dubiously. "More than once?"

"Now, Tom, I'm not going to talk any more," Mother answered. "I want you to go to sleep—and you've all to-morrow to ask questions."

But he knew that to-morrow she would find some fresh pretext for putting him off. "I can't go to sleep like this," he complained. "I'm far more likely to go to sleep if you tell me about it first."

Mother looked at him and hesitated. "I *have* told you," she said, "all that there *is* to tell."

"Oh, Mother dear!" Tom protested.

"But what do you want to know?" she asked, half laughing. "There's no *secret*! I never saw such a boy for weaving mysteries and romances out of nothing!"

"I want to know about walking in my sleep," Tom replied. "Did I do it more than once?"

"Once!" Mother exclaimed. "Once a night would be more like it." Then, as he lay gazing at her with a frown puckering his forehead, she resigned herself to the inevitable. "It was like living in the house with a small ghost," she said, "and I got so accustomed to it that I used to look at the clock if you were a few minutes late. Luckily it didn't have to be midnight; between half-past ten and eleven was when we expected you, and it never occurred twice in the same night. As soon as you had had your little perambulation, that ended it, and you were all right till morning. Now, are you satisfied?"

Tom lay pondering. "How long ago was it?" he asked.

"Three—no, it must be more than three years ago. At least, that was when it started and when it was really bad. Later it

88

became less frequent, and in the end we believed you had out-grown it. Doctor Macrory always said you would. And so you have, really; to-night's performance was an exception and only happened because you weren't very well."

"Why didn't you tell me before?" Tom questioned suspiciously.

"I don't know—except that Doctor Macrory thought it might be better not to."

"You weren't even going to tell me now," Tom reproached her, but he was too much interested and too curious to dwell on that aspect of the matter. "It was queer," he went on, "that I didn't wake when I came down to the study. I woke up to-night the minute Daddy grabbed hold of me—that is, if I was really asleep."

"We didn't grab hold of you," Mother said. "We were always very careful. And now——"

But Tom interrupted her. "What did I do?" he asked.

"Nothing," Mother answered. "You were as good as gold. You used to open the door and come into the room—that was all. As I say, exactly like a little ghost. You took no notice of us, and when we'd turned you round, back you'd march to bed again without the least trouble."

"But didn't you speak to me?" Tom still pressed her. "Why didn't you? Are you sure I was asleep?"

Mother sighed. "That's the worst of telling you anything! There's never an end to it. You know *yourself* that you must have been asleep, or you'd remember about it. *You* sometimes spoke, but we didn't."

"And can't you remember anything I said?"

"No, I can't," Mother answered. "You didn't talk to us at all, you didn't even know we were there. . . . There's nothing wonderful about it," she added, "lots of people talk in their sleep now and then. I dare say most people do."

Tom turned on the pillow so that he faced her. "Weren't you cross?" he asked.

"Cross!" Mother repeated uncomprehendingly.

"Well, it must have been a nuisance if it happened so often."

"Oh, I see! No, I wasn't cross."

After that he lay quiet for so long a time that she began to think he must have dropped asleep, when suddenly he said: "I'd like you to sing to me."

She was accustomed to abrupt changes of mood, but this one was more surprising than usual. "Sing!" she exclaimed. "That would be a nice thing to do at this hour of the night—and wake up the whole house!"

"You need only hum," Tom coaxed her. "That won't wake anybody."

His face was flushed now—even his forehead—and when she put her hand against his cheek it felt hot and dry. She didn't know precisely what lay behind his odd request, but she could guess perhaps, so she began to sing in hardly more than a whisper, and instantly he smiled. This made her want to kiss him, but she was afraid it might disturb his drowsiness if she did, so she sang on, in the lowest voice she could produce—lower even than her speaking voice. And outside in the garden other voices presently were raised, though it was barely dawn. But by this time she could hear him breathing and knew that he must really be asleep.

CHAPTER X

Tom wasn't ill at all—at least nothing to signify—though Mother insisted on getting Doctor Macrory to see him, and Doctor Macrory, just because he had been called in, wrote a prescription and kept him in bed. He was sitting up, with several pillows behind him, on the afternoon of the third day, when Mary opened the door and announced Master Pascoe. Master Pascoe thereupon entered, and from the foot of the bed gazed at the invalid commiseratingly.

Tom put down his book and said: "Hello!"

He had not expected this call, and for some silly reason its first effect upon him was to make him feel embarrassed. This was partly due to Pascoe's attitude, which was exactly that of a visitor at the Zoo. He kept on staring as if the bars of the bed were the bars of a cage, till Tom at last advised him to go down to the study and get the field-glasses; then he stopped.

"I only wanted to see how you were," he apologized. "You don't look too bad. What's the matter?"

"Nothing. . . . Just I wasn't well."

Pascoe seemed satisfied with this diagnosis, and came round to the side of the bed. He had a parcel in his hand, and in silence he proceeded to remove the string and paper, revealing within the outer wrapper yet another paper—a paper bag—while Tom watched the performance with curiosity.

"I got you these," Pascoe explained, "because I thought they'd be strengthening, being filled with wine."

Tom, still more surprised, expressed his thanks.

"They're wine gums," Pascoe continued. "I don't expect you've ever tasted them before."

"Why?" Tom asked. "I mean, why shouldn't I have tasted them? Are they expensive?"

Pascoe, being a truthful boy, hesitated. "As a rule I expect they are," he compromised. "But these weren't—so very. . . . I mean I got them more or less a bargain."

"Oh," said Tom, noncommittally.

"It was for the very queer reason, too, that they had been in the shop for some time."

To Tom, however, the reason appeared quite comprehensible, though he did not say so, Pascoe's eyes being fixed upon him.

"Of course, that only makes them better," Pascoe pointed out, "because wine improves with age. In fact it isn't really good till it *is* old. Everybody knows that."

"The man in the shop can't have known it," Tom mentioned guardedly.

"No. People like that don't drink wine; they only drink beer or stout. Anyway it wasn't a man, it was a woman, and Daddy says women are never judges of wine."

Tom did not dispute the opinion. Pascoe's father, he knew, was a wine merchant; in fact generations of Pascoes had been in the wine trade—Pascoe, Wine Merchant, established 1802—he had seen the place often, down town—dark but attractive-looking —old-fashioned—with a low doorway, low windows, and a brown dusky interior within which, amid casks and flagons and cob-webby bottles, somewhere lurked Pascoe senior, rubicund and genial, though Tom had never actually been introduced to him.

Still, wine gums weren't just the same as wine, he thought; they must consist of a variety of materials, not all of which would be improved by keeping. Meanwhile Pascoe junior placed the open bag on the counterpane between them, and since he could hardly refuse, Tom rather gingerly selected a specimen and began to chew it. It tasted better than he had expected, for viewed in the mass the wine gums looked distinctly unappetizing, with a tendency to coalesce, even to liquefy; but taken singly they proved not so bad—sticky and soft and sweet—eatable at any rate. "Thanks awfully," he repeated. "It was jolly decent of you."

Pascoe did not deny the decency. He too helped himself, and then sat down beside the bed, after which, amid fragmentary talk, they munched the wine gums for some time.

The bag indeed was more than half empty when Pascoe pro-nounced these astonishing words: "We'll stop the minute we begin to feel the effects. It doesn't matter with you of course, but I have to ride home."

Tom's jaws slowly ceased to work as he turned an uneasy gaze upon his friend. "What effects?" he asked, with a dawning con-sciousness that he had begun to feel them already.

"We may get tight," Pascoe replied, "with any luck."

Tom was startled. That Pascoe, of all people, should express such a desire, was bewildering. It must be inherited. It detracted too, he couldn't help feeling, from the generosity of the gift, reducing it at once from an act of sympathy to a mere experi-ment of dubious disinterestedness. Anyhow, he didn't see why Pascoe need smack his lips in such a fashion, and told him so.

92

"I'm tasting," Pascoe said. "You always make a noise like that when you're tasting."

"I don't," Tom contradicted, "and it's pretty awful! You don't eat your meals in that way, I hope."

"No. You don't understand. I don't mean ordinary tasting. You only taste like this with samples—when you're trying a new wine. I've seen Daddy doing it heaps of times. Sometimes you spit the wine out again."

"Well, you needn't do that here," Tom exclaimed quickly. "It's disgusting enough as it is."

Pascoe was not offended. "All right," he said; "I wasn't going to." And with that he stopped tasting, or at least stopped making a noise. "The exams began to-day," he presently observed. "I did rather well in the maths papers. Have another wine gum."

"No, thanks," Tom muttered, turning his head round towards the window and lying very still. His voice, too, had acquired an unusual, muffled sound, and something in his aspect—a slight haggardness, a peculiar hue perhaps—appeared to strike Pascoe, who leaned forward, looking at him hopefully. "Do you feel ——" he was beginning, when Tom with a sudden upheaval of the clothes half scrambled, half tumbled out of bed. On his knees he groped frantically beneath it, and then, before the solemn eyes of his visitor, was painfully and emphatically ill.

Pascoe, quickly retreating, watched the catastrophe from a distance. "Hard luck!" he murmured.

But Tom, with the sweat trickling down his forehead, and his hands clutching the counterpane, could not answer for some time. "It's your beastly wine gums," he at last managed to gasp, hurt and annoyed by the calmness of Pascoe's tone. "You'd better ring the bell," he added, getting back shakily between the sheets.

Pascoe crossed the room, but at the chimney-piece he paused in thought. "What are you going to say?" he inquired.

"I'm going to say I've been sick," Tom answered impatiently. "Unless you want to take it away yourself."

Pascoe didn't, so he rang the bell, and immediately afterwards announced: "I think I ought to be going."

"All right," Tom answered coldly, for he knew well enough why Pascoe wanted to go, and indeed Pascoe himself made no secret of it. "Your mother will think it was my fault," he explained.

"So it was," Tom replied.

"I couldn't tell that *this* would happen," Pascoe murmured deprecatingly. "I really thought they might buck you up a bit. Honestly I did. That was why I got them."

"You got them to see if they'd make us drunk," Tom told him. "And you jolly well waited till I'd made myself ill before you mentioned a word about it."

Pascoe's gaze was still fixed upon him. "You're surely not going to tell her *that*!" he expostulated.

"I'm not going to tell her *anything*," Tom answered. "Because for one thing she's out." And with this he shut his eyes and kept them shut till Mary appeared in the doorway. Then he opened them and looked at her. "Mary, I've been sick," he said.

Mary, who had actually brought them up tea, hastily set down the tray. With unerring instinct—though possibly helped by the sight of the paper bag—she at once grasped the situation. "My goodness, Master Tom, what rubbish have you been eating at all? I'd have thought you'd have had more sense!"

So for that matter would Tom, and he did not defend himself; but Pascoe detected a reflection on the quality of his gift. "As it happens, what he was eating was perfectly harmless," he interposed loftily. "And people are never sick unless they require to be."

Mary gave a kind of snort. "Oh, indeed!" she retorted. "It's well there's somebody that knows everything! Of all the conceited little brats!" And she flounced out of the room, bearing with her the evidence of calamity.

Tom chuckled feebly, but Pascoe's face was crimson. "She oughtn't to be allowed to speak like that," he spluttered. "You ought——"

"How can *I* help it!" Tom interrupted. "I expect she and Phemie were in the middle of their tea when the bell rang, and it's not the sort of job anybody likes at such a time. You were jolly lucky that she didn't box your ears."

He chuckled again, and Pascoe stalked to the door with a frigid "Good-bye."

"Good-bye," Tom called after him. "Thanks for coming."

Pascoe stopped. With his hand on the door-knob he stood wavering. At last he turned round. "I *may* come to see you again or I may not," he pronounced doubtfully.

"If you don't," Tom reminded him, "you won't be able to dam the stream."

Pascoe instantly returned to the bedside. He particularly wanted to dam the stream, and had even planned the construction of a new channel. Anyhow his exit was all spoiled by Tom's indifference, so it was with a complete return to affability that he asked: "When do you think you'll be well enough?"

"I don't know. In a day or two. At the moment I believe I'm going to be sick again."

"Oh, here!" Pascoe remonstrated, drawing hurriedly back.

"Well, I can't help it," Tom grumbled, though he was still half laughing. "I feel rotten."

"I'll tell that woman," said Pascoe. "And I dare say I'll come to-morrow."

This time he really did go, and a minute or two later Mary reappeared. "I'm most frightfully sorry, Mary," Tom apologized humbly. "It was a false alarm."

But when he was alone again he shut his eyes and lay quiet. He was glad Pascoe had gone, for he wanted to lie still, without talking to anybody. In a little while he might begin to read, but just now it was more comfortable to lie thinking. Pascoe's visit had reminded him of school and Miss Jimpson, and that his absence must have interfered with her plans concerning Mr. Holbrook. Not that he could really have helped her much. Mother, to whom he had imparted his impressions of Miss Jimpson's romance, had told him it was all nonsense and that he was on no account to say or do anything. She had been very positive about this, and for some reason not particularly pleased. . . .

Dash it all, he might have talked to Pascoe about the holidays!

Those beastly wine gums had put it out of his head. Pascoe usually spent his holidays with an ancient aunt who lived in the Manor House at Greencastle in Donegal, and it was to Greencastle that Tom and Mother and Daddy were going—to an hotel there. Of course he had already told Pascoe this, but they hadn't had time to discuss it properly and there were all sorts of questions he wanted to ask. However, he was pretty sure Pascoe would come back to-morrow. . . .

He wondered if he would see much of Pascoe after the holidays. Not nearly *so* much, anyhow, for Pascoe, like Brown, was leaving at the end of term, and at his new school he would be a boarder. Tom half wished that he was leaving too, though he dreaded changes. Still, he would have to leave fairly soon in any case, and it might as well be now—Daddy had even suggested it, but had somehow let the matter drop. On the other hand he would like to stay on till after the Christmas concert, and he would hate saying good-bye to Mr. Holbrook: there were difficulties both ways. . . .

Presently he took up his book. He did not open it, but holding it in his hands still lay thinking. The book didn't interest him, it was stodgy and dull—a story of the Peninsular War, and war stories always bored him. There was a book downstairs in the study, however, which did interest him, and he felt suddenly tempted to go and get it. The temptation was strong, and it was undisguised, for Tom knew very well that it was temptation. He had discovered this book some weeks ago, quite by chance, on the top shelf of a locked bookcase, and had first been attracted by the queer pictures it contained. These had to do with magic, but not the kind of magic described in fairy tales. This was utterly different, and, whether true or false, was propounded seriously, while the magicians mentioned were persons who had actually lived— Nicholas Flamel, Schroepffer of Leipsig, Cagliostro, Doctor Dee and others—wizards and alchemists, evokers of spirits, searchers for the Elixir of Life and the Stone of the Philosophers. The book told of black magic and white magic, of the doctrine and rituals; it explained ceremonies and symbols, it described experiments. Tom had kept his discovery to himself, feeling sure, before he had read many pages, that though this book must belong to Daddy, Daddy certainly would forbid him to read it. He *had* read it however; there could be no going back on that. He had not only read it but pored over it, and at present he wanted to pore over it again. Yet in another way he didn't, because he knew that he would hide it under the bedclothes the moment he heard Mother coming in, and that was rotten. Besides, there were things in the book—— He didn't quite know what some of them meant, though he could guess vaguely, and that, somehow, helped to keep them in his mind. It might have been this book, too, that had first made him begin to think queer thoughts about Henry.

What he didn't understand was how it could ever have come into the possession of Daddy. He could understand Daddy's borrowing it, and glancing through it perhaps, out of curiosity, but not keeping it. For one thing, he wouldn't believe a word of it: in fact it was exactly the sort of stuff that would irritate him most, with its fantastic statements unsupported by proof, and its mysterious hints at secrets that must not be fully revealed. Of course, Daddy might have bought it with a lot of other books at an auction, or it might have been given to him. It was at any rate a strange book for him to have; and Mother, Tom was sure, would think it wicked.

Abruptly he decided that he wouldn't look at it again. Yet still he didn't feel happy. There wasn't much virtue in so late a resolution—nor much use either, since his memory could now supply all that his imagination needed. He felt that perhaps he ought to tell Daddy about it: he felt that he wasn't quite what either Daddy or Mother believed him to be. And that was to put it mildly! Anyway, he resolved that he wouldn't look at the book again, or, if he could help it, think about it. . . .

This determination brought him relief, and gradually his mind emptied and stilled. His feeling of sickness, too, had completely gone; he felt now only languid and comfortably drowsy. The soft summer murmur floated in to him through the open windows. The afternoon sounds, the afternoon silence, were different from the morning, he thought—or was it only the light that was deeper? He would think of pleasant things. Mother said Donegal was lovely. That was easy to believe, but Mother had never been in the particular part of Donegal they were going to, so had been unable to give him any details. He lay making pictures of the sea; and behind the pictures he called up, and washing through them, was a low endless music, for he could not look at even imaginary waves without also hearing them. . . .

"Well, have you had a nice sleep?" Mother was home again, and bending down over him with her hat still on, so that she must only this moment have come in.

"I suppose so," he smiled.

"And are you feeling better?"

"Yes, a great deal better, Mother dear." And this was true: half an hour's sleep had revived him marvellously. But he knew from the way she had spoken that her inquiry had merely been a general one, and that she had heard nothing about the wine gums. Probably she had come straight upstairs without seeing Mary.

"That's good," she said. "Would you like to get up? I don't mean now, but after dinner. I shouldn't think it would do you any harm to get up for an hour or two then."

"I will," said Tom. "Have you just come in?"

"A few minutes ago," Mother answered. "It's nearly half-past six. What have you been doing?"

"Nothing much," said Tom. "Pascoe was here for a bit. What have *you* been doing?"

"Interviewing Mr. Pemberton part of the time. I think we'll try to get away as soon as we can—perhaps early next week—and I wanted to explain things to him."

"But will Daddy be able to go next week?" Tom inquired.

"I don't know; we'll talk it over this evening." She sat down on the side of his bed.

"Where did you meet Mr. Pemberton?" Tom asked, after a moment.

"I didn't meet him, I called at the school."

"But——" His brow puckered a little.

98

"I saw your friend Miss Jimpson too," Mother went on, "and had a talk with *her*."

This was getting serious, and Tom's face reflected his anxiety. "You didn't mention what I told you, I hope?"

Mother looked at him curiously. "About her troubles? No: she struck me as being a singularly heart-whole young woman, and quite capable of attending to her own affairs."

Still he wasn't completely reassured, for he knew Mother had a habit of saying whatever came into her head, without caring a scrap to whom she said it. "What *did* you talk about?" he persisted.

"Chiefly about you," Mother teased him. "Miss Jimpson seems very fond of you."

Tom blushed. "Oh!" he muttered, taken aback. He waited for her to tell him more, but she didn't, so he was obliged to ask: "What did she say?"

"That she thought you were a dear little boy, though at the same time rather peculiar."

Tom blushed again. He didn't believe Miss Jimpson had said that—at least not just so plump and plain, nor in those words. "Did you tell her I wasn't?" he demanded, for Mother had another of her pauses.

"No, why should I? I entirely agreed with her."

Tom glanced up quickly, and then for a little lay silent. "Did you talk for long?" was his next question.

"Not very; a quarter of an hour perhaps. Much can be said in a quarter of an hour." She still smiled down at him, and then suddenly asked: "Why are you so suspicious? What do you *imagine* I may have said to her?"

"I *can't* imagine," Tom murmured doubtfully; "that's just the trouble."

He became conscious that Mother was looking at him with an ironical expression in her eyes, and he turned away. "Would you rather people *dis*liked you?" she said, but he made no reply. He knew that she knew he hated people to dislike him, and indeed next moment she proved it by adding: "So you see!"

She stooped down and Tom put his arms round her neck.

"Why are you such a silly?" she whispered.

99

He didn't know why, and he didn't know that it *was* silly. Pascoe, he was sure, would have hated to be thought a dear little boy, and still more to be called one; and though he hadn't any particular wish to resemble Pascoe, neither was there any need to be sloppy. He wondered if he *was* sloppy? He was afraid it looked very like it—sometimes. Secret sloppiness didn't so much matter; at all events you couldn't help it; but open sloppiness was another thing, and the difficulty was to keep it secret—at least with people like Mother, who didn't pay the slightest attention to what you said, but went bang behind your words to what they outwardly denied. He felt very contented now, for instance, though there was no doubt that she was petting him. In fact it was pretty awful, and she herself of course was quite shameless. But then, he liked it, and she must have guessed that. He sighed, and thought of the reserved and austere Pascoe. Also he thought that he wasn't a "dear little boy", and perhaps he ought to tell her so. He wasn't particularly little to begin with, and, though he might be dear to Mother, that wasn't what either she or Miss Jimpson had meant. What they had meant was something quite different, and it wasn't true. It might be true in some ways—at least he hoped it was—but it certainly wasn't in all.

Part Two

CHAPTER XI

The house was to be shut up, though William of course was to look after the garden as usual. But Phemie and Mary were going to stay with their own people near Downpatrick, and this had created the problem of Henry. Henry had no people, or none that anybody knew about, and obviously he couldn't be taken to an hotel. It was decided therefore to leave him, like the garden, to William, until Phemie at the last moment thought he would be more comfortable at Downpatrick. Why, nobody quite knew, and Mother was doubtful if Henry would want to go; but Phemie was sure he would. She made ready a travelling-basket, and after all, though everyone had forgotten about it, she had a kind of proprietary right in Henry, he was *her* cat, or at least it was she who had first opened the door to him. So that was settled, and it was remarkable how confident Phemie was, even going the length of showing the basket beforehand to Henry, who glanced at it and yawned. "You see, Master Tom, it will be quite easy."

Thus speaking, Phemie placed the basket on the kitchen table, with a sort of "this-is-how-we-do-it" air, like a conjuror about to perform a trick that has never yet failed.

"Wouldn't it be better to shut the window?" Tom suggested, but Phemie ignored his advice. She smiled and shook her head. Then she approached Henry, who having recently finished a plate of fish was in a lethargic mood, and allowed her to lift him in her arms and set him standing up in the basket. True, she had to hold him there, but his struggles were perfunctory, there was really nothing more to do except to get him to lie down so that the lid could be closed and fastened. That was a simple matter, and to accomplish it Phemie, still smiling complacently, laid a large flat hand on the middle of Henry's back. Tom at this point breathed

"Look out!" but Phemie pressed firmly and at the same time tried to pull down the lid. It was only then that Henry awakened to her intention. His whole body stiffened; he neither spat nor swore; but he drew one lightning incision about two inches long down Phemie's wrist. There was a scream; the basket was knocked flying; and Henry, like a black streak, disappeared through the kitchen window.

Phemie wept, which in so strong-minded a person struck Tom as disappointing. It struck Mother in the same light, for there was nothing to cry about, though the scratch was a nasty one and had to be treated with iodine. After that nobody pretended to have any further qualms about leaving Henry behind; William was told to fix up a bed for him in the wood-shed; and though it was practically certain that Henry would occupy another bed, of his own choosing, human duties were felt to be fulfilled.

Henry in the meantime was gone, and after such behaviour you wouldn't have expected him to reappear till the house was shut and the coast clear; yet actually he turned up half an hour later, when Phemie and Mary had departed to catch their train. Daddy and Mother were still upstairs, but the luggage had been brought down and packed into the car, and Tom was merely waiting in the hall when Henry strolled in through the open front door just as if nothing had happened. He walked straight up to Tom, his tail in the air, and began to rub against his legs, purring loudly. "No," Tom scolded, rejecting these overtures. "You're a bad cat and I don't want you. You can have the house to yourself since you're so determined; but it will be the outside of it."

He had no sooner said this, however, than it struck him as premature. Nothing was more probable than that Henry would contrive to find a way into the house if he wished to. Just now he seemed to be very affectionate and anxious to make friends, but hadn't he already achieved the first of his purposes, which simply was to be left behind?

And Henry, between Tom's legs, purred louder and louder, rolling up his eyes sentimentally. There weren't any whites, but if there had been, nothing else would have been visible, so Tom looked into the "greens" and pondered. There must be something behind all this—some object—and though he failed to guess the object, he sat down on the floor and absentmindedly began to stroke Henry, without realizing that he was doing so.

Henry arched his spine and gave a tiny guttural cry from the back of his throat. It was really quite a touching picture of the emotional interval before bidding farewell; and also, Tom felt, it was a direct invitation to him not to go with the others, but to change his mind and stay on, when he and Henry would have the house to themselves.

"I must be getting frightfully suspicious," he thought. And, "We're a nice pair!" he added to Henry. "Though it's mostly your fault and I'm not just going to let you have it all your own way."

At these words Henry hid his face, thrusting it against Tom's jacket, while simultaneously the grandfather's clock struck eleven, and Tom couldn't help thinking there was warning in its voice, and, when he looked up, in its kind old face also. It was a clock of the highest principles—anybody could see that—and he turned Henry round so that he might get an object lesson. But Henry didn't look—wouldn't look—which in itself was a bad sign. The clock, Tom decided, ought to be wound up the very last thing, so that for eight days at least, even if Henry did succeed in breaking in, the house would have a proper guardian. The only drawback to this scheme was that he had been strictly forbidden to wind it: Daddy always wound it himself; and there wouldn't be the least use in trying to explain the present situation to Daddy.

He *would* wind it. He hesitated only for a moment, then quickly crossed the hall, opened the case, and proceeded to do so —after which he felt better. He listened to the comfortable ticks, and each tick assured him that the clock was pleased and would try to keep awake as long as possible. "I believe he will, too," Tom said; and to Henry: "Now—he'll tell me everything that happens while we're away, so you'd better be careful!"

"And goodness knows what he's up to at this moment!" he concluded aloud, for he had merely been going over all this part-

103

ing scene in memory; actually Henry and the clock were far away; Tom, Daddy, and Mother had been in Donegal for more than a week now, staying at the Fort Hotel at Greencastle; and at the present moment he was climbing the hill to Glenagivney.

Or not exactly that, because he had come to a temporary halt, and for the last five minutes had been sitting on a stone bridge resting. The climb was a long one, and the hill—though the other afternoon when they had driven over in the car it had seemed nothing—this morning had proved to be one of those wearying and deceptive hills whose summits retreat at the same rate as you advance, so that you always have another final stretch in front of you. Tom's jacket was slung over his left arm, a luncheon basket was on the bridge beside him, and the day, as he reflected, beating off the flies with his handkerchief, was about the hottest day he could have chosen for his excursion.

Not that he really had chosen it, or for that matter been given any choice. He wouldn't be here now if he hadn't received a post-card from Pascoe to announce that Pascoe himself would be arriving to-morrow, and would be staying with Aunt Rhoda till the end of the holidays. That had settled it: it must be to-day or never.

Yet when he had mentioned his plan, giving the reason why it would have to be carried out at once, it had called forth un-favourable comments from both Daddy and Mother. Also untrue and unjust, for it certainly didn't imply, as they appeared to think it must, that he wouldn't be glad to see Pascoe or didn't want his company. It only meant that on his last visit to Glena-givney he had felt very much attracted by the place, and had decided that he would like to return to it some day by himself. He didn't know exactly why he wished to do this, though it was partly because it had seemed so secluded and deserted, even with Daddy and Mother there, that he couldn't help imagining how completely solitary it would be if he were alone. It would be strange; it would be exciting; it would be an adventure; possibly he mightn't like it as much as he expected, but far more probably he would. . . .

Yet that was not all—was not even the chief thing. Only the

104

chief thing could hardly be expressed even to himself. It was—
wasn't it?—a feeling, ever so deeply and mysteriously alluring,
that there was just the remotest, just the faintest chance that he
might meet somebody. This, in a way, perhaps appeared contra-
dictory; but it wasn't really—not with the kind of meeting, the
kind of person, he had in mind. Possibly there *was* no such person
—outside dreamland—but possibly there was, and *if* there was,
then this place was as close to dreamland as solitude and loveli-
ness could make it. Naturally, however, he couldn't tell Daddy
and Mother such things, though he had often thought them and
sometimes dreamed them. Anyhow, by coming alone, he didn't
see what harm he would be doing to Pascoe. . . .

He listened to the stream trickling far down below him, under
the road. He began to print his name on the stone, but the point
of his pencil broke. He had rested long enough, he must be getting on, and he slid down from the bridge and caught up his
jacket and basket.

The road was thick with dust and so steep that in places horses
and donkeys had to draw their carts from side to side in a zig-zag
track. Here and there it was actually solid rock, which must make
it frightfully slippery in winter, especially for the small feet of the
donkeys. Tom's own feet were big, and so were his hands. He
ought to have pointed this out to Mr. Holbrook, for it might be a
hopeful sign. . . .

On either side of the road stretched the heather, purple and
brown and dark olive-green, with black patches where the turf
had been cut. There were no trees, but only the wide gentle
curve of the hill rounded against the sky, very simple, and somehow soothing.

Now that he had left the bridge and the stream behind him, he
wished that he had taken a drink while he still had had the
chance. He had been a long while on this road, partly because of
donkeys who weren't working and therefore had time for a little
gossip, and partly because of stones in his shoes. Every time he
got a stone in his shoe he sat down on the bank, and every time he
sat down on the bank he found it hard to get up again. It was so
hot, with that cloudless sky and not a vestige of shade, and he

very much doubted if carrying his jacket was really a good plan. The grasshoppers made as much din as if they were being broiled on frying-pans. He wished that he hadn't brought a basket at all, though at the time, when Miss Forbes had suggested it, he had been pleased. Already he had examined the contents. It contained a thermos flask, a bottle of milk, a knife, a spoon, a cup, cake, sandwiches, bread, biscuits, cheese, bananas, sugar, butter, salt— and some of these things were pure luxuries, he could have done quite well without them.

The sun was almost directly overhead and so fiery that if you looked at it through your fingers it was like a solid ball of white flame. Well, he must be near the top now—and—yes—here it was! And there down below him, though still some distance off, was the sea.

It looked intensely blue under a glittering haze of light. It looked as if it were absolutely unvisited and unknown. The descent on this side was much shorter and steeper than the hill he had just climbed, and the country was greener, being mostly pasture land. There were two or three white cottages, but he saw no human beings anywhere.

Near the bottom of the descent, the road, which had been growing narrower, branched off sharply to the left, and became a grassy track, winding between thick fuchsia hedges to the entrance of a rocky gorge, from which rose a low murmurous noise of water. Where the hedges were broken, Tom caught a glimpse of high grey rocks threaded with silver streaks. Under the shadow of the hedge the grass was thick and long, and the golden pollen of the buttercups brushed off on to his shoes. There was a pungent scent of wild vegetation everywhere—quite different from the heavier, sweeter scent of a garden—and some of the fields were so white with daisies that they looked as if they were deep in snow.

"I'm going to rest here," Tom made up his mind, "and get cool again." So he lay down in the grass under the hedge—lay on his back as close to the hedge as a half-hidden ditch would allow —and after the hot glare of the sun it was like being in a green twilight.

"This would be a good place to camp out," Tom thought.

It would be easy enough to do it, too—with Pascoe. Pascoe was what old Pemby called a resourceful boy. He had mended the spring of Pemby's gate for him one afternoon, while Pemby himself had stood watching and beaming through his glasses. Tom also had looked on, and not been resourceful. In that respect he took after Daddy, who, according to William, "had no hands". "The master has no hands," William had explained confidentially to Tom; and this after poor Daddy had spent nearly half an hour trying to adjust the lawn mower. "I'm not sure that it's much better than it was, William. Perhaps *you* can find out what's wrong." William had merely stood silent and supercilious, and the moment Daddy was gone: "The master has no hands," he had said. "These learned people's all like that."

Pascoe had hands, and if a tent could somewhere be borrowed he would be sure to be able to rig it up and do the other necessary things. Yet in spite of his resourcefulness Pascoe wasn't the companion Tom imagined as sharing his adventure. He wasn't like him in any single way: which was indeed easy to see, for at that moment the companion appeared.

He had scrambled through a gap in the hedge, and when he saw Tom he stopped short as if in half a mind about scrambling back again—a very ragged boy, with bare feet, no jacket, and rents in his shirt and trousers through which his skin showed. He had hair the colour of the bleached ears of wheat, and the brightest eyes Tom had ever beheld.

While he stood hesitating, neither advancing nor retreating, Tom sat up. Then the boy, though still keeping at a distance of two or three yards from him, sat down facing him. He had a home-made fishing-rod in his hand, which he laid on the grass beside him, and a basket filled with damp dark watercress. He gazed at Tom in alert stillness.

There was something in this fixed gaze that Tom found unusual. It was not rude, but it was very much interested, and the interest was of an oddly impersonal kind, just as if he were confronted with an experience entirely new to him. But they couldn't sit staring at each other for ever, and to break the silence, and because he could think of nothing else to say, Tom pointed to the watercress and asked: "Where did you get it?"

"Down there," the boy replied, without removing his gaze from Tom's face. "There's plenty in the stream. Fishes, too, if you can catch them." He lifted off the top layer of watercress and revealed beneath it three speckled trout. "You could cut a willow rod that might do."

Tom shook his head. "I haven't a line, or a hook, or bait."

"I've a line," the boy said, "and the bait's only wor-r-rms."

He pronounced the last word slowly, and put so many "r's" into it that Tom thought he must be Scotch. But the rest of his speech wasn't Scotch. Besides, dressed as he was, he must be a native, a farm-boy very likely, belonging to one of the thatched cottages Tom had passed a quarter of a mile back, for there were no others between this and the sea. He decided to ask the boy if he lived here, and was very much astonished when he answered "No".

After this he began to laugh, and when Tom wanted to know what he was laughing at, he said "At you", and instantly became grave.

The strange thing was that Tom didn't feel a bit offended by this speech, it merely quickened his curiosity. "Why?" he questioned. "Because I asked you where you lived? I don't see anything funny in that!"

"No," the boy agreed, "it wasn't funny." Yet he said this, too, in an unusual way, as if he were only accepting Tom's word for it; and he still kept on looking at him inquiringly. "I don't know what 'funny' is," he presently added. "I was really laughing for practice."

This was a very strange boy, Tom thought. A little astray in his wits probably—only his eyes, his whole face, seemed to deny that. And he just sat there, without speaking again, but watching Tom intently and looking rather lovely. It was queer, but he *was* lovely—really lovely: his beauty seemed to shine through his rags, and he sat with a most peculiar lightness, like a butterfly poised on a leaf.

"Where *do* you live?" Tom tried again, and the boy, without turning, waved his hand.

"Over there," he said; but the gesture was vague, and might have included the whole sky and sea. Tom, at any rate, could make nothing of it.

Neither could he very well go on asking questions; it would be better to mention something about himself; so he did this, and told where he was staying and about his walk that morning, and ended by telling his name.

"I have a name," the boy at once replied; and when Tom asked him what it was, he said: "Gamelyn."

Tom repeated the syllables to himself. He had never heard the name before, and it might be either a Christian name or a surname. "That's only one of your names," he said aloud. "What's the other?"

Then the boy answered: "I have no other."

Tom said nothing except "Oh!" After that he sat thinking. The bright clear eyes were still fixed upon him, and now he shrank a little from their light. Surely it had increased! Not a word had Tom uttered, nevertheless the boy answered just as if he had spoken: "I was sent to you. I am what you asked for."

"I didn't ask for anything," Tom denied, but his voice had a quaver in it, and it was with an effort that he went on more firmly: "I don't think I can wait here any longer. I must go down to the sea."

Then the boy smiled at him and immediately his uneasiness vanished.

"Why did you say that?" he asked. "I mean about being sent to me. It wasn't true, was it? How could you have been sent to me?" Yet it might be true, he reflected; he might have been sent from one of the cottages.

The boy shook his head. "I was sent because you wanted me. I was told to come. *Didn't* you want me?"

There was a pause before Tom's reply came, very haltingly: "I don't know. I don't know who you are."

"I'm an angel," the boy smiled. "*Your* angel. You must have imagined me and wanted me. You must have imagined me very strongly, because if you hadn't I couldn't have come."

A still longer silence followed, and then Tom muttered unhappily: "I imagined a boy."

"I'm a boy," the angel said—"the boy you thought of."

"You're not," Tom answered. "It was a human boy I thought of."

As he spoke the last words it seemed to him that the figure before him quivered and grew less distinct. The voice too was now hardly more than a sighing of the wind. "Once—twice—a third time—and then no more. . . ." But Tom could not be sure that he had really heard these words, and now that it was too late he cried out: "Don't go away. . . . Don't. . . ."

There was no boy—no angel—only a vanishing brightness in the air, soon indistinguishable from the sunshine.

Simultaneously there sounded a music as of the chiming of innumerable tiny bells. It came from the fuchsia flowers above his head, and it was wakening him, though he tried not to awaken. But something else was awakening him also—a touch, a warm breath on his hair. Abruptly he opened his eyes and found himself staring straight into the long narrow face of an inquisitive old goat.

CHAPTER XII

"Go away!" said Tom sharply, and the goat, who had been bending down over him, was momentarily startled, and backed several paces. There she paused to size Tom up. This did not take long, and, the result being reassuring, she approached again.

She had managed to uproot the peg to which she was tethered and it trailed after her at the end of a rope. Tom distrusted goats. Moreover this particular goat had a sardonic gleam in her eye which boded little good. He would have retreated had it been possible to do so, but it wasn't, and the goat realized this. It may have been sheer playfulness, but suddenly she rose half sideways on her hind legs in an extraordinary fashion, and Tom, without an instant's hesitation, rolled backward into the ditch.

Luckily it was dry, so he got only a few nettle stings. But the goat, surprised by his abrupt disappearance, advanced to the edge of the ditch to see what had happened. Once more they stared at each other face to face. Then—and actually leaning over him to do it—she began to pluck sprays of ivy from the bank on the other side. "This really was the limit!" Tom thought. "Only what could he do?" And she showed no sign of moving on. He was obliged to crawl along the bottom of the ditch on hands and knees, encountering further nettles and brambles, while the goat, quite regardless of the trouble she was causing, continued her meal. Then, to crown all, when he judged it safe to clamber out again, she immediately gave chase, so that he had to take to his heels.

The pursuit, it is true, was brief, and on the goat's part not very serious, but it was none the less alarming to Tom. Besides, he had left his basket behind and didn't see how he was going to retrieve it. The goat, he felt sure, still had her eye on him. Without the least inconvenience she could watch his movements and continue to eat at the same time. It was most annoying. Perhaps if he were in his turn to attack—to advance boldly and with loud shouts—— But he didn't think so: a peace-offering would be better. Only the rich greenness of the lane seemed to make any additional offerings rather superfluous. Everything she could possibly desire was there already and within easy reach. The lane was a kind of caprine Paradise. All she had to do was to stretch her neck and she seemed jolly good at that. The grass was long and juicy; the hedge was full of honeysuckle, ivy, and convolvulus; there were pollard willows above her, and cow-parsley and wild strawberry plants under her feet. There was also deadly nightshade, Tom perceived, but nothing was deadly to goats. She was now sampling some furze prickles. Still, an offering was his best chance, so he chose vetches as being easiest and quickest to gather, and collecting a large bunch of these, intermixed with

111

willow-tops, and holding the bunch at arm's length before him, he returned.

The goat seemed surprised to see him. It was as if they were meeting for the first time. She gave conventional little bleats of astonishment as he approached. What a dear little boy! And so kind! Where *had* he got all those lovely things? Surely they couldn't be for her, and really they were far too pretty to eat! She took jolly good care all the same to gobble them up as quickly as possible, and in the process made them sound so crisp and succulent that Tom felt half inclined to try a mouthful himself. He cast the remains of his bouquet at her feet, lifted the basket, and this time walked away with dignity.

He had come out of that rather cleverly, he thought. A resourceful boy—like Pascoe! Only there was never anybody to *see* his resourcefulness, or to be impressed by the way he managed things. . . .

As he proceeded, the sound of the stream grew louder, and another turn brought the whole valley into view. Tom scrambled down to the water's edge. The stream splashed its way swiftly, the stony channel narrowing in places to form miniature rapids, and again widening out into sandy pools. In several of these pools he found watercress.

His dream, driven out of mind by the encounter with the goat, was thus brought back to it, though he couldn't remember the boy's name. A queer name—beginning with an "L". But he wasn't a boy, he was an angel—*his* angel—which meant, Tom supposed, his guardian angel. The only names of angels he could think of were Michael, Raphael, and Gabriel, and it hadn't been any of these; nor, he thought, like them. And was it true that he had imagined an angel before he fell asleep? He was sure it wasn't, though certainly he had been thinking of somebody to camp out with—somebody not like Pascoe. This seemed unkind, but then Pascoe *wasn't* his ideal friend, and there was no use pretending he was. On the other hand, an angel wasn't his ideal friend either, no matter how nice he might look. An angel wasn't right at all, Tom felt: he couldn't be a friend; he was at once not enough and too much.

In the meantime he might as well have his lunch before going any further. Sandwiches usually made you thirsty, and the stream water would be pleasanter to drink than tea out of a thermos flask. So he unpacked his basket, ate a few sandwiches and a banana, and when he had finished took a deep drink. The water was brownish in colour, but clear and cold. Probably it contained iron, in which case he'd better have another cupful, for iron was a tonic, as he knew, having been ordered it after more than one illness by Doctor Macrory.

He repacked his basket and followed the stream down to the shore. Here it became shallower and wider, flowing in several channels, and though it still ran swiftly its voice was lost in the roar of the breaking waves. For a while Tom threw pieces of wood into the current and watched them being carried out to sea, but presently he tired of this amusement and began to walk along the beach. The place *was* as lonely as he had imagined it would be. Perhaps even lonelier, for it seemed to him almost like an undiscovered world. Or an abandoned world maybe—with that black broken hull of a boat half buried in the sand. "The world will be like this," Tom mused, "when all the saints have been caught up into the air."

No sign of a human being: not a soul could have been here to-day; the only marks on the long brown stretch of sand were the thin strange footprints of sea-birds. The entire crescent of the bay must measure more than two hundred yards, and it was shut in behind and at both ends by cliffs which rose nearly perpendicularly to a height of some hundred and fifty feet. These cliffs were covered, but not densely covered, with grass, through which fragments of grey rock thrust forth. The sun was still well above them in spite of Tom's loitering, and the tide must be nearly at its lowest ebb. When it was full, the water would reach almost to the foot of the cliffs, he supposed, because except at the edge the sand was not white and powdery, but brown and smooth.

And it was the most fascinating shore he had ever seen. Below the unbroken stretch of dry sand, the lower, ridged sand was strewn with rocks of many colours—bluish, pink, and every shade between light and dark grey. It was as if in some remote past these rocks had been thrown up by an earthquake; and the water churned between them, and ran up the beach in foam. There were glittering pools and delicate seaweeds—seaweeds moss-green, and seaweeds more brightly green than grass; seaweeds branching like coral and coral-pink; seaweeds brown and purple. There was very little of what he knew as wrack, but there were seaweeds, clinging to the lower flatter rocks, with long smooth slippery blades that were exactly like the razor-strop hanging up on the door of Daddy's and Mother's bathroom. He supposed that all these weeds really had their own individual names, like land weeds, though people just called them vaguely sea weed. It would be interesting to make a collection of them— with Pascoe. Something caused him to add this little tail to his thought—something very like a precaution, though he wasn't sure what the precaution was against. Perhaps an angel. He glanced round, but saw nobody. . . .

The pools were fascinating. They were like small lagoons. There were tiny fishes in them, and crabs, and other creatures. Tom wondered how they managed not to be carried out by the tide. He took off his shoes and stockings, but some of the pools were deeper than they looked, so he took off his trousers as well. He explored the pools for a long time. He'd have bathed, only perhaps the bathing here was dangerous. Anyway, secretly, he much preferred paddling.

Many of the rocks were stained and patterned curiously with beds of minute mussels, purple and black. The colours were clear and beautiful. He stood watching all this vivid sea-washed beauty and listening to the waves. He could have listened to the waves for hours without tiring. Their sound was like no other sound, though the wind in a wood might sometimes remind you of it. He thought he liked the sea better than anything, but it was really the sea running up the sand or breaking against the rocks, really the music of the sea, that he liked; for when he was out in a boat he didn't much like it—in fact it soon bored him. But when you were on the shore it was different, and the sound hid away everything else, and was like an endless lullaby. . . .

114

Gamelyn, his name was. It didn't begin with an "L" after all. . . .

A small and very tickly green crab was walking over Tom's foot. He drew his foot out of the water with the crab still on it, and then turned to look back at the cliffs. He wondered if he could climb them. "Not that I'm going to," he added prudently, "and perhaps get stuck half-way up."

Several sheep had come to the edge and were looking over. Somehow they made the whole scene less lonely. It wasn't exactly as if they had been human beings, but it was very nearly the same, whereas the seagulls hadn't made any difference at all. This was puzzling. . . .

The cliff was in shadow now, and there was a line of shadow along the shore at the foot of it. Mother had lent him her watch. It was a wrist-watch—a rather silly little thing and a very distant relation indeed of the clock he had left in charge of the house—but still it told you the time, and what it said now was four o'clock. He wished he had a spade so that he could dig channels between the pools, but there weren't even any big shells. Suddenly a dark round head rose out of the water to look at him. "That's a seal," said Tom, and remembered having read somewhere—but it might only have been in a fairy story—that seals are passionately fond of music. If they are, he thought, they must get precious little of it except what the waves make. So he sang to the seal, and the seal really did seem to listen, though he wouldn't come out of the water.

It was lovely singing here: it was like singing with an orchestra. "What I'd like most of all," Tom decided, "would be for all animals and all birds, and even all fishes and insects, to want to be friends with me. And they would too," he thought, "if they only knew. Some do know—some dogs and donkeys—but there are so many that don't. It would be fine to be friends with a seal." And he began an adventure in which the seal came close to the rocks and took him for a ride on his back. He imagined Daddy and Mother and Pascoe and Miss Jimpson and Brown—a whole crowd of people—standing on the shore in amazement. Nor was it really so impossible. It would have been quite possible, and

115

even quite easy, if things had been just a little different—if animals could speak a human language, for instance. . . .

He wondered if ships ever came into this bay. He hadn't seen one, but he supposed they must. . . .

"Was this the face that launched a thousand ships?" Pascoe had made a mess of that; he had said "boats", and been offended because Pemby had talked for five minutes about how the change of one word could rob a line of all its character. "Ships," Pascoe had amended. "Silly old ass," he had added under his breath. "Steamers, rafts, canoes, barges." And though Tom had appreciated the wittiness of this, he had felt all the same that Pemby was right. There *was* a difference, though he didn't know what made it, and Pemby hadn't explained. But "ships" meant more —meant masts and yard-arms and great white sails, and even a look-out man at the bow, shading his eyes with his hand—and a wide, heaving sea.

It was rather mysterious: he wished Pemby *had* explained it. . . . But perhaps he ought to be going home soon. He had enjoyed himself frightfully, though he wouldn't object at present if a fisherman or somebody were to come down to the bay, or even appear at the top of the cliff. It had begun all of a sudden to be a little *too* lonely. He put on his trousers and walked back along the shore, while the seal accompanied him, or at any rate swam in the same direction. Tom followed the track of his own footprints, but they somehow looked now so solitary on that deserted beach that they gave him a queer feeling and he was not sorry to reach the end of the bay.

Here he had another meal, to fortify himself for the homeward climb. Also another drink out of the stream—more iron. The basket was lighter and Tom heavier when he began to toil up the ascent. He reached the place where he had gone to sleep, but the goat was no longer there. . . . Yes, this was the exact spot—where the grass was crushed—and that was where the angel had sat. A sudden thought made him stoop lower and examine the ground carefully. It showed no superficial marks, but actually Tom was not looking for marks, he was looking for a sprig of watercress.

But there was nothing. He sighed faintly and resumed his

116

journey. When at last, plodding stubbornly, he reached the beginning of the wider road over the hill, there was a cart loaded with green rushes drawn across the way, and beside the cart was a man with two dogs. Tom was glad to see all three of them, and as the man wished him good evening, he thought he might stop to talk with him, and pat the friendly sheepdogs. The conversation lasted while the man finished his pipe, but Tom talked most, for the man hadn't much to say. He was a good listener, however, and Tom made a lengthy and circumstantial story of his rambles. The goat was in it, and so was the seal; only the angel was not mentioned. Then he told the man about Daddy and Mother and the expected Pascoe. Henry came next, but this was because the man asked him if he had a dog of his own. And the dogs pricked up their ears, Tom fancied, at this point, listening with far more attention while he was describing Henry's antics than they had shown before. "Well, I'm afraid I must be going," he concluded at last, quite reluctantly, "but I'll very likely be back with my friend soon; in fact I'm sure to be."

"That's right," the man replied, "I'll keep a lookout for you."

CHAPTER XIII

He arrived home, tired and dusty, to find Daddy and Mother entertaining visitors. To Tom they were not interesting visitors, and when after dinner they were taken out for a drive, he was quite content to be left behind, though he had nothing particular to do. But he did not want to do much, feeling a good deal more tired than he would admit, and for a while he sat on a bench watching a very noisy and hilarious game of golf-croquet which was being played by two young men and two girls. All four were staying at the hotel without adding to its attractiveness, Tom felt; and while he watched their game his actual thought was that they were awful! So presently he climbed up on to the battlement and stood with his back to them, gazing over the parapet.

Below him the ground dipped and rose again, forming a narrow ravine which ran on to the sea. On the opposite side of this ravine, and on a level with the Fort, were the grey ruins of a castle. The castle had been built in 1313, Daddy said, and little remained of it now except the lower walls, and here and there the fragments of a spiral staircase. The floor was solid rock, however, though partly coated with grass; and looking through a broken archway, her pale mild face turned towards him, Tom perceived a sheep reposing in solitude.

He waved his hand and smiled (he was getting to know quite a number of animals), and the sheep bowed. There were plenty of rabbits moving among the rocks and bracken down below, but the sheep appeared to be the sole proprietress of the castle, a white and woolly chatelaine, gazing out with the prudent inquisitiveness of her race. She somehow had an exclusive, old-maidish appearance, and Tom wondered if that ever happened with animals. Rather prim, she looked, but affable—quite different from those girls anyhow, who were certainly bent on not remaining old maids.

The sun was sinking, and the rich warm flood of light, filling empty spaces and washing crumbling stones, had a curious effect of spiritualizing the scene. From the precise spot where he now stood, Tom two or three times a day had looked across at this castle—also he had climbed up and explored every inch of it— yet never before had it suggested to him anything beyond itself. Now its altered aspect awakened a vague stirring in his mind, as if a submerged impression were trying to force its way upward to consciousness; but unsuccessfully, for it produced in him only a dim sense of being reminded of another scene, a place still unidentified, but which he had at some time visited, though he could not tell when. Yet it ought to be easy, he felt, for he knew very few ruins—Inch, Greyabbey, Bonamargy, Dunluce—he could remember no others. And then suddenly he knew that it wasn't a real place at all he was thinking of, but only a place in a

118

dream—that queer dream which he was convinced had been repeated several times, though it still obstinately eluded his waking efforts to recall it. He saw, too, that even the fancied resemblance was an illusion. There was no resemblance; the house of his dream had not been like that. Moreover, it had not been near the sea, and the ravine itself had been different, a kind of wood, a kind of glen—like the glen beside his own house at home. . . .

The glen at home! Could it be? The thought brought him up with an abrupt little shock of discovery. But it was true, though it seemed very strange that recognition should only have come now, and in so roundabout a fashion. On the other hand his dream-house had not been like the house at home either, and certainly it had been the castle, perched up there with the steep drop beside it, which had set him pondering. Surely he ought to be able to remember everything now. But he could not: it was just as baffling as ever. Only that one brief glimpse of a vanishing scene—as if he had entered a theatre at the very moment when the curtain was descending—and then—Henry scratching at his bedroom door. . . .

Tom turned round, and immediately perceived that he must have been gazing at the castle for a long time. The croquet players were gone, yet he had not heard them going. It was latish too—he could feel that—though perhaps not more than half-past nine or ten. At all events Daddy and Mother had not yet returned, and since the moment they did so he probably would be sent to bed, it might be just as well to move a little further off while he had the chance.

He came down from the battlement, and passing round by the kitchen quarters and through the vegetable garden, descended a rough path to the shore. The falling dew had made the grass slippery and enticed crowds of snails from their hiding-places. Tom, careful not to tread on these adventurers, walked along a beaten track, with bracken on either side of him and the rocky shore below. He climbed a stile and skirted the wall of the Manor House, where Miss Pascoe lived. It was a low stone wall, scarcely three feet high on Tom's side, and almost level with the strip of green sward within. The garden stretched at the foot of tall rocks; which were split here and there into narrow crannies suggesting the entrances to secret caves. It was a brilliant garden in the daytime, but the colour was draining out of it now. And behind house and garden and rocks there rose steeply a dark plantation.

An overflow of flowers from Miss Pascoe's garden bordered the path along which Tom was walking. Some had even seeded themselves close to the shore—white, yellow, and purple foxgloves, and Saint John's-wort, with its yellow flowers and green and deep-crimson leaves. At the end of the wall the ground widened out on both sides and the coastline was broken into a series of small bays, each with its smooth sandy beach. The tide was full or nearly full, and Tom scrambled out as far as he could over the lichened barnacled rocks, till the water was lapping at his feet. The thickly crusted rocks were the colour of tarnished silver, and up the numerous channels between them the water swelled and sucked backward with a hollow melancholy sound.

The sun had vanished nearly an hour ago behind the hill Tom had climbed on his way to Glenagivney, but it was still reflected in the clouds, and the reflection was mirrored in a crimson track, almost the colour of blood, across the tumbling sea. On the opposite shore, soft as a pastel drawing, the hills were outlined in dark slate-blue against a paler sky.

The light was fading fast.

The Manor House, large and square and white, had become like a phantom house glimmering against the black background of the wood. Further along was the grey mass of the Fort, with the round Martello tower, at the foot of which was a stone staircase leading to Tom's bedroom (for he had a private staircase all to himself), and further still was the castle. Up the faint blue sky there rose a heavy column of cloud, like a genie escaping from a jar. Cloud upon cloud, the sky was strewn with them, loose and floating, those underneath tinged to gold, those nearer earth grey or faint mauve, with deep translucent wells between them of pale pea-green and silver-blue. But on the farther shore darkness was descending like a curtain, blotting out the pattern of the

hills; and a peculiar mystical happiness had descended upon Tom
—dreamily peaceful—almost ecstatic—for it was only remotely
related to this world.

CHAPTER XIV

He had been right about that at least; undertaken with
Pascoe the walk to Glenagivney became quite different.
Pascoe, with a specimen-box and a press he had manu-
factured for drying flowers, turned an idle excursion into a
scientific expedition. He had even brought a botany book with
him, borrowed from Daddy, whom he had consulted, and who
had given him a sort of introductory lesson on how to use the
book, while Pascoe all the time had hung on his words with a rapt
interest and attention that ought to have been flattering. It had
made Tom, at least, think how extremely satisfactory a son
Pascoe would have been for Daddy; and this in turn made him
wonder what kind of father would have found *him* satisfactory.

Not one like Daddy, he was afraid, though perhaps sharing the
same tastes and interests was less important than he imagined.
It couldn't be the only thing, at any rate, for he and Pascoe
shared very few, and it didn't prevent them from being friends.
They were much happier now, for instance, going this walk together, than either of them would have been with any of the
other boys they knew, and yet each probably was getting a quite
different kind of enjoyment from it. Pascoe was busy collecting
flowers; Tom, though he too plucked a flower occasionally, was
really thinking all the time of what had happened on his last
visit here. It was in this very lane that he had dreamed of his
angel, and in this lane that he had met the goat. *She* certainly
had not been a dream, and he kept a lookout for her, wondering
if she would remember him. The lane, however, proved to be
empty of goats and angels alike.

"Let's get over to the other side of the hedge," Pascoe suggested. "It looks as if it was mostly heather there, but we may find some small flowers, and anyhow I want to press the ones we've got while they're fresh." So they jumped the ditch, crawled through a gap, and picked their way on stepping-stones across a shallow stream.

They were now on the edge of the ravine above Glenagivney Bay. Here and there, marking the track of the lane, a few slender half-grown trees grew, chiefly birch and willow, but all the open ground was rocky and deep in heather—dry, brittle, and fragrant. Tom sat down among it; Pascoe, who had work to do, sat on a stone.

"I love this place," Tom thought, expressing the immediate feeling of contentment that flowed in to him through all his senses. What stretched before him was a kind of pageant of summer at its height—an intensity of heat and light, of colour and growth and movement, filled with low stirrings and secret calls. The sea was visible when he sat up; indeed, though considerably below them, it was quite close as a bird would fly. Then, when he lay back in the heather again, it disappeared, and looking up he saw nothing but a bluish quivering haze that veiled the deeper blue of the sky.

Pascoe at once got busy. He opened his tin specimen-box and unscrewed his press, between the boards of which were a dozen sheets of blotting-paper. Tom admired the neatness with which he manipulated his flowers. He must have a very delicate sense of touch, for his fingers seemed never to bruise anything, never to fumble or make a slip. Watching him, Tom felt a momentary desire to assist, but knew that he wouldn't be allowed to do so, and relapsed again into laziness. The slope on which he lay supported him at exactly the right angle for comfort; in spite of the buzzing and humming, no flies molested him; and the fair-haired Pascoe, with his mouth pursed up and an intensely serious expression on his whole countenance, looked somehow both amusing and attractive. "Would you be surprised if we saw an angel?" Tom asked him, but it was the kind of question Pascoe evidently regarded as merely symptomatic, for he neither stopped working nor answered.

"The worst of botany books," Pascoe presently remarked, "is that unless there's a coloured picture, or you happen to know the name of the plant already, they don't help you much. That is, if you're a beginner. Your father told me I might find it a bit complicated at first."

It was at this moment that a large woolly dog joined them.

Neither of them had seen him approaching; he hadn't been there a second ago, and now he *was* there—that was all. Probably a sheepdog of sorts, though he bore a marked resemblance to a bear, for his eyes were small, his muzzle blunt, and his unusually thick blackish-grey coat, to which a long streamer of goose-grass was attached, seemed to contain the accumulated dust of a lifetime.

He sat down facing Tom and Pascoe, nearly closed his eyes, and opened his mouth sufficiently to allow three or four inches of pink tongue to protrude. His breath came with the quick, panting sound of a small gas-engine, and his tongue dripped slowly drop after drop of moisture on to the ground. Pascoe, looking up from his work, frowned thoughtfully at him in silence. Then he said, with what was rather like a sigh: "There's no doubt it's much easier to identify animals than flowers."

Tom supposed it was, though at the same time he was finding some difficulty in regard to this particular specimen. "You mean you'd know he was a dog?" he pondered.

"Well, wouldn't you?" Pascoe replied; "and yet there's far more difference between him and lots of other dogs than there is between you and a monkey."

"Thanks," said Tom, while he continued to study their visitor.

"I didn't mean you in particular," Pascoe explained. "I meant *us*—human beings. What breed would you say he was?"

"That's just what I've been trying to make out," Tom murmured doubtfully. "He *isn't* so easy to identify. I don't think he's any breed at all. He's just Dog. He looks to me like the first dog."

"Yes, he does rather," Pascoe agreed. "And I expect they were all the same once, like pigeons. I think that's pretty clever of you."

Tom was pleased, for Pascoe did not often pay compliments. He tried to be clever again. "I think I know his name," he said.

Pascoe looked at him sceptically. "What is it?" he asked.

"Bruin," said Tom, though the moment he had said it, it struck him as feeble. "Bruin! Bruin!" he called.

Yet marvellous to relate, he had guessed right, for a bushy heavy tail immediately thumped the ground. Tom was delighted. "I nearly always know dogs' names," he added imaginatively.

Pascoe did not answer, but suddenly he called out: "Chrysanthemum! Chrysanthemum!" and the tail once more thumped recognition.

Tom changed the subject. "Anyhow, he's joined us," he said. "And he's going to stay with us all day. You can see that." And indeed Bruin, or Chrysanthemum, or whatever his name was, did show every sign of intending to remain.

"Go home, sir!" ordered Pascoe, but this time it didn't work, and Tom murmured: "Sucks to you!"

"It's no good," he went on; "he's just friendly and frightfully determined. He knows quite well we're having a picnic, and he knows we can't do anything if he makes up his mind to stay. He'll eat most of the sandwiches too: dogs like that have awful appetites. I bet he could eat a whole leg of mutton."

"I bet he won't eat *my* sandwiches," replied Pascoe simply.

He began to screw up his press, and Tom waited till he had finished before rising to his feet. "Well, what about going on?" he then proposed. "It'll be nicer down at the sea."

They picked their way back to the lane, the woolly dog preceding them, looking round over his shoulder every few seconds as if encouraging them not to lag behind.

For some reason this air of leadership began to displease Pascoe, who wasn't particularly fond of animals. Tom merely found it amusing, and Pascoe's attitude amused him also.

"It's because he's so beastly full of himself," Pascoe grumbled. "Besides, I know he's going to be a nuisance. Just look at him! You'd think he was taking charge of us! It's what *he* thinks, anyhow. For two ticks I'd turn round and go the other way."

"So would he," Tom answered gaily; "you won't get rid of him like that, and we want to get down to the shore."

There was something in what Pascoe said, all the same, and the nearer they drew to the sea the more urgent became Chrysanthemum's signals. For an oldish dog he was behaving very oddly. He kept running on ahead and then running back again, showing all the time more and more excitement. Tom half expected to be grabbed by the jacket at any moment, and though this didn't actually happen it came as near to it as possible. Pascoe deliberately slackened his pace.

"He *is* leading us!" cried Tom with sudden conviction. "I wonder what's the matter!" For he had read about Saint Bernards, and other philanthropic dogs, organizers of rescue parties, inveterate humanitarians. Yet it seemed hardly likely that there could be any question of a rescue here, unless somebody trying to climb the cliff had sprained an ankle or fallen.

"There's nothing the matter," Pascoe told him. "Don't take any notice; he sees he's impressing you. If you stop taking any notice of him he'll soon get tired."

But Tom was doubtful, and he ran down the last slope and on to the beach, where he waited for Pascoe, with Chrysanthemum jumping round him in the most extraordinary fashion.

It couldn't be a rescue, however, for there wasn't a living soul in sight. Besides, Chrysanthemum never so much as glanced at the cliff, but devoted all his attention to Tom. In another minute Pascoe had joined them.

The tide was out and they walked at the sea's edge till they reached the end of the bay. Here, on a flat rock, Tom put down the basket and Pascoe his botanizing paraphernalia.

"What *is* the matter?" Tom exclaimed again, all his curiosity returning as Chrysanthemum began to dig wildly beneath the very rock they had chosen. He showered the sand out in a thick storm, and in a very short time had scraped a hole about a foot deep. "He'll soon be in Australia," Tom murmured, but he had begun to feel a share of the excitement himself, half hoping for romantic developments—a big brass-bound box—even a little one would do.

"Perhaps it's a smuggler's hiding-place," he suggested to the less impressionable Pascoe. "Do you think it could be? Or it may be treasure out of a wreck."

"It's much more likely to be a dead body," returned Pascoe gloomily, and this unpleasant view was somehow so plausible that it instantly dispersed Tom's dream of treasure-trove.

He wished Pascoe had kept quiet: he wished they had gone to the other end of the bay. Side by side they stood watching Chrysanthemum, who was now so plastered with sand as to be more like some unclassified marine object than a dog. The hole he was making grew deeper and deeper; at any moment a stiff dead hand or foot might gruesomely appear.

"I wish we hadn't come," Tom whispered. "Do you think it would be wrong for us to go away?"

"No, I don't," returned Pascoe emphatically, "and I'm going." He lifted up his own personal belongings as he spoke, and Tom lifted the basket.

"We're not the police," Pascoe went on. "It's none of our business to go hunting for corpses. And if there *is* a corpse, it must be of somebody who was murdered."

This also seemed a logical conclusion: Pascoe would make a very good detective, Tom thought. So they retired nearer the cliff and chose this time a rock above high-water mark.

The curious thing was that Chrysanthemum, after a single parting glance at his unfinished labours, immediately joined them and began fresh excavations in the new spot.

They were equally vigorous too, and Tom, though he was several yards off, got a shower of sand in his face. Yet in spite of being half blinded he felt relieved. "It's all nonsense!" he cried. "There can't be dead bodies all over the place. It's not a cemetery."

Then he tried an experiment. He lifted a stone and threw it. Chrysanthemum instantly ceased digging and raced after the stone with deafening barks. At last they'd grasped what all along he had wanted, and from that moment he jumped about them and barked without ceasing. The rocks reverberated. It was a marvel how one dog—even a big one—could make so much noise. There was little question now of sea-music and lonely shores. Nothing less like his last visit could Tom imagine.

"He's going to spoil the whole thing," he said, beginning to share Pascoe's opinion. "We may as well give it up and go somewhere else. We can try up there on the cliff. If we get further away from the sea he may stop barking, and he won't be able to dig."

"I'm not going away from the sea," Pascoe declared obstinately. "I'm not going to let any dog upset my arrangements. What's more, I'm going to bathe before lunch."

"He *has* upset them, whether we like it or not," Tom replied; but when Pascoe began to undress, he did so also, and they ran down to the water's edge. The blue sea glittered in the sun, and big rounded waves came tumbling in, foaming past the rocks and hissing up the smooth brown sand. Chrysanthemum bathed with them: that was to be expected. But it didn't matter much; it was only surf-bathing anyhow; for even quite close to the edge the waves were as high as their shoulders and carried them for yards up the beach. Chrysanthemum was swimming most of the time; Pascoe tried to swim; but Tom waited for the waves, sitting in the shallows and letting them lift him up and sweep him on with squeals of delight, leaving him stranded high and dry. It was fine sitting on the sand in ten inches of warmish water, with bubbles of spray melting on your legs. Presently Pascoe came into the shallows too; and then Chrysanthemum—they were all together now. Pascoe looked extremely naked beside Chrysanthemum, whose coat was as dense as, and much longer than, a sheep's. Chrysanthemum was really a good name for him, though Tom knew it had been chosen by Pascoe as the most unlikely he could think of. But really it was much better than Bruin, which was stupid. The kind of chrysanthemum that has long loose petals, Tom decided. For the hair of his coat, mixed with sand and sea, was hanging down now in tangled clusters exactly like petals.

"I don't see why we need dress," he said, burying his feet in the sand. "Not a soul ever comes here, and it's more interesting to have no clothes on; it makes you behave differently."

127

"It doesn't make *me* behave differently," Pascoe contradicted, "and you always behave as if you were naked."

This remark puzzled Tom. It sounded as if it ought to have a meaning, and perhaps it had—yet he couldn't discover any. He gazed at Pascoe in uncertainty.

But Pascoe was doing exercises—touching his toes without bending his knees. "Are you hungry?" he asked. "We'll not dress if you don't want to."

"Middling," Tom thought, abandoning the question of nakedness. "But I'll get hungrier when I begin. I always do."

"Then let's have our grub," Pascoe said, "because *I'm* starving."

The unpacking of the basket was of absorbing interest to Chrysanthemum. With a slowly moving tail he sat down about a yard from Tom and directly facing him. To Pascoe he paid no attention whatever. "How does he know?" Tom wondered. "He heard him saying things, of course, but he can't have understood. It's very mysterious how they know. They must get thought-waves or something." He held out a sandwich of ham and brown bread. Chrysanthemum leaned forward and the sandwich disappeared. It was exactly like posting a letter.

Tom looked at Chrysanthemum and Chrysanthemum looked at Tom. The pendulum movement of his tail seemed as automatic as if he had some clockwork arrangement inside him. "After all, he's not as big as I am," Tom mused, "and yet it takes me two minutes, I should think, to eat a sandwich." He glanced at Pascoe half guiltily as he offered another, but Pascoe was feeding as hard as he could, his jaws working as regularly as Chrysanthemum's tail. "You're a silly to give him all your lunch," he remarked with his mouth full. "He's probably better fed than we are; at any rate he's about twice as fat. I'm not going to give him *any*thing—not so much as a crumb."

He had said this before, and Tom didn't care. Besides, it wasn't true that Chrysanthemum was fat. He wasn't any fatter than Pascoe himself; they were both about right, and Tom wished he was the same.

It was strange, nevertheless, how Chrysanthemum had

divined immediately whence the source of blessings would flow. He never so much as looked at Pascoe until the latter offered him the shell of a hard-boiled egg. "I wouldn't do that," Tom advised. "You might want it later."

Pascoe had begun on the tomatoes, which were overripe and inclined to spread; in fact they *had* spread—there was tomato on his chin and on the tip of his nose—but this didn't trouble him, nor did Tom's sarcasm. "I don't want him," he replied, "and I'm not going to encourage him. You didn't want him yourself a few minutes ago. It's only weakness now, and because you're silly about animals. I suppose you think *I'm* being stingy."

Tom didn't think so; he knew Pascoe was acting upon principle. But then he didn't share the principle and had begun to like Chrysanthemum; how could you help liking anybody who was so friendly!

He mentioned this, but Pascoe said it was only cupboard friendship.

"It began before he ever *knew* there was any grub," Tom declared. "It began the moment he found us."

"Which was the moment he sniffed the basket," Pascoe replied. "You said yourself he knew we were having a picnic."

"Even if he did," Tom argued, "I don't see that it makes any difference. He came because he wanted our company, and he wouldn't go away now if we stopped feeding him: he wouldn't say a word; he would still be friends."

Pascoe went on eating, unmoved.

Luckily Chrysanthemum didn't care for tomatoes, so Tom had his full share of these. During this course Chrysanthemum disinterred a long-deceased crab, which he crunched and swallowed with apparent relish. "The eggshells were at least fresh," Pascoe pointed out dispassionately. "It just shows you what he's like." But Pascoe didn't understand Chrysanthemum any more than he understood Tom. Tom and Chrysanthemum understood each other. And in the end Pascoe *did* give him a sandwich, though he was careful to explain that it was really to Tom he was giving it.

They had left enough for a second if smaller meal, and now they repacked the basket. "What do you want to do?" Tom asked; but Pascoe had eaten too much to be immediately energetic.

"Nothing for a bit; then either bathe again or else dress and explore along the top of the cliff. What would *you* like to do?"

Tom had no special wishes, so this programme suited him well enough. Clothes were arranged as pillows and Pascoe went to sleep almost at once. So did Chrysanthemum, with his heavy damp head on Tom's stomach—selected after several trials as being the only really soft spot in his body. Tom did not feel sleepy—only lazy and content to lie on his back and listen to the waves. Besides, he didn't want to go to sleep; it was too pleasant lying here like this; and the pleasantness somehow included everything—Pascoe and Chrysanthemum—the sea and the sun and the earth. He thought of his angel, but very lazily, and the angel reminded him a little, though only a little, of a boy who had once spoken to him at a party, and whom he had never seen again. Eric Gavney his name was—quite a big boy. He went to the school Pascoe would be going to after the holidays, and to which Tom himself would be going, he supposed, next year. . . . If not sooner; for there had been some talk of that recently—chiefly, he thought, because Daddy and Mother seemed to have an idea—a quite ridiculous idea—that Pascoe looked after him, and that it would be better if they were to go together. . . .

It was queer—this getting to know people. Sometimes it made a difference, though usually it didn't. Three years ago he hadn't known Pascoe. And there was Chrysanthemum, lying with his head on Tom's stomach—and yesterday neither of them had had the least suspicion that the other existed! When he went to his new school he would get to know a whole crowd of boys whom he now couldn't even imagine, though they must all be alive and doing something at this very moment. With some of them he might become friends: with one he might become great friends —have the kind of friendship he sometimes dreamed of: not that he would ever drop Pascoe. He couldn't conceive of happiness without friends; they were much more important than anything else, he thought; and even the earth he would have liked to be as nearly human as possible. Though human wasn't exactly what he meant: Chrysanthemum, for instance, wasn't human. What he meant was more just having feelings and the power to communicate them—a capacity for friendship. . . .

Pascoe wasn't like that, he knew. As a matter of fact Tom was the only boy with whom Pascoe ever associated. Of course, Tom didn't associate a lot with other boys either; but he would have liked to, he couldn't feel indifferent in the way Pascoe seemed to feel. He didn't *really* dislike Brown, for example. At the present moment he couldn't think of a single person he disliked. True, the present moment was hardly to be relied on, for he was in a peculiar mood—a rather sloppy mood, he fancied—one at any rate in which he felt capable of finding passionate romance in limpets and beauty in a woodlouse. . . .

And the waves curled over and ran up the sand; and a little puff of wind came from the sea and moved in Pascoe's hair. . . .

A long time elapsed.

"Wake up!" cried Tom at last, for it looked as if Pascoe and Chrysanthemum would lie there for ever.

Pascoe opened his eyes, but very drowsily.

"It's getting late," Tom told him. "You've slept for hours."

The sun had indeed dropped visibly, but at the same time it was moving round the side of the cliff, which was lit up now where before it had been in shadow, while the whole sea lay in a rippling glory. Chrysanthemum was the first to move; sleep had refreshed him and he began to dig. Pascoe jumped up with a shout and ran down to the breaking waves. Pascoe was knee-deep in the Atlantic.

And it began all over again. Pascoe's voice was raised in a tuneless chant; Chrysanthemum's voice was raised: Tom, though he squatted in the shallows as before, joined in the chorus; the cliff's edge was lined with interested sheep. They plunged in and out till they were cold; they ran along the sand till they were hot; they threw stones for Chrysanthemum; they dressed and ate everything that remained in the basket.

"We ought to be going home soon," Tom supposed regretfully, for he didn't want to go home, and suddenly realized that he was

131

feeling very tired. He might have been wiser, perhaps, to have had a sleep like the others.

"We'll go now," Pascoe said, "and then we can collect more flowers." He gathered up the botany book, the specimen-box, and the drying-press as he spoke. "If we could only make *him* carry something," he added, with a glance at the unencumbered Chrysanthemum. "I don't suppose he's ever done a stroke of work in his life."

"I don't suppose he has," Tom agreed, "though he *may* work for a shepherd, and this may be just his day off."

The walk back he found very heavy going, for the tide had come in a long way and they had to plough through soft sand. Pascoe and Chrysanthemum seemed to find no difficulty.

When they reached the stream he explained about its tonic quality, which he had forgotten to do before, and Pascoe said there *might* be something in it, though Tom's deduction, made from the colour of the water, was unscientific. At any rate all three drank from it—Tom and Chrysanthemum close together, Pascoe higher up.

"You can get a most frightful thing from dogs," Pascoe mentioned when they stood up again—"a thing that grows on your liver till it kills you. It's quite common among the shepherds in Scotland, because they allow their dogs to eat off the same plates as they use themselves. I'm sorry I didn't remember about it sooner, though it's very unlikely you'll get it. He *was* below you, wasn't he?"

"Yes," said Tom rather faintly.

"Then that's all right; you're safe. I wouldn't have told you, only it's just as well that you should know in case you ever get a dog of your own."

They had begun the ascent through the now familiar scene, though in the evening light all the colours were deeper. The fields of still unripe oats were vividly green, but the hay was already cut and stacked. Pascoe—who always seemed to be a few yards ahead—did not find many new flowers, and Tom found none. On the other hand, he lingered to watch half a dozen black bullocks standing dreaming in the shade, knee-deep in long grass, their tails alone moving, switching away the flies. He knew it was partly an excuse to rest, and Pascoe, he was afraid, must have guessed this, for he stopped at once, and asked him if he were tired. Tom didn't answer, because he wasn't sure whether Pascoe was tired or not. Then this struck him as stupid, so he said he was, and sat down on the bank with his arms round Chrysanthemum.

Pascoe sat down also. "I am too," he declared, but he couldn't be so very, for he immediately began to work with his flowers. Pascoe was very nice in ways like that, Tom pondered dreamily; lots of boys would have boasted that they weren't tired even if they were. But Pascoe wasn't like that, and he was the only boy who never called him Skinny. . . .

He could have sat there for a long time just thinking such thoughts; he could even have gone to sleep, and would have liked to do so; but in a few minutes they resumed their journey. The last faint sound of the waves had been left behind, but there was a constant ripple of hidden water near. At length they emerged out of the lane and the smoother road across the hill began— bare, and without hedge or bank or wall. Before them was an unbroken outline, as of an immense curving bronze-green barrow—smooth, naked, and dark against the evening sky. On either side the turf bogs stretched, rich and sombre, covered with heather and sprinkled with bog-cotton. Greener beds of moss and flowering rushes showed where the land was soft and treacherous, while the light caught an occasional gleam of stagnant water. At wide intervals, and branching off at right angles from this ascending road, cart tracks diverged across the heather. These tracks were firm yet soft under foot, being composed really of powdered turf, and they were grey in colour, except where a darker patch showed that a stack had recently been removed.

Suddenly Pascoe gave a little squeal and stood still.

"Good!" murmured Tom, immediately subsiding.

"Look!" cried Pascoe, grabbing him by the arm and pulling him to his feet. "There they are! I'd forgotten all about them."

Tom looked obediently, but saw only a couple of turf-cutters, with their carts, far away across the bog.

"I'm sure it's them," said Pascoe eagerly. "I don't see Kerrigan, but I'm sure those horses are Blossom and Welcome."

"Blossom and Welcome?" Tom repeated, unenlightened.

"Yes—Aunt Rhoda's horses. . . . Kerrigan was to come over with the two carts this afternoon for turf."

"Oh," murmured Tom, beginning to understand.

"We'll not have to walk home after all."

"Good!" said Tom again.

They had got so used to the company of Chrysanthemum that it was only at this point that they realized he oughtn't to be there, and that they must have passed his home long ago. Immediately a new problem was raised, altering everything.

"He picked us up away down near the sea," Pascoe said, "and that must be where he lives. What are we going to do about it?"

Tom didn't know. But he knew that, stuffed with grub and after hours of friendship, Chrysanthemum wouldn't want to leave them.

"*You'd* better tell him to go home," Pascoe said. "It's really you he's following, and he won't take any notice of me."

Tom said nothing, but he gazed back down the hill. He was pretty certain that he couldn't do that climb over again. "Go home," he said to Chrysanthemum, but he didn't say it in the right way. It sounded weak, more like a suggestion that he might have made to Pascoe himself, and as such Chrysanthemum considered it, with his head on one side and an amiable expression on his face. He wagged his tail.

"Oh, well," said Pascoe good-naturedly, "I suppose we'd better keep him and bring him back to-morrow."

So, with Chrysanthemum still of the party, they set out across the bog, striking a diagonal line to the nearest track.

The horses and carts and the figures of the two turf-cutters were clearly silhouetted against the sky, but it was not till they were quite close that they perceived a third man, for he was reclining on the ground on the farther side of one of the carts, leaning his back against the wheel and smoking.

"They haven't done a thing, of course," Pascoe murmured in an undertone, "except take out the horses and stand there yarning. They're always like that: Kerrigan would sit there talking till to-morrow morning."

Certainly nobody was working at the moment—or looked like beginning to work. Blossom and Welcome were browsing on such scattered tufts of grass as they could find among the heather; Kerrigan was talking through a haze of tobacco smoke; and the two turf-cutters, leaning indolently against the stack, were also talking, while at the same time they watched the approaching trio. The whole scene had an atmosphere of leisureliness that fell in marvellously with Tom's own mood and inclinations: he felt quite ready to sit down and join in the conversation, or at any rate listen to it.

"Shall we go or stay?" Pascoe continued to whisper. "Kerrigan doesn't really want them to hurry. They haven't even taken off their coats, and we may have to wait for hours."

"I'd rather stay," Tom whispered back. "Does it matter?"

But Kerrigan at this point must have discovered what they were discussing, for he took his pipe from his mouth and called out: "Now sit you down, Master Clement, and take your ease. A rest will do you good, and the mistress will know rightly where you are."

"We didn't promise to be back at any particular time," Tom put in persuasively. "I'll stay if you will."

Meanwhile the turf-cutters were being greeted as old friends by Chrysanthemum. "And where might you have picked up Mrs. Reilly's Mike now?" one of them asked. "Sure it's two desperate dog-stealers you have there, Kerrigan, an' you'd do well to keep a watch for the police when you'd all be riding home together in the light of the moon."

This was a joke, and a good many others followed, during which Tom noticed with relief that Pascoe had become absorbed in the botany book. He himself began to stroke the soft cheeks of Blossom and Welcome: Blossom dappled-grey, and Welcome chestnut-brown; both wearing stockings. He had always felt a particular liking for carthorses with stockings: the stockings

135

seemed somehow to add to their powerfulness. Blossom and Welcome were solid as mountains, and Tom thought far more attractive than slender highly-strung thoroughbreds. They moved slowly and ponderously, and looked as mild as old-fashioned nurses. He could even imagine them answering advertisements, and putting in "fond of children" at the end. But he was really very tired, and seeing that the turf-cutters, so far from being spurred to activity by the arrival of Pascoe and himself, had now actually sat down, he followed their example, and stretching himself on his back in the smoky clouded purple of the heather, listened to the slow lazy talk. Pascoe had produced a pocket-lens and with his penknife was performing some kind of botanical dissection; Chrysanthemum was searching for rabbits; Blossom and Welcome continued to nose about for provender; while Kerrigan and the turf-cutters smoked and pursued a desultory conversation interlarded with humorous yarns. Everyone was doing exactly what he wanted to do, Tom reflected, and not interfering with anybody else; and this seemed to him to be exactly the way life ought to be conducted. . . .

Kerrigan and the turf-cutters had drifted into reminiscences of supernatural visitations and warnings, suggested by Tom's account of the fright Chrysanthemum had given them when he had first begun to dig. They were chiefly tales of hearsay—one leading to another—but they all had a local background, being the experiences of friends or relations, and the cumulative effect was persuasive. Pascoe probably was the only sceptic present. . . .

It was Chrysanthemum's tongue licking his face that made Tom open his eyes. And astonishingly he found that everybody was ready to go home. The turf-cutters were putting on their coats, the carts were loaded, Pascoe was on Welcome's back, and Kerrigan, knocking out the ashes from a last pipe, asked Tom whether he would like to ride on one of the loads or on horseback.

Horseback, he decided, feeling now quite rested and energetic; so he was set up on Blossom, and slowly the journey home began.

Probably he would have been a good deal more comfortable sprawling on top of the load, but nothing would have induced

him to make this change. Pascoe had begun to sing—his usual
kind of tuneless song—and the two turf-cutters walked with
Kerrigan beside the carts till they reached the road. There they
said good-night, and with Chrysanthemum, turned back towards
Glenagivney.

Kerrigan didn't know what time it was. Neither did Pascoe,
and neither did Tom, for to-day he hadn't Mother's watch with
him. But it wasn't moonlight, though a wraith of a moon was in
the sky. Far below them was the grey shadowy sea, and across it
—a sign that it must be fairly late—the revolving lights had
begun to flash their signals.

CHAPTER XV

Tom and Pascoe, after a religious discussion, had decided
to read the whole Bible through, chapter by chapter, from
Genesis to Revelation, but it was Pascoe to whom it had
occurred that this spiritual effort might be turned to material
advantage. And strange to say, mentioned in a carefully thought-
out letter to the wine merchant, it *had* actually produced a postal
order for five bob, though Aunt Rhoda, perhaps because she seldom went to church, would only go the length of half a crown,
and even that in the unsatisfactory form of a promissory note
payable on the accomplishment of the task. Fired to emulation,
Tom had tried what *he* could do, but either he lacked Pascoe's
adroitness or else possessed the wrong kind of parents, for Daddy
had simply looked at him and sighed, while Mother, with a
wretched sixpence, had given him a lecture on the ignobility of
seeking pecuniary reward for good actions. It appeared that there
were even specific warnings in the Bible against this very plan of
Pascoe's—texts about serving two masters, about God and
Mammon. Pascoe, Mother seemed inclined to think, was serving

only one master, and that one Mammon; whereupon Tom instantly, though it was their first encounter, had a clear vision of this Mammon—called up out of Limbo by the mere sound of his name—a sort of debased demi-god, with a large stupid face, a fat smooth dark-grey body, and a dirty tail. He didn't like the looks of Mammon at all.

But as yet the reading had not progressed very far; the first three chapters of Genesis, subtracted from the grand total of chapters in both Old and New Testaments, leaving so large a number that it became a question as to whether Aunt Rhoda oughtn't to pay interest on her half-crown. In the meantime there had been much to argue about. Tom remembered talking of these very chapters with Mother, in the garden at home, on the evening preceding his sleep-walking adventure, but Mother hadn't got nearly so much out of them as Pascoe. Pascoe—by means of logic and pure mathematics—had actually deduced, not the area indeed, but the exact shape of Eden. He went over the proof with Tom. It was quite clear, wasn't it, where the Tree of Life stood? You were told that bang off: it stood in the middle of the Garden. But the Bible, you were also told, was absolutely true, and the only absolute truth is mathematical truth.

"I don't know whether it is or not," Tom said, feeling all the same that Pascoe was about to produce something remarkable.

"Well, you ought to know," Pascoe replied. "Everybody else knows; all mathematicians at any rate."

"Miss Jimpson?" Tom suggested.

"Miss Jimpson!" Pascoe echoed pityingly. "Miss Jimpson isn't a mathematician. She knows just about enough to teach a few kids." But he added: "You needn't mind my saying that, because maths, of course, isn't your subject. You're good at other things, and nobody can be good at everything."

"All right," said Tom, leaving Pascoe to proceed with the argument.

"I suppose you admit that the only mathematical figure which has a centre is a circle?" was the next question.

Tom thought of a square and a triangle, but did not mention either.

"You do admit that?" Pascoe went on. "Well then, since we're dealing with absolute truth, which is mathematical truth, and since we're told that the Tree of Life was planted in the centre of the Garden, it follows that the Garden must have been circular in shape."

"There were two trees," Tom objected after he had recovered a little. "There was the Tree of Knowledge as well as the Tree of Life, and I don't see how they both can have stood in the same spot."

"No," said Pascoe, "they didn't; and you aren't told that they were both in the centre; you're only told that the Tree of Life was."

Tom had no further arguments, and indeed ever since then he had pictured Eden as Pascoe described it. "It's a huge circle," he said to himself now, after he had blown out his candle. And having decided this, he thought for a minute or two of Chrysanthemum, and then of the ride home. But very soon his mind slid back again to Eden, which had always interested him, and had been made by Pascoe more interesting still.

Why, for instance, when forbidden to eat of the Tree of Knowledge, had nothing been said to Adam about the Tree of Life? Pascoe had a theory explaining this also, though he admitted himself that it was not based on such pure reasoning as the other, and therefore could be regarded only as a probability. His theory was that there was no *need* to warn Adam against tasting the Tree of Life, because the Tree of Life was invisible to him until after he had eaten the apple of knowledge. Then, of course, his eyes had been opened, just as Siegfried's ears were opened when he tasted the dragon's blood. And this really was frightfully clever, for it exactly bore out what the Bible told you—that as soon as Adam had eaten the apple, or whatever it was, God had begun to be frightened that he might find the other tree and eat one of its apples too. "They were both magic trees," Pascoe expounded, "therefore one of them might easily have been invisible. Only their magics were different. The Tree of Knowledge showed you things and taught you things; the Tree of Life had the same power as the pillar of fire in *She*. . . . Not," he added, "that I believe at all in either of them."

139

The last words were a disappointment; in fact they left Tom distinctly annoyed, for he had been on the point of accepting these conclusions. But Pascoe was always giving you surprises like this, and he looked at him reproachfully. "You've just *said* that the Bible is absolutely true," he grumbled.

"I didn't," Pascoe returned. "I said people *told* you it was absolutely true; and I said that if it was, then it must be mathematically true. In my opinion it's neither the one nor the other."

"Then you're an agnostic," Tom declared. "Or an atheist," he added more thoughtfully, struck by what would ultimately happen to Pascoe. "Daddy, I don't think, believes it all," he presently admitted, "though he won't argue about it. But Mother does: she told me so."

"A lot of it's nonsense," Pascoe replied. "Just as much nonsense as the story of Saint Columba learning to read by swallowing a cake with the letters of the alphabet printed on it. You don't believe *that*, do you?"

"No, I don't," said Tom, "and I never heard of Saint Columba."

"Well, a lot of the Bible stories are just as silly."

"Who told you about Saint Columba?" Tom asked suspiciously.

"Aunt Rhoda told me. And she says the lives of the saints are crammed with things like that."

"The lives of the saints aren't in the Bible," Tom pointed out. "And anyhow I don't think the Tree of Life is silly at all."

Pascoe looked at him. "Why are you fixing so specially on the Tree of Life?" he said. "There were two trees."

"I don't know," Tom confessed. "Except that I saw it and not the other one. I mean I saw it for a minute when you were speaking about it." He paused to pursue a private cogitation. "*Can* you see a thing if it isn't real?" he wondered aloud. "I mean, could you see an oak tree in your thoughts if there never had *been* an oak tree? Where would the thought come from? Not that this was like an oak tree. It had flat leaves of a kind of silvery grey, and nearly white on the under side. They were big leaves too, for the size of the tree, which wasn't really a big tree; and they moved very easily—not with the wind, but as if they *wanted* to move. The trunk was smooth, and like the trunk of a birch, only thicker, and——"

"Oh, stop!" cried Pascoe, almost choking. "You're about the biggest little——" He left the rest unspoken, but Tom had no difficulty in supplying the word "liar".

"It's queer that we should always call each other 'little' when it comes to disputes," he thought, pulling the bedclothes up under his chin. "And it's queer the way Chrysanthemum dug in the sand. . . . I wonder how Henry would like it if I brought Chrysanthemum home with me? Not at all, I suppose. I wonder what Henry's doing at this moment, and if the clock has stopped yet? . . . I wonder if I could really bring Gamelyn again?"

But this was a proposition he could test, and it brought him up abruptly. "He *said* three times," Tom pondered. "Or anyway I thought he did. . . . Which means of course now only twice. . . . He had fair hair, but not so fair as Pascoe's, which is practically white.

"Fair hair," he murmured sleepily. "I like fair hair best." And then, somehow, there was a window open to the dawn—a garden, and birds singing endlessly. Another voice, a human voice, but not really Tom's voice, though he was making it come out of him and it sang—sang ever so much better than Tom could sing. . . .

Suddenly he was wide awake.

"I think I *will* try," he determined, sitting up in bed. "Just where that streak of moonshine is."

And even as he said so, the moonlight quivered and Gamelyn was there.

Like and unlike the boy in the lane; but this time not in any disguise, really an angel.

He certainly *had* altered. He looked even nicer than before, though he was now such a big boy that Tom felt qualms about having called him. He had better explain how it had happened, find an excuse. "I'm afraid I didn't *really* need you," he apologized. "I was just trying——" And then he was silent.

The angel waited: he did not seem to understand. For all that,

141

Tom still felt that he had done wrong. The angel was a guardian angel and at present·Tom had nothing to be guarded from, in fact he had brought him for no reason whatever—at least no serious reason. If only he were a real boy! He looked so like one, and Tom so wished he was one! The angel watched him with bright steadfast eyes, like pools with the sky mirrored in them: his body was silvered by the moonlight, and he had no wings. "This is the second time," he said. "Let us go."

"Go where?" Tom answered.

He slid out of bed nevertheless, and stood in his pink striped pyjamas on the floor. The angel had opened the door, and now beckoned to him before passing on down the stone staircase. It was very like a picture Tom had·seen of Saint Peter escaping from prison, and next moment they were out on the grass.

The angel climbed on to the ramparts and Tom climbed up beside him. The ruins of the castle were clear in the moonlight—everything was marvellously clear. Down in the ravine he could see the rabbits playing.

And if anybody should happen to be awake, he suddenly remembered, and should happen to glance out of a window, both he and his naked companion would be plainly visible. But at that moment Gamelyn caught his hand and their flight began.

It was so swift that Tom felt and saw nothing—so swift that he seemed only to have drawn his breath once before they were standing in a hollow misty land between mountains. Or at least he thought they were mountains, though they might only be gigantic clouds, for it was very dark, and through the darkness there leapt streaks of scarlet flame. Presently his eyes grew more accustomed to the gloom, and peering through it, he could make out two immense shadowy forms moving rapidly and soundlessly backward and forward. In the right hand of each was a long thin scarlet flame that wheeled and darted, cleaving the mist this way and that; and Tom knew that these were the flaming swords, and that those grey shadowy forms were the sentinel cherubim; but they were of colossal proportions, and in the dim light he could not see their faces.

A voice whispered in his ear: "Not much chance of getting in that way!"

Tom answered "No," for he felt scared, and also surprised. The voice somehow did not sound right—sounded far less like the voice of an angel than the voice of a boy.

"Don't be frightened," the voice went on. "They don't see us, and even if they did we could get away. They never leave the garden and they're not nearly so close as you think."

This was a comfort at any rate, though Tom would gladly have been further off still, and presently he said as much.

"I thought you wanted to get in," the voice answered. "It can be done."

"I don't think we ought to try," Tom murmured uneasily. "I don't think they want us to try."

He had never, indeed, felt surer of anything in his life, and the boldness of Gamelyn implanted another misgiving, and this time one which awakened not only opposition but reproach. "It's very strange," he said, "that you should talk like that—seeing that you're supposed to be my guardian angel. I'd have thought you'd have tried to keep me *out* of mischief—especially dangerous mischief like this. Are you sure you're an angel at all?" And he turned to Gamelyn suspiciously.

But there was no reply: no Gamelyn.

And this was natural, because for a second or two he was sitting on the bank of the river at home, though he had hardly time to realize it before he was back again in the hollow misty land; and it was not the river at home that was rushing in an inky blackness beneath him.

"That is the way," Gamelyn pointed, "if you have the courage and will trust me."

Tom sighed. He hadn't much courage, he thought; but he had a great deal of trust, so perhaps it came to the same in the end.

"Put your arms round my neck and hold tight," Gamelyn whispered, and Tom obeyed him. He gave just one tiny cry, barely audible, but which he couldn't quite repress, as they plunged down. . . .

Down—down—down—through the soft black rushing water.

They sank like stones, and Tom held his breath. But if you know *how* to hold your breath it is quite easy, he found, and he felt no discomfort at all. He simply didn't breathe out any of the breath he had drawn in, and therefore everything remained just as before, and he could have gone on for hours. Actually, they weren't a very long time under water, and it wasn't cold—perhaps because they were moving so quickly. For when he came to the surface again no mountains or cherubim were in sight, and he was in broad sunshine. Gamelyn, too, had disappeared, so Tom scrambled out on to the bank—alone in Eden.

But if it was a garden, it was a garden grown wild, and was far more like a wood, though there were plenty of flowers. And birds and butterflies and bees. Animals, too, for that was a giraffe over there, nibbling the tops of some shrubs. Tom sat down to collect his thoughts, and it was not till he felt his seat gently rising and sinking beneath him that he found he had sat down on a hippopotamus. The hippopotamus was reclining on his side in a bed of purple irises, and seemed so comfortable, that though Tom scratched him under his ear—always the best place—and scratched his hardest—he only opened one small eye and closed it again.

So this was where Adam had lived! Tom stood up to take stock of his surroundings. But here on the river bank, even when he stood on the hippopotamus, he was too low down to see much. The right spot would be that hill, or mound, about two hundred yards away—and there was something else about the mound which caught and riveted Tom's attention.

It rose in grassy smoothness to a height of some fifty feet—green sward all the way up till you reached the very top; but on the top, in conspicuous isolation, stood a tree. Tom gazed at this tree with round and ever more credulous eyes. No tempter was there to beguile him; he had no such excuse as had been found by his greatest grandmother; the dire result of the Fall can never have been more convincingly illustrated than by his instantaneous resolve: "If there are any apples on that tree, I'm going to have one." And he had no sooner reached this determination than he set off at a run.

Climbing the mound did not take long, and in another minute or two he was standing under the dark-green spreading branches, peering up eagerly between them. Yes, there were apples, early as the season was. But before he could take a further step, with a loud whirring noise, ten times more startling than the rising of a pheasant, a great white bird, surely some kind of albatross, flew out, uttering a strident metallic cry. Tom got a terrible fright, which was only natural. "It's so silly for a big bird like that to build in a tree!" he exclaimed half angrily. And it was a nuisance, too, for now if he were to climb the tree, the albatross would very likely think he was going after her nest, and might attack him. What was he to do? For though he could see that there were lots of apples, they were all on the upper branches where he could not reach them. And they looked small and unripe. The tree itself, he felt sure, was not the Tree of Life, but the Tree of Knowledge. Still——

There! She *had* come back, and was standing watching him, not more than five yards away. "I'd better not climb, but throw a stick," said the prudent Tom. "She can't very well object to that!" Luckily there were several good-sized sticks lying about.

So he chose the largest, and taking careful aim—and trying not to think of the albatross—he flung it as hard as he could at the nearest clump of apples. Instantly there was a commotion in the brushwood below, and a large shaggy dog—the born image of Chrysanthemum—came tearing up the hill to retrieve it.

But not before a shower of little apples had come pattering down on Tom's head and shoulders, rebounding thence on to the grass. The dog, having brought back the stick, dropped it at Tom's feet, and then backed a few paces, where he stood, with his red tongue lolling out and his eyes rolling affectionately. The albatross also watched, but she made no movement. It was really not a bit like the Bible—or at least not very.

Tom picked up an apple. "Hard as a board!" he muttered; and indeed it was. It had a thick wrinkled rind, too, and when he forced his teeth through this, he found the inside very dry and bitter. He screwed up his face, for the apple tasted worse than the worst medicine, and he could hardly keep from spitting it out.

But he got it down at last, and then stood waiting for some mysterious change to take place within him.

Nothing happened. Once he had actually swallowed the apple its bitterness vanished, but that was all. No fresh knowledge dawned upon him; nothing new about either good or evil; his mind was precisely what it had been before. "I'd better test it," Tom decided, only it was difficult to think of a satisfactory test. "I wish I had an algebra here," he whispered to himself; "then I could have tried a sum and I'd soon have known."

As he stood puzzling his brains the shaggy dog came sidling up to him. He caught a flap of Tom's pyjama jacket between his teeth and gave it a little shake to attract attention. After which he said shyly: "I'm the first dog. I'm Dog."

Tom instantly remembered his theory about Chrysanthemum. Pascoe had thought it clever at the time, and now it was confirmed—Dog's words confirmed it—and it occurred to him that perhaps everything in the Garden was the first of its kind.

"I'm the first dog," Dog said again. "My name's Dog."

"I know, I heard you," Tom replied.

"You wouldn't have heard me if you hadn't eaten the apple," Dog reminded him; and from the sound of his voice Tom was afraid his feelings were a little hurt.

Hastily he patted Dog's head. "That's quite true," he told him. "At least, I'd have heard you, of course, but I wouldn't have understood you."

"Now I'll be able to understand Henry too," he thought, "and not just pretend I do."

Meanwhile the albatross had waddled over to them. "Here he comes!" she scolded, and in so pugnacious a tone that Tom instinctively stepped back a pace. But it wasn't with Tom she was angry. "Look!" she cried, giving him a nudge with her wing, so that the tip of a feather narrowly escaped his eye.

"Don't," said Tom peevishly.

The albatross apologized, but at the same time she stretched her right wing out to its full extent, till it almost covered him. It was the first time Tom had ever been taken under a wing—

146

literally at all events—and he struggled to free himself. "I can't see anything when you do that," he muttered in excuse.

"Well, keep close to me, and don't let him fascinate you," the albatross said. "Keep as close as you can."

Tom did as he was told—partly because the albatross seemed to be really uneasy, and partly because he felt a little nervous himself. For a large and beautiful serpent, his long sinuous body burning in the sun, was leisurely climbing the mound. His colour, except for some jet-black markings, was more brightly green than the grass, and his raised, flattened head was swaying slowly from side to side as he advanced, with jewelled lidless eyes fixed upon them.

Neither Dog nor the albatross spoke a word, but Tom could feel them, one on each side of him, quivering with disapproval. Yet the serpent showed no sign of hostility, nor did he seem embarrassed by the marked silence in which he was received. "Well, Adam," he said softly, in a low pleasant voice, "so you've come back at last, and without Eva."

Tom felt very absurd. Really it was ridiculous! He had always pictured Adam as at least middle-aged even thousands of years ago; and now to find himself actually mistaken for him!

"I'm not Adam," he answered, turning away.

"Not in the least like him," snapped the albatross. "Quite different in colour, shape, and size. No more like him than a wren is like me."

She drew still nearer to Tom, and so did Dog, though goodness knows they had been near enough before. All three were now as firmly united as the ace of clubs, but the serpent merely coiled himself round them, and with his head raised to the level of Tom's face, gazed straight into his eyes.

"I didn't really think he was," he murmured in a voice that had a kind of sleepy music in it. Tom had never before heard a voice so beautiful—so caressing and persuasive. "I didn't think he was—in spite of those ridiculous things he's got on." He touched the ridiculous things with the tip of his forked tongue for only a second, yet the albatross ruffled all her feathers. "If he's not Adam," he went on, "why is he wearing them?"

147

"They're my pyjamas," Tom answered, blushing; while the albatross muttered "Manners!" loud enough for everybody to hear.

But the serpent paid no attention to her. "Take them off," he said to Tom, and seemed to expect him to do so.

"I won't," Tom replied, astonished at his own boldness.

"Why not?" said the serpent. "They're very ugly."

Tom looked down at them with diminishing confidence. They certainly *weren't* particularly beautiful. Mother had bought them at a cheap sale, and compared with the albatross's soft plumage, and the serpent's enamelled skin, and even Dog's rough fur, they looked both gaudy and common. "Do you really want me to?" he asked in a wavering tone. "I mean if you——"

"Of course," said the serpent. "What are they for? Why shouldn't you look nice?"

"Why indeed!" Tom thought. But aloud he said: "I don't know that I *will* look nice. . . . It's not that I *mind* taking them off. Only——" He proceeded to do so, however, and felt that they were all watching him with the liveliest interest, not excepting the albatross, in spite of her remark about manners.

He pulled off the jacket slowly, and then the trousers, and there followed a pause in which nobody expressed admiration. It was just as he had anticipated; he was a disappointment; and he sat down on the grass, resigned but sad.

"You're far too thin, poor child!" cried the albatross fussily; and now that Tom was naked she appeared more than ever bent upon mothering him.

This seemed to arouse a latent jealousy in the serpent. "Don't coddle him," he sneered. "He's a boy, not an egg."

The albatross trembled with annoyance. She rose threateningly, and Tom was afraid there was going to be a battle. But the serpent was either too cautious or too lazy, and to Tom's relief the dangerous moment passed. The temper of the albatross remained ruffled, however, and when, with those snowy pinions closely enfolding him, Tom couldn't help fidgeting a little, she gave him a peck and said quite sharply: "Sit still!"

Tom repressed a squeal. It hadn't really been a very hard peck, but on the other hand she had a beak of iron, and he certainly didn't want a second one. So he sat as quiet as he could, and it was more with a view to effecting an escape than anything else that he presently made a suggestion. "Now that there are four of us," he ventured timidly, "we might have a game of something perhaps."

"Why so?" inquired the albatross, and Tom indeed had no particular reason to offer. "Making up a four you know," he explained rather feebly. "It was just the words that put it into my head."

"The child has very little sense," the albatross observed. "It's kinder to take no notice."

"I'll play a game with you, if you like," Dog whispered in Tom's ear, but the albatross overheard the whisper and her wing pressed tighter than ever.

"He doesn't want to play games," she snapped. "He's tired. If anything, he ought to have a sleep, and in the meantime we'll sit as we are."

Dog did not insist. There was something very nice about Dog, Tom thought. Though he mightn't be as clever as the other two, or have so strong a character, you felt at your ease with him, which you didn't quite feel with either the serpent or the albatross. Dog was like the Rock of Ages: he evidently hadn't changed in one single quality since the very beginning; so that knowing successive generations of dogs was really just knowing Dog.

"It seems strange that nobody is asking questions," remarked the albatross inconsequently. "I suppose it is because the child is extremely well-mannered—either that or else unusually shy."

Now Tom had been thinking of a question at that very moment. Unfortunately it was an extremely personal one, having to do with the loss of the serpent's legs, so in spite of this encouragement he still hesitated to ask it. The albatross broke the ice herself. "What is your name, child? I expect you have a special name, like Adam and the angels."

"Tom is my special name," he said.

"Tom!" they all repeated, and it had a curiously different sound coming from each. Dog turned it into a short sharp bark;

149

with the albatross it sounded more like a cry, plangent and harsh; with the serpent it had a low breathing sound that was half a love word.

And then suddenly a most pertinent question occurred to Tom, and he asked: "Does God ever walk in the Garden now?"

Possibly he had said the wrong thing: it very much looked as if he had. The serpent's eyes glittered; the gaze of the albatross was fixed on a point so remote that Tom wouldn't have been surprised to learn that her home was at the South Pole. Only Dog remained untroubled as ever. "I don't think so," he answered cheerfully. "I've never seen him." Then he added, with a sort of quaint innocence: "Sometimes I bark at the angels and their swords."

Tom could quite believe it. All the same he thought it was brave of Dog, and said so.

Dog looked pleased. "They take no notice," he remarked modestly. "Besides, I keep on our side of the hedge. It's just for something to do, and because there's nobody else to bark at, but it'll be different now you've come; I'm very glad you've come."

Tom was sorry to disappoint Dog, but he felt he ought to mention that he was only paying a visit and wouldn't be staying long. . . . Though how on earth he was to set about going home again, he had as yet no idea.

"Of course he won't be staying," chimed in the albatross, in her possessive domineering way. "I'm going to take him to the sea in a few minutes."

"Then your nest *isn't* in that tree," Tom exclaimed, "and I needn't have been frightened to climb it after all!"

"Do I *look* as if I would have a nest in a tree?" the albatross replied impatiently. "Use your wits, child."

"I *am* using them," Tom retorted, for he was getting rather tired of being treated in this fashion. "And it's ridiculous of you to talk of carrying me. You couldn't possibly do it even if I was only half as big as I am."

The albatross looked as astonished as if a linnet had attacked her. "Well I never!" she cried, spreading out her wings like great white fans and taking a few leaps from the ground as
150

though to show him. Tom felt that perhaps he had spoken too impulsively, and to change the subject he asked her where she *did* live.

The albatross settled down again, but he wasn't sure that she had entirely forgiven him, for it was rather coldly that she answered: "I live beside the Pacific Ocean."

"Near the top of a cliff," Dog supplemented.

"The highest cliff," continued the albatross. "If you were there you could look out over the water all day long. And when there was a storm you would see waves as high as that tree, rolling in and bursting and thundering up the rocks. At night you would watch the clouds scudding across the moon, and listen to the howling of the wind, and perhaps see a great ship foundering."

"I don't want to see a ship foundering," Tom told her.

"Don't you?" said the albatross, surprised. "Why not? It's most exciting. There's nothing so exciting as a good shipwreck, with plenty of screaming and struggling. And in the morning at sunrise you fly over the place where the ship sank and search among the floating wreckage and dip down to the green waves and let them carry you along, up and down, up and down—like the rocking of a cradle—with nothing but the sea all round you and the sky above you for miles and miles and miles."

"I couldn't do any of those things," said Tom quietly, "because I can't fly. And I can't even stay in the water for more than a very few minutes without getting benumbed."

"Benumbed!" repeated the albatross. But she was really so moved by her own picture of the joys of the sea that she had hardly listened to him. "I must be going," she cried restlessly. "I only looked in—I don't remember why."

"Only birds and fishes *can* get in or out," Dog whispered to Tom. "The rest of us have to stay here."

The albatross now stood with her head lifted and her eyes fixed on the sun. She stretched out her wings, beat them twice, and then, seemingly without an effort, rose into the air and glided away over the tops of the trees, higher and higher, till she was only a minute white speck in the sky; and finally that speck too vanished.

"And she never even said good-bye!" Dog marvelled. "After all the fuss she made about you too!"

Yet with the disappearance of the albatross he himself seemed to find that they had talked long enough, for he yawned, and presently dropping his head down between his outstretched paws, closed his eyes.

And all this time the serpent had been looking at Tom. It was as if he had been waiting for this moment, as if he had anticipated it, for now he drew his green coils in a little, and his narrow head found a pillow on Tom's legs, while his eyes remained bright and wakeful.

"You are the youngest thing here," he breathed, "and I am the oldest. I am older than Dog and the albatross, older than Eden, older than the earth."

"I don't think I can be the youngest, surely," Tom replied, having just seen a very small squirrel peeping down at them between the leaves.

"You are the youngest, because nothing has been born here since the gates were shut. Nothing has been born and nothing has changed."

"But you said just now that birds and fishes could get in," Tom reminded him dreamily, for the serpent's voice had a strangely lulling influence.

"*I* didn't say it; Dog said it. Birds and fishes might find a way in, but nothing that was not here at the beginning could live in this air."

"The albatross," Tom murmured.

"The albatross is Albatross and was named by Adam."

"Then is Adam himself still alive?" Tom questioned wonderingly.

"No. But on the other creatures there was no curse, only upon Adam and me. Besides, old age came on very slowly here, not at all as it does with you; and sooner or later most of the animals and birds and creeping things ate the berries of the Tree of Life. After that they remained for ever as they were."

"Is that a secret?" Tom asked eagerly. "I mean, can I tell

152

about it when I go back? I'm sure nobody else knows, and it may be frightfully important." Not that he could quite see the importance, but he was sure it would cause a sensation and possibly make him famous. Not only scientists like Daddy, but people like bishops and Dean Inge—— And then an objection occurred to him. "How is it that *I* can live here?" he asked. "I wasn't here in the beginning and yet the air hasn't done me any harm." He drew in a deep breath to prove it.

"Didn't an angel bring you?" said the serpent softly. "I too am an angel."

"A fallen angel," Tom very nearly reminded him, but luckily checked himself in time.

The serpent looked sad, which made Tom feel sympathetic. He began to stroke the smooth glittering coils. Then the serpent raised his head and pressed it tightly against Tom's cheek. Fallen angel or not, Tom had begun to like him. "I never cared for Eva," the serpent whispered, so close to Tom's ear that it was like the murmur of a sea-shell. "That was the cause of it all."

Tom, who had no great affection for Eva himself, was neither surprised nor shocked, only interested. "What had she done?" he asked.

"I don't know really that she had done anything," the serpent answered plaintively. "You see, she didn't need to do very much, she was a misfortune in herself. Everything was so much nicer before she came. Afterwards Adam grew different. It was because she didn't really care about anybody *except* Adam, though at first to please him, she pretended that she did. And before long she got so great an influence over him that he could see only with her eyes and think only her thoughts. Of course he didn't know this. She would ask his advice, she would consult him, she would look at him with eyes full of admiration, but all the time really she was making him say and do exactly what she wanted. And he was flattered and pleased and weak and foolish, and he thought there was no one like her."

"Nor was there," the serpent presently resumed in a more sombre tone. "Poor old Dog was the first to find the difference, though he was too simple to understand what had caused it. Eva

153

in a way, was simple also. I knew exactly the depth of her intelligence, and it exasperated me to see Adam hanging on her words."

"How deep was it?" Tom inquired curiously.

"A dewdrop would be an ocean in comparison."

Tom could not help fancying that there must be some personal feeling here, but he did not say so. "Adam's must have been still shallower," was what he said.

"So far as she was concerned Adam's didn't exist," the serpent replied. Then he paused, but soon went on sadly: "It was at no time remarkable, but before Eva came there was at least enough of it to make conversation possible. We used to talk in the evenings—Adam and I—when it was coolest and pleasantest. It was rather like talking to Dog, but Adam wanted to learn, he took an interest in most things, and I became very fond of him. Later he was interested only in Eva, which made his conversation monotonous. To her, however, this seemed natural and right: she wished to have him wholly to herself, and when he came to talk with me—as he would still do sometimes, though more and more rarely—she would find an excuse for calling him away. There would be something she wanted done, something she must ask him about, something she must tell him. Failing this, she would come with him, and that was worst of all. Picture it—little Tom! Since she couldn't be ignored, everything had to be reduced to the plane of her interests. Adam would sit silent, listening to her. I would be silent too. And she would babble on. But, unlike Adam, I used to think, when I wasn't too bored to think anything, how sweet it would be to wring that soft little neck. Anyhow, it was all utterly changed from what it *had* been. And then one day, when Adam was doing something or other she wanted him to do, I thought of a plan to get rid of her. I knew it needn't be elaborate; I didn't think it would be difficult; as a matter of fact I decided only to remind her that this tree was forbidden. There was no need to do more, no need to persuade her to taste an apple. If I had tried to persuade her she might even have refused. So I simply watched—watched her eating it—taking silly little bites that I could hardly keep from pushing the whole thing down her throat. This I know was mere impatience, and when she had finished I no longer felt any grudge against her, and was even prepared to be friendly with her. I knew she would be banished from the Garden, and Eva as a memory would be not unpleasant. What never for a moment occurred to me was that she would run straight off to Adam and get *him* to eat an apple. Perhaps I ought to have guessed, but I imagined she would keep the whole thing secret, if not for her own sake, then for his."

"I've eaten an apple," Tom could not help interrupting.

"Yes, I saw you; but they've lost most of their power now."

"Oh," said Tom, a little regretfully. "They're like musk, I suppose. You know how the smell of musk has gone." Then he asked: "Has the Tree of Life lost its power too?"

"Do you wish to live for ever?" the serpent questioned him.

Tom hesitated. "I don't know. . . . Yes, I do. I do wish it."

"It only means for ever in that body," the serpent said. "It would be a foolish choice. You will live for ever as it is, though it will not always be the same life. But that is better."

"Do you think so?" Tom pondered doubtfully.

"Much better," said the serpent. "How do you know that your present life will not become a burden to you? I could show you lives you have already lived, and I don't think you would wish to return to them."

"Tell me about them, you mean," Tom corrected him. "You couldn't show me."

"Show you," the serpent said.

"But how?" Tom argued. "If a thing is past it isn't any longer there. You can't show me the snow house Pascoe and I built last winter. I could show *you* a photograph of it if I was at home, but the house itself isn't there."

"Where is it then?"

Tom wondered. Where *was* it? Where was anything you didn't happen to be looking at? "I suppose," he said, puckering up his forehead, "I suppose it has gone into the invisible world."

"There *is* no invisible world," said the serpent.

"But that can't be true," Tom answered, frowning still more. "Lots of things are invisible. Sounds are invisible—and smells."

155

"There *is* no invisible world," the serpent repeated.

Tom made no reply, and presently the serpent continued: "There are degrees of perfection in the organs of vision—that is all."

It was a puzzling doctrine. But then, many things were puzzling, and it was not the first time that something rather like it had occurred to Tom himself. At all events, even if it wasn't true, he couldn't prove it wasn't. He remained silent until he said: "You mean that all that has happened *is* still there."

"Yes; all that has been; all that is; all that will be. Time is an illusion. Shut your eyes and look."

Tom shut his eyes, and, as he did so, he felt the air filling with the serpent's peculiar odour, felt the serpent's coils twining about his naked body like a climbing plant, felt the serpent's face pressing, smooth cheek by cheek, against his own. There was a minute of dizziness—a blank—and then he was in a large bare stone room hung with black curtains and decaying tapestries. Or was it he? A boy was in the room, waiting beside an old man clad in a white woollen robe, with a wreath of leaves upon his silver hair, and a short naked sword at his feet. The old man was shredding herbs into a chafing-dish poised above a lighted brazier, and a blue smoke wound up to the roof. There was a white marble altar with strangely shaped alchemical vessels upon it, and the boy, who was Tom and yet not Tom, knew the names though not all the purposes of these vessels, and he heard the old man muttering as his hands moved like fluttering pigeons above the chafing-dish.

"To-night, half an hour after midnight, the great work will be accomplished," he muttered. But the boy had heard those words before, and he knew the old man's hopefulness, and he thought: "The great work will never be accomplished. He has been saying that for years. He was saying it before I was born. He will be saying it when he is dying. Always it has failed, something has gone wrong before the appointed time was reached. And I think it was well for me perhaps that this happened. I do not like to leave him, because he has been kind in his way, and he is old and lonely; but I will leave him before the hour strikes."

156

He could hear the wind in the dark trees outside, and a black cat, crouching beyond the magic circle drawn upon the floor, watched him with fierce green eyes. Then the boy thought, as he had lately come to think, that the cat was an evil spirit, for he knew that the old man was a wizard. "The cat will try to keep me from escaping," he thought. "He is here for both of us. Why else should he have come? But my master does not know this. Or if he knows it, then the cat is his familiar spirit. I am not sure which is true, but I am sure that it is time for me to leave him—now while I am still able to do so."

The smoke drifted slowly through the room, and as it spread out, the different objects it touched began to waver and to lose their substantiality, and the mirror behind the altar became clouded. There was no light now except from the fire burning in the brazier, and this fire glowed and dimmed as if it were a living creature breathing. The air grew sensibly colder, and the boy felt an increasing lassitude in all his limbs, and a numbing drowsiness that weakened his will. And suddenly there came a knocking on the heavy oak door. The old man did not hear it, for he had begun his incantations in a louder voice. But the cat heard it and growled angrily. His fur bristled, his tail switched from side to side, his eyes glared and he looked as if he were about to spring. Then the knocking came again—louder, louder, louder. The cat sprang; it was tearing at Tom's doublet—trying to reach his throat. It had grown large and heavy; it was shaking him. Tom gasped, choked, cried out—and suddenly he was back in his bedroom at the Fort, with Pascoe standing over him in the sunlight, his hands still grasping Tom's shoulders.

"Goodness, you're hard to wake!" Pascoe exclaimed. He had a towel and a bathing suit, and he looked very "early-morning" and energetic. "I'm going to bathe before breakfast," he said. "Down below the castle. Do you want to come?"

But for a moment or two Tom could not answer. "What time is it?" he then asked weakly. "And how long have you been here?"

"About an hour," Pascoe said, "shaking you as hard as I could. It's after eight, but there's still plenty of time if you hurry up."

Tom heaved a deep sigh, though it was a sigh of relief and he disguised it as a yawn. He stretched himself under the bedclothes and smiled. "I've had the queerest dream," he couldn't help beginning, but Pascoe would not listen.

"Are you coming or not?" he asked impatiently. "When I say there's plenty of time I don't mean there's time to waste. You can talk about your dream on the way."

Tom would rather have talked where he was. He didn't particularly want to bathe—the water would be as cold as ice at this hour—only still less did he want to go to sleep again. But he could see that Pascoe wasn't in the mood for dreams: he seldom was, for that matter. "Yes, I'll come," he said, making up his mind. "But I'll not dress. I'll just put on a coat and come as I am."

CHAPTER XVI

Leaning over the stern of the boat, Tom dabbled his hand in the water and wished that the holidays were not so nearly over. Pascoe was in the bow among the lobster-creels—which contained more wrack than lobsters, for the haul had been a poor one—and old Danny McCoy was rowing, with little dips of strokes, and chewing a plug of tobacco. Tom and Pascoe had rowed round from the harbour to the lobster-pots; Danny was bringing the boat back. . . .

Only three more days for *him*—though Pascoe would be staying longer. But on Saturday Tom would be going home— Mother had actually suggested going on Friday—and two weeks later (it had all been settled in an extraordinary hurry) he and Pascoe would be going to their new school.

Not that Tom had any apprehensions about that, and he was still to keep on his music lessons with Mr. Holbrook. . . . Mr. Holbrook might now be engaged to be married. At any rate there had been plenty of time: it seemed to Tom ages since that afternoon when he had sat with Miss Jimpson in the teashop.

He gazed down idly through the water. The boat was passing over a shoal of jelly-fish. He had never seen a lot of them together like this before, and he hoped they were drifting out to sea. Possibly jelly-fish served some useful purpose—Mother said everything did—but he doubted it, and in a swarm they looked repulsive. Ambiguous creatures at the best, on the border line between two kingdoms, hardly more animal than vegetable. Pascoe said they could move in any direction they pleased, by a process of suction and contraction—Pascoe was always interested in how things worked—but to Tom it looked as if they merely drifted on the current or the tide, trusting to encounter a bather. . . .

Danny rowed on in silence. The only sound was a cloppity noise—like little slaps—made by the sea against the bows of the boat. Pascoe had taken a small book from his pocket and was reading it. It was called *Spinning Tops*, but, in spite of this rather gay title, was in reality a scientific primer. Pascoe was unique—absolutely single-minded; Tom couldn't imagine anybody else who would bring *Spinning Tops* with him when going out on a lobster hunt. . . .

He listened dreamily to the cloppity clop. The sea was lovely. When he grew up he wouldn't live in a town or near a town, but by the sea. Danny McCoy shifted his plug of tobacco from the left cheek to the right. Why did he do that? Danny's brown hands, rough and wrinkled as oak-bark, tugged at the oars with little jerks that had not much weight behind them. He was a strange old man—"touched", people said—and Tom had once seen him the worse for drink. But he had been told that two pints of stout could produce this effect on Danny, and anyhow, even when drunk, he was never objectionable. He might stagger a bit, and talk to himself out aloud, but that was all, and it did not happen very often. He lived alone in a thatched cottage at the end of the village, and the country people said he was odd because he had been "away" when a boy. This meant, Tom knew, that he had been taken by the fairies. He was burning to question Danny on

159

the subject, but had been cautioned against doing so. The old man never spoke of his experience himself, and got angry if anyone else alluded to it.

Daddy, of course, said it was all nonsense—at least the fairy part of it. This, and one or two similar tales which Tom had picked up, Daddy said were the inventions of ignorance and superstition embroidering on what probably were ordinary cases of hysteria. Pascoe was equally incredulous, but Tom himself had seen a young man—Sam Grogan—who had been chased for more than a mile by a ghost. Along the high road, too! He had been on his bicycle, and riding as hard as he could, yet the ghost had only given up the pursuit at the edge of the village. Outside the Post Office Sam had fallen off his bicycle exhausted. He had been taken into the Post Office by several friends—for it was a spot where most of the boys and young men gathered in the evenings —and somebody had brought him a drink from Casey's public house opposite. Tom had not only seen Sam Grogan, but he had also seen and talked to one or two of those who had assisted him, had seen the bicycle, had seen Casey's public house, had been in the Post Office—had seen everything in short except the actual ghost, and *it*, save for Sam's first impression of a tall shadowy figure approaching through a gap, nobody had seen. But its screams had been bloodcurdling, and it had screamed the whole time it was chasing Sam—screams of murder.

Tom felt tempted to ask Danny's opinion of this story: he felt particularly tempted to ask him what he thought of Port-a-Doris. For Tom had recently visited that lonely little shut-in bay and had not liked it. To say he had not liked it was indeed a mild statement of his feelings. He had hated it. He had felt uncomfortable the whole time he had been there. Port-a-Doris had seemed to him ugly, gloomy, and even sordid, which was remarkable, since it was a kind of show spot, and supposed to be most picturesque and romantic. You got to it through a little tunnel in the rocks. There was nothing but a narrow stony beach, the sea, the black rocks, and a high sloping grassy cliff. Yet while everybody else was exclaiming how charming it was, Tom had got an impression of something sinister and depressing. It had been a most unpleasant feeling, as if a cloud of ugliness, gloom, and evil, were pressing down upon his mind. And—which was stranger still—the ugliness was the same kind of ugliness he had seen once in a crude woodcut Brown had brought to school, showing a man, in a squalid bedroom, hacking with a razor at the throat of a half-naked woman.

What produced this sense of ugliness, and why should he alone feel it? It had not been there for Daddy or Mother or Pascoe. Pascoe had bathed, and while he was still in the water two young lovers had come along to look for cowrie-shells on the beach. Mother in the end had got quite cross with Tom because he couldn't help suggesting every now and again that they should go away. They had brought a tea-basket with them, and though at last she had given in to his persistence, she had said that she would never go another picnic with him. And Tom loved picnics. But not picnics to Port-a-Doris. . . .

While he was thinking these thoughts he kept his gaze fixed on Danny's face, and old Danny rowed in meditative silence. His eyes were nearly shut, but what you could see of them was greenish-grey. He wore an old blue jersey; his hair was white; his face and throat were mahogany brown. And myriads of little crinkles, fine as threads, radiated from the corners of his eyes. Tom liked these, perhaps because they showed more clearly when the old man smiled. His smile made you smile back again, and, though his teeth were very much discoloured, it had all the engaging innocence and immediate friendliness of a baby's.

The sea dropped in glittering showers from Danny's dipping oar-blades. The blades themselves were hardly wider than the clumsy shafts. There was a gurgle of water under the floor-boards of the boat when she tilted, and the mast and the rolled-up patched sails lay along the bottom under the seats. Danny rarely sailed her except when he went out fishing at night or across to Magilligan. Perhaps a little smuggling went on. Pascoe was sure there was a great deal, which was why Danny had not invited them to go out with him at night, in spite of several pretty broad hints. The hints had been dropped by Pascoe, but

Tom hadn't bothered, because he was sure that anyway he wouldn't be allowed to go. . . .

The shore glided slowly past: the Manor House glided past; the Fort was gliding past, when Danny rested on his oars and gazed up at it. Pascoe went on reading, but Tom looked up too, though only for a moment, because really he was watching the old fisherman's face. "Strange things do be on the sea at night," Danny pronounced slowly, "and strange things on land. I've seen a light rising out of the sea like a thousand holy burning candles, and I've climbed the hill to Glenagivney and seen a glory of saints and angels in the sky."

"I've seen that too," Tom said, and the old man looked at him kindly.

"You're living up there," he went on mildly, nodding his head towards the Fort. "And I seen a strange sight there too—not so long back."

"Yes," Tom answered softly.

"It was a night it might be two or three weeks ago when I seen it," Danny went on.

"From here?" Tom asked. "From the sea?"

But Danny shook his head. "That night I wasn't on the sea. It was from up yonder—from the castle. I'd been resting my bones there in the early evening, and sleep came on me, and when I woke the moon was up and throwing a light you'd see clearly by it to read a book. But the sight I'm tellin' you of was two figures on the battlement, and one might be like yourself in your night clothes, but the other bigger—and the big one was in his pelt. The little one was ordinary like, but the other had a shining round him that was more than the shining of the moon. Maybe you'll be thinking I had a drop taken, and maybe I had before I lay down. But it had passed off, and I was as sober then as I am now. I didn't offer to rise up from where I was, and I didn't stir hand or foot unless maybe it was to cross myself. Not that there was danger for me or anyone in that shining boy, and him with the beauty of an angel of God. I just looked for while you'd be holding your breath, and then they was gone."

162

Beyond the old fisherman Tom could see Pascoe, but Pascoe had not even stopped reading.

"I'll take you in here," said the old man pleasantly, "and it'll save you the walk round from the harbour."

He put the boat in close to the rocks, and Tom and Pascoe jumped ashore. But even when they were alone Pascoe made no comment on Danny's story, though he must have heard it. On the other hand, he didn't know what Tom knew, for Tom had not told him his dream. Interrupted at the time, he had never told it later, so perhaps there wasn't really very much for Pascoe to say.

CHAPTER XVII

On the level ground above the rocks they separated, and Tom climbed the path to the kitchen garden of the Fort. He was dining at the Manor House that evening for the first time, and Mother had told him that he must put on a clean shirt and collar and his Sunday clothes—a black jacket and light grey trousers. Miss Pascoe, it seemed, would expect nothing less, though Tom was sure, from the odd glimpses he had caught of her, that she wasn't the kind of person who cared at all about dress. She rarely went outside her own garden, and she must be as old as the hills, being not really Pascoe's aunt but his father's.

Dinner was at seven o'clock and Pascoe himself opened the door when Tom arrived. He gazed at the immaculate attire without comment, but also, Tom felt, without approval, his own appearance being precisely what it had been an hour ago when they had stepped out of Danny McCoy's boat.

"You're in plenty of time," he said. "Aunt Rhoda's having a bath."

Tom, a little disconcerted by this frankness, murmured that he was sorry. "I mean," he explained, "if I'm too early." He *was*

163

on the early side, he knew, and Mother had warned him that he would be. But he hadn't thought it mattered, and anyway Pascoe's greeting ought to have been different.

Pascoe was still taking in the details of the Sunday clothes, when a stout florid gentleman, in a crumpled grey flannel suit, descended the stairs, whistling. He, also, cast a glance at Tom, and then immediately turned to his son. "Now you just run along and dress properly to receive your guest," he said. "This is a civilized country and *somebody* must keep up appearances."

"Come in, come in," he went on breezily to Tom, shaking hands in such a manner as to propel him at the same time into a large, low-ceilinged room. "Run on now," he repeated over his shoulder to the motionless and reluctant Pascoe. Then, shutting the door, he turned to Tom with what was remarkably like a wink, and said: "He'll blame this on you, I expect."

Tom, from the last glimpse he had had of Pascoe's face, thought it very likely, but he couldn't help it and didn't very much mind. He looked about him curiously. This was the drawing-room, he could see, and it contained a frightful lot of furniture—cabinets with glass and china in them, high-backed chairs, and round polished tables. There was a black woolly hearthrug of the kind he liked to lie on, a grey patternless carpet very soft underfoot, a grand piano, an ornamental gilt clock flanked by Dresden china shepherds and shepherdesses, a beautiful Japanese screen in four panels, and a sprinkling of Yorkshire terriers.

"Seven of them," said the wine merchant, who had been closely following Tom's gaze. "Companionable little beasts. Usually find one or two of them on your bed in the morning. There *were* eleven, but she screwed herself up to parting with four. . . . You wait," he went on, with a quick glance at the clock. "It's now ten minutes to seven. You just wait!"

Naturally he would wait, Tom thought; and it seemed to him a strange thing to say, seeing that he had been asked to dinner. But the wine merchant continued to look at the clock as if it held some secret. He had not invited Tom to sit down, and they were both standing facing the chimney-piece when there arose a remarkable though distant noise, as of demons struggling in a cataract. "The bath water," said the wine merchant, cocking an ear. "You'll find this a house of surprises. Makes the deuce of a row, doesn't it! Whole place needs going over from chimneys to drains—particularly the drains—only she won't listen to advice. . . . By the way, we've not met before," he suddenly recollected. "Better introduce ourselves."

"I know who you are, sir," Tom said politely.

"And I know who you are. Call it a draw, and start at scratch. . . . Six minutes now."

It seemed to Tom that the wine merchant was a most unusual person, and especially surprising as the father of Pascoe. Of course Pascoe was unusual too, but not in the same way—not nearly so genial and off-hand.

"You're Clement's great friend, aren't you?" the wine merchant said. "At least, his *only* friend, which mayn't be quite the same thing. I'd ask you your opinion of him only I don't believe you'd tell me."

Tom didn't tell him, and the wine merchant hardly gave him an opportunity before he added: "You're having great times, I understand. It's just the place for that. I had great times here myself when I was a boy, and I wouldn't mind having them over again. . . . Three minutes more."

His gaze was still glued to the clock, and Tom found himself staring at it too, though without the faintest comprehension. Even the companionable dogs seemed infected by the mysterious expectancy, for they had gathered round, with their seven little faces lifted.

"Ah!" murmured the wine merchant at last, raising both hands to his ears as the first silvery note of the chiming hour floated out. But one note only was audible, for with that there arose from the seven Yorkshires such a nerve-shattering acclamation as Tom had never heard in his life. They stood in a crescent before the chimney-piece, their heads thrown back, their lungs expanded, and the din while it lasted was appalling. It was all over in less than a minute, however, leaving Tom slightly dazed. The wine merchant withdrew his fingers from his ears, laughed briefly, and looked at him with rueful, comical eyes. "She's trained them to do it," he said apologetically. "Miss Pascoe, I mean."

Tom drew in a breath. "Trained them!" Then, recovering, he added half incredulously: "Every time the clock strikes?"

"Yes," the wine merchant sighed. "Every time. It's their star turn—and there used to be eleven of them."

"Eleven!" Tom echoed.

The wine merchant nodded. "They only do it if they're in this room, you know; but then they usually *are* in this room, except at night. Still, it's a comfort that they don't do it for other clocks. There are clocks all over the house, you see—even in the bathrooms—and few of them agree about the time."

"But how very——" Tom was beginning, and then stopped.

The wine merchant's eyes met his in a glance of complicity mingled with warning. "Unusual—eh?" he suggested. "I'd call it that—till you get home at any rate. The old lady likes you to be surprised, but not anything more. Not a word of criticism, remember: the dogs are sacred. I asked Clement if he had told you about them, and he said he hadn't."

These last words were enlightening; they explained to Tom why he had been brought into the drawing-room with such eagerness. Pascoe's father, he was beginning to think, must be rather an anxiety for Pascoe the son. Perhaps that was why he had not been introduced before, though Pascoe had been on familiar terms with *his* people for ever so long. "No," he said, "he didn't. Maybe *he* wanted me to be surprised too."

The wine merchant looked at him. "D'you think so?" he murmured. "Hardly in his line, I should say. Not the sort of thing he approves of—though he holds his tongue about it because he and his aunt are as thick as thieves. . . . Clement—you know—that was *her* idea. He was Edward at the font—called after me—only better not mention that I told you. The old lady when she began to take an interest in him wanted him to be called after *her*. Difficult, naturally, but luckily she had a second name, Clementina, for if she hadn't she'd have done her best with Rhoda. She's an old lady of character, you see, and what she wants she usually gets."

166

"Well," Tom exclaimed, "I don't think she'd any right to make a change like that. He's your son, not hers, and I expect you'd have liked him to be Edward."

"Ssh!" the wine merchant cautioned, for there were sounds outside the door, and next moment it opened to admit Miss Pascoe herself, followed by her grand-nephew in the unaccustomed elegance of an Eton suit. The Yorkshires rushed tumultuously to greet their mistress, and, more or less entangled in the group, Tom was introduced.

Aunt Rhoda was a slight, small, and wiry-looking old woman, visibly of extreme energy both of mind and body. Tom had hitherto seen her only from a distance and through bushes, digging in her garden; on which occasions she had been wearing a kind of purple tam-o'-shanter, top-boots, and a very short skirt. She was now wearing a wig, though not with any attempt at deception, since obviously it had been chosen as a compromise between the age she felt and the age she actually was. The wig was piebald, and the small wizened mobile face beneath it reminded Tom irresistibly of a monkey's. The dark, observant eyes, younger than the wig and ever so much younger than the wrinkles, increased this resemblance. And perhaps the strangest thing about it all was that Tom did not think Miss Pascoe ugly. The standard might be simian, but the effect was sympathetic and attractive. She was dressed in black, with a lot of soft black lace at her throat. Her hands, yellow and dry as parchment, were even more wrinkled than her face, but they flashed with emeralds and diamonds, for she wore at least half a dozen rings. She welcomed Tom in the most gracious manner—not without a hint of ceremony—and they went in to dinner, one of Miss Pascoe's jewelled claws resting lightly on the wine merchant's sleeve.

Tom got a nudge in the ribs from his own partner. "What did you want dressing yourself up like that for?" Pascoe whispered. "Now we'll have to sit in the drawing-room all evening, I suppose—looking at picture-books."

"I didn't dress myself up," Tom whispered back.

"You did; you've got on your Sunday things, and that's why I was made to put on mine."

167

"They look very nice," Tom told him, but Pascoe answered with disgust: "Oh, for goodness' sake! . . . I'd all the stuff ready for a bonfire, too. All the garden rubbish for months and months, and a lot of stuff that's been there for *years*! I got Kerrigan to dump it all over the wall this afternoon, and it's there waiting, about as high as a haystack. You told me you liked bonfires."

"So I do; I love them," Tom replied.

But this muttered conversation was interrupted by the wine merchant's voice, raised from the dining-room: "Come on— come on—you two. What's keeping you out there?"

So they entered, and took their seats, as if no dispute had arisen, both looking very proper and well behaved.

All through dinner Tom received constant attentions from the Yorkshire terriers, who gradually converged in an ever closer circle about his legs. Every time he put his hand down it was met at once by a tongue or a cold damp nose. But nobody minded his feeding them: Miss Pascoe indeed was clearly pleased, and passed him tit-bits from her own plate. In fact it was the nicest dinner-party Tom had ever been at. Both Miss Pascoe and the wine merchant seemed to like him, and were interested in all he said. Not politely interested, but really interested, so that he couldn't help feeling he was a success. In this congenial atmosphere he expanded happily, for it was never difficult to make him talk, though it might be easy enough to shut him up. He talked now —talked quite a lot.

After dinner they returned to the drawing-room, leaving Pascoe's father over his port. But almost immediately he joined them, coffee was brought in, and the wine merchant lit a cigar. Tom, anxious to hear the next performance of the dogs, had looked at the clock the moment he had entered the room. But they had sat so long over dinner—which had been late to begin with—that the hour was past, and he saw he would have to wait until nine. The dogs, indeed, were perfectly aware of this themselves, and seeking the more comfortable chairs, they scattered themselves about the room in attitudes of repose. After one wavering glance at the hearthrug, Tom sat down on a straight, tall, very high-backed chair, probably valuable, and certainly

168

uncomfortable. The Yorkshires had been wiser or more experienced, for Tom's was a chair in which you could only sit bolt upright and look and feel like a graven image. But having once made his choice, he didn't like to change it.

"I hear from Clement that you're a very good singer," Miss Pascoe said to him; "much better than any of the other boys."

"What about going out?" Pascoe immediately called from the window, but was as quickly squashed by the wine merchant.

Tom, himself, thought the interruption rude: Miss Pascoe took no notice of it whatever.

"I should very much like to hear you sing," she went on. "Don't fidget," she suddenly told her nephew, turning round so sharply that Tom was reminded of the albatross. "Clement, I'm sorry to say, takes no interest in music, and has no ear. He must get that from his mother's side, for all our family were musical."

"Mother does like music," Pascoe contradicted. "She likes military bands."

Miss Pascoe ignored this reply. "We were a large family," she continued, lapsing into reminiscence, "and my father had us all taught either to sing or to play some instrument. What he liked best himself was chamber music—trios and quartettes for strings and piano. I used to play the piano parts, and I sang a little too. But my youngest sister sang really well. Her voice wasn't big enough, or perhaps she might have become a professional. But she was sent to London, to have lessons from Tosti."

Tom was at once interested. "I learn from Mr. Holbrook," he said, "but I know one of Tosti's songs—'Serenata'."

Miss Pascoe had risen from her chair. "The great drawback to living in a place like this is that one has no opportunity to hear music."

"Couldn't you get a gramophone?" Tom suggested, watching her as she went to the piano.

"I don't care for gramophones," Miss Pascoe answered.

Tom was surprised, and wondered how long it was since she had heard one. "Mr. Holbrook says the recording is ever so much better now than it used to be," he ventured, "and it goes on getting better and better."

169

"I dare say it does," Miss Pascoe agreed, "but even if the records were perfect they could still only repeat themselves, and that's what I don't like. Every shade of expression coming always in exactly the same place. . . . I wonder now if there's anything here that you know." She opened a box of music and began to rummage amongst it. "My fingers are rather stiff, I expect, but I ought to be able to manage an accompaniment if it's not too difficult. Unfortunately the only songs I have are those my sister used to sing when she was a girl. If I'd thought of it sooner I'd have got you to bring your music with you."

"I couldn't have," said Tom. "We didn't know there'd be a piano in the hotel and didn't bring any music."

"Well," said Miss Pascoe, "just have a look through this, though it's hardly likely that you'll find anything." She brought him a volume bound in limp dark-blue morocco, with the initials "A.F.P." stamped in gilt letters on the front cover.

Tom took it on his knee and turned over the pages, glancing at the words more than at the notes.

"List, pilgrim, list! 'tis the harp in the air."

"The green trees whispered low and mild."

"Stay, stay at home, my heart, and rest."

All were unknown to him, forgotten drawing-room ballads, much more old-fashioned even than Mother's songs, and the paper was quite yellow. Yet, as he turned the leaves, a faint music seemed to float out into the air, thin and ghostly, like the tinkling notes of a musical-box.

"Say, must ye fade, beautiful flowers. . . . Stars of the earth, why must ye away? Stars of the earth, why must ye away?" Absent-mindedly he glanced over it, till something familiar in the rhythm arrested his attention. He looked then at the notes, and, though his ability to read music was rudimentary, he knew these notes, and turned back to the title and the composer's name on the front page. The title was strange to him, but the composer was Donizetti, and, in small letters underneath, the title Tom knew was given, with the name of the opera, *La Favorita*.

"I know this," he cried, strangely pleased by his discovery, which was like the finding of an old friend. "Only I don't know these words. But the music's the same."

"Let me see," said Miss Pascoe curiously, as she stooped over his shoulder.

"Mr. Holbrook made me sing it in Italian," Tom continued; "but I don't think this is a translation. In fact it can't be; it doesn't mean the same thing at all."

"Dear me," murmured Miss Pascoe, "what an accomplished little boy you are!"

Tom blushed. "It's not that," he protested hurriedly. "It's just that Mr. Holbrook likes the sound of the Italian words, and so I learn them off by heart."

Miss Pascoe had taken the book from him. "Of course!" she exclaimed abruptly. "It's from an opera. . . . The tune was a favourite with my father, and he used to play it on the fiddle. . . . Do you think you can remember *your* words?"

"Oh, yes," said Tom. "It's the last song I learned."

The wine merchant was puffing at his cigar in friendly silence; Pascoe was silent too; and Miss Pascoe smiled at Tom. "Shall we try it?" she asked, returning to the piano. "But I'd better just run over the accompaniment first to see how it goes."

Tom complied at once, and leaving his chair, crossed the room to stand beside her.

Aunt Rhoda's beringed hands looked strangely ancient and withered on the ivory keys, he thought, but she needed no glasses to read the music, and she played quite well. Not with the careless assurance of Mr. Holbrook, naturally, who could improvise an accompaniment if he didn't know the right one, but certainly better than Mother.

Pascoe came over from the window to get a closer view of the performance, and Tom frowned at him to go away. He wished Pascoe wasn't in the room at all, because, though he didn't mind in the least singing to Aunt Rhoda and the wine merchant, Pascoe made him nervous. Especially when he came so near and stared solemnly like an owl. Tom frowned again, but it had no effect.

Meanwhile Aunt Rhoda played the four introductory bars. "Now," she murmured—just like Mr. Holbrook.

171

Tom moistened his lips with the tip of his tongue, opened his mouth, and then suddenly spluttered: "I can't if you keep on staring at me."

These words were not addressed to Miss Pascoe; nevertheless the accompaniment stopped as abruptly as if they had been. "Come away, Clement," called the wine merchant from the other side of the room, and Pascoe obeyed. The accompaniment began again.

Tom tried to think he was singing to Mr. Holbrook. He shut out the others from his mind; shut out the room; shut out everything but the sound of the piano—plaintive, soft, and clear. There was just the slightest pause, and then:

Spirto gentil, ne' sogni miei brillasti un dì, ma ti perdei, fuggi dal cor, mentita speme, larve d'amor, larve d'amor, fuggite insieme, larve d'amor!

He loved the sound of it—caressing and sad—the floating, liquid curves of sound, lingering like a pattern drawn on the air; then melting away. . . .

"You sing beautifully, dear, and perfectly in tune," said Miss Pascoe when he had finished, her hands still resting on the keyboard. "Doesn't he, Edward?"

"Like a lark," the wine merchant agreed, relighting his cigar, which had gone out during the performance.

Tom felt flattered and pleased. He thought he had sung well, and he would have liked to go on and sing better still, with such an appreciative audience, but Pascoe approached and drew him firmly by the sleeve towards the door. Tom had to go; anyway it was most unlikely that he knew another of Miss Pascoe's songs; he was very lucky to have found even one.

Pascoe led him into the hall and closed the door behind them. "Come on up," he said. "I'm going to change, and then we'll light the bonfire."

They went up to his room, where Tom sat on the bed, while Pascoe hastily removed the Etons and got into his everyday clothes. He had two boxes of matches, one of which he presented to Tom; and as they ran downstairs Tom could hear Miss Pascoe still playing over softly the air he had sung.

The moment they opened the hall-door the sound of the waves reached them, but the evening had clouded over, and a gusty breeze was blowing from the sea.

"There's the stuff," said Pascoe, pointing to two heaps of garden refuse—one of them much larger than the other. "We'll light the small one; it's as dry as tinder; and pile on the other by degrees. You light this end and I'll light that."

They wasted a few matches in their hurry, but soon a thin blue smoke, accompanied by a light crepitating noise, rose waveringly into the air. The foundation, however, was so dry and inflammable that almost at once it burst into a blaze. The danger was that it might burn itself out too rapidly, but there was a pile of fir-cuttings, and these caught too. Using the pitch-forks which Kerrigan had left for them, Tom and Pascoe built up their pyre, working as hard as they could, while the flames rushed up, licking the air and dropping round them in scarlet flakes. Then, before they knew what was happening, a gust of wind swept the flames backwards, and with a rushing, roaring sound, their whole store ignited. A clear blinding sheet of golden flame leapt at them, and so quickly that they had barely time to jump back. There was no more stoking to be done, everything was burning at once, and for a minute or two, even to Tom, it was rather terrifying.

Pascoe was in an agony. "I hope the old wall doesn't go!" he cried, beating with his fork at descending showers of sparks, while Tom stood rooted to the spot in a kind of trance. The whole house was lit up—and the shore, and the rocks, and the edge of the sea.

"You're doing nothing!" screamed Pascoe, who was still making desperate and futile efforts to keep the surrounding bushes from catching, though the heat was too intense for him to get near the actual fire. Tom beat out a few sparks, but it was useless, they could do nothing, and he dropped his fork. He retreated a few paces, and then stood still, lost in a rapture that was dreamy yet exultant. Through it, after a while, he became dimly aware of other figures, other voices, than Pascoe's—the wine merchant's, Aunt Rhoda's—and all the voices sounded excited, and the wine merchant's angry. But Tom was only half conscious of them, like far-off sounds heard in a dream. The growing brambles and furze-bushes had caught now: it looked as if the whole shore would soon be ablaze. And the shifting uncertain wind swayed the fire sometimes towards him, and sometimes away. Through the smooth, rushing sound there came numerous explosions; blazing fragments fell; and showers of sparks floated far and wide like burning rain. . . .

The fire seemed to have divided Tom from the Pascoe family. It had thrust them back to an immense distance; they were no more than gesticulating marionettes. They were outside his world, but the fire was in his world. He heard the seagulls crying, and a startled rabbit ran almost over his feet. The whole world was burning, with bright wings of flame that rushed up the sky, while far above Tom's head, pale and remote and spectral, a white moon hovered like a gigantic moth, appearing and disappearing as the clouds drifted across it.

The red flare reached no further than the foam at the edge of the sea, but it was still increasing, and the flames were still mounting higher. Kerrigan and another man had now appeared, and they and the two Pascoes were exerting every effort to keep the fire from spreading through the garden inside. But Tom did not notice this till a dense cloud of white steam suddenly hissed up. Then he saw what was happening; they had turned on a hose; and in a minute or two the enchantment was ended. To Tom it was like the slaying of a beautiful great beast. The beast

174

—a dragon—still heaved its rosy coils here and there, but they were dying rapidly, and as they died they sank back in an ashen grey. Soon only smoke and cinders and steam were left—charred black branches and sodden ashes—while the vanished colour-notes of dim green and bronze crept back into the evening land-scape.

Then, and not till then, did Tom really awaken to the disaster. At the same time he felt his arm grasped and shaken; and an angry voice almost sobbed into his ear: "Why didn't you help? There's going to be the most frightful row about this. All Aunt Rhoda's ramblers are burnt, and the trellises with them."

"Are they?" said Tom, beginning to feel a little scared. "I don't think they can *all* be burnt."

"All that were on this side of the garden," Pascoe wailed. "She's pretty mad about it, I can tell you, and Daddy's worse. You'd better go home. There's no use your saying good-night to them; they saw that you didn't do a thing."

Tom shook off Pascoe's hand. He hadn't done much, he knew; but what *could* he have done? He made a detour, with Pascoe gloomily following him, and then scrambled over the low wall into the garden. The remains of the fire had been beaten down, but the flattened mass of embers still glowed dangerously when the wind swept over it, and Kerrigan was still plying the hose. Tom walked straight up to Miss Pascoe and the wine merchant, who watched his approach in silence. He didn't know what to say, and, since nobody else spoke, in the end he held out his hand to Miss Pascoe, murmuring involuntarily: "Thank you very much for a pleasant evening."

The wine merchant coughed, and Miss Pascoe replied rather grimly: "I'm glad you enjoyed it, though I suppose we ought to thank you and Clement for the chief entertainment."

"I'm sorry about the garden," Tom said uncomfortably. Dusk hid the full extent of the ravages, but he could see that they had been considerable.

"Yes, we're all sorry about that," the wine merchant put in; and for a moment or two they stood looking at each other—Tom with very grave and serious eyes.

175

"It was an accident," he said.

"But it made a fine show—eh? Clement, I'm afraid, will have to be more careful in future about the pleasures he arranges for his friends. Something a little less Neronic perhaps."

Miss Pascoe's dark eyes, very bright in the small wizened face, had been all this time fixed on Tom in a close scrutiny. "Do you know, I believe the child was hypnotized!" she now abruptly exclaimed. "He *was*! You can see it!" She gave a sudden little cackle of laughter which astonished everybody, though it drew a sigh of relief from the depressed Pascoe.

"Come in," she cried, grasping Tom's arm tightly. "You must have some supper before you go home. The men can look after the wreckage." And she drew him towards the house, leaving the wine merchant and Pascoe to follow.

"Are you really sorry?" she questioned, peering at him curiously; "because I never saw anybody who *looked* more rapt in enjoyment. Tell me the truth, please; it's the least you can do."

"I'm sorry *now*," Tom told her. "I'm very sorry about your garden. But at the time I don't think I was sorry. I mean I *did* enjoy it."

"Well, you gave *me* something to enjoy when you sang to me," Miss Pascoe answered, "so perhaps we'd better leave it at that."

"Would you like me to sing again?" Tom asked her.

Miss Pascoe laughed quickly. "Yes, I would," she said. "I'd like you to sing that song again before you go. Then you'll be able to tell your mother that the evening was a complete success." She gave his arm a sudden squeeze that was almost a pinch as she spoke; adding however, with just the faintest sigh: "She'll require all the assurance you can give her, I expect. That is, if she happens to look over my wall to-morrow morning."

Part Three

CHAPTER XVIII

A peculiar thing was, that though it had several times occurred to Tom that he might be asked to stay on at the Manor House after Mother's and Daddy's departure, and return with Pascoe at the end of the holidays, this evidently had occurred to nobody else. Or perhaps it had, and they didn't want him. At any rate, whatever the cause, no invitation had been given; yet the wine merchant was gone, and even if he had been still there, there must be heaps of empty rooms.

Nor was it much good, he found, trying to make the most of his last two days. They weren't days at all; he had no sooner got up than it was time to go to bed again. Possibly these days contained, as usual, twenty-four hours, but it was difficult to believe it. Time was a cheat. If you watched the hands of the clock you could hardly see them moving, but the moment you turned your back and got interested in anything they simply raced. Breakfast —a bathe—and then the clatter of the lunch bell to announce that the day was half over. And always a melancholy feeling that there were only so many hours more; with gaps—great empty blanks—to be deducted for sleep.

On the last night of all, as he looked out of his window before getting into bed, he saw that it had begun to rain. Not heavily, but a feeling of gathering rain was in the air—the weather was breaking. And then, with a sudden pang of conscience, Tom realized the frightful selfishness of his thought. He couldn't help the thought, but he could make amends for it by adding a special petition for fine weather to his prayers, and he did this, leaving the rest to Providence.

When he awoke the sun was shining brilliantly. Part of his prayer at least had been answered, if not the Aunt Rhoda part. The whole place was looking its best, and the knowledge that he would be leaving it in another hour or two added to its attractiveness. He dressed and went downstairs. He almost wished that they were starting at once, for he had a feeling of restlessness, which nevertheless wasn't in the least like the restlessness he had felt when they were leaving home. It had no excitement in it: he merely felt unsettled. . . .

At breakfast both Daddy and Mother were fussy. Practically all the packing had been done overnight; only the last few things remained to be put in; and directly the meal was finished Mother went upstairs to do this while Daddy waited to pay the bill. Tom went out into the garden.

He expected Pascoe, but no Pascoe appeared. Presently the luggage was brought down and stowed away in the car. This was too sad to watch, so Tom hung over the wall and looked down at the sea. He imagined Pascoe running in at the last minute with an invitation from Aunt Rhoda. That would be a real answer to his prayer—far more to the point than all this sunshine. "Come along, Tom, and get your coat on," Daddy called out; while Mother asked, as he slowly approached: "Are you sure you've left nothing behind you?"

Yes, Tom was sure. He put on his cap and his overcoat. Here was the lunch-basket—a good big one—for they were going to picnic by the roadside. Then came the last good-byes, shakings of hands, prognostications for next year—which might or might not come true, and anyhow were cold comfort—and he took his place beside Mother in the seat behind. The door slammed; more waving of hands; Daddy started cautiously, yet for all that managed to uproot a croquet hoop with the left back wheel as he turned the sharp corner through the gateway.

But it was better now that the journey had begun. Strange, however, that Pascoe hadn't turned up. He had said he would: he must have overslept himself. Tom pictured him enviously, with the whole long summer day before him—nearly a fortnight before him. Lucky Pascoe! And there he was, racing down the road, waving and shouting! Tom waved, so did Mother, but Daddy wouldn't stop. How pleasant it would be if by some miracle Daddy and Mother, like Saint Paul, were suddenly to be converted, change their minds, and decide to stay on for another week. Only it was too late now, he supposed: their rooms would have been taken. . . .

They drove on—past the Post Office—through the village— past Danny McCoy's cottage—nothing before them now but the empty road.

"Well, so far so good!" Daddy remarked, with what seemed to Tom an unnecessary air of joviality.

The statement wasn't even true, so he found a faint pleasure in contradicting it. "I've forgotten my bathing things," he said.

The car slowed down. Tom knew he had been pretty careless, but somehow his mood was not apologetic. "And I particularly *asked* you if you'd got everything!" Mother exclaimed. "Besides going through all your drawers myself."

Bathing things weren't usually put in a drawer, Tom thought, but he kept this to himself. "I know," he said. "They weren't in my room; they were on the garden wall, drying. And I've left my racquet up in the tower; and the tennis balls are there too, and my tennis shoes."

Daddy laughed, but Mother didn't. She told him he was the most provoking boy she had ever met, adding in a tone of resignation: "I suppose we'll have to go back." Daddy turned the car.

This time he didn't bring it in to the Fort, but waited at the side of the road, and Tom had to run on by himself and make his collection. The place was deserted; everybody had disappeared— gone golfing, or bathing, or whatever the morning's programme might be. He wouldn't think about it: it was too depressing. He got his things and returned to the car.

The second start was accomplished without spectators or good wishes. Tom had a flat sort of feeling, as he scrambled back into his seat, that the Fort and all connected with it belonged to the past.

He was not in a talkative mood; neither was Mother; and Daddy never talked while he was driving. Mother made an occasional remark, but only of the kind to which you answered "yes" or "no" out of politeness. Nor were they even remarks about the recent holidays, but about home matters, about Phemie and Mary, and the hour of arrival. Tom leaned up against her, snuggling into the most comfortable position he could find.

The journey was uneventful, and even on the barest and straightest stretches Daddy demonstrated clearly that he was not one of our Speed Kings. "Step on it!" Tom urged him, but the request was received and intended merely as a mild little joke. They were not a motoring family; Mother probably came nearest to it of the three.

Towards one o'clock they began to look out for a suitable place to have lunch—eventually drawing up in a lane. It proved, however, to be less suitable than had at first appeared, for they had scarcely unpacked the basket before the car was surrounded by an audience of released schoolchildren. "They all look so hungry, too!" Mother exclaimed, torn between compassion and a desire for privacy. "Give that little girl a sandwich, Tom."

"If they're hungry, it's only because it's their dinner time," Daddy said unsentimentally. "They're perfectly ordinary, well-nourished, greedy children."

Mother, nevertheless, insisted on distributing cake and bananas to those she fancied—a most unfair arrangement, Tom considered—for obviously there wasn't enough to go round, and he could see the little boys were getting nothing. He gave the last banana to a boy of his own size.

During the second part of the drive he felt pleasantly sleepy, and it was only when Mother began to recognize landmarks that he sat up and looked out. They were within a few miles of home now, and as the road grew more and more familiar Tom's alertness increased. Soon they were within walking distance, and a few minutes later the car slackened speed before turning in at their own gate. The journey was over.

And there was William—there was everything in fact—looking exactly as if they had never been away. William had cut the grass, too, and marked the tennis court, which was surprising. All the windows in the front of the house were open.

Mary must have been on the look-out, for she was at the hall-

180

door before Tom could scramble from the car. Mother and Daddy were slower. Then Phemie appeared, and William began to take out the luggage. Mother went straight on into the house, but Daddy, William, Mary, and Phemie collected bags and suitcases before following her. Tom brought up the rear, carrying Daddy's golf-clubs.

The first thing he did on entering the hall was to look at the clock. It had stopped. He left the golf-bag in the cloakroom and came out to have another look. Yes, it had stopped—and at three minutes to twelve. "Three minutes before midnight," he added darkly to himself, though he knew it was just as likely to have been three minutes before noon. And it didn't really matter anyhow; all that mattered was that from three minutes to twelve on a certain day or night the house had been left unguarded.

Everybody else had gone upstairs carrying luggage; Tom was left alone in the hall. He had wound up the clock once before and he determined to wind it again. But he must act swiftly, before Daddy came down: the clock might have something to tell him in private. He opened the door; he wound the clock and started the pendulum; then he stepped back and looked inquiringly at the round mild face. The clock regarded Tom with an air of recognition, but it said nothing. It really *did* look different from the way it had looked a minute ago. Its ticking, too, seemed laden with unconfided secrets. If only it would hurry up, for time was so important! Here was Tom back again! it ticked; and doubtless it would be as well that he should know what had taken place during his absence—certain things, certain doings, more than odd. At any rate he would be able to judge of that for himself. The clock cleared its throat and——

Of course William must appear and spoil everything! Down the stairs he came clumping, and didn't pass on, but stopped beside Tom. "You've set her going again, Master Tom," he observed. "You weren't long!"

"It's not 'her', it's 'him'," answered Tom rather crossly, as the clock discreetly struck twelve in the perfectly conventional manner of ordinary clocks. William waited till the last note had sounded. "No," he then said, "clocks is always 'her'; same as

181

boats. You haven't moved the hands: it should be eight minutes past four." He had spoiled everything any way, Tom thought, and he was sure the opportunity would never occur again. It *couldn't*; he didn't know why, but he felt sure that it couldn't. This had been the one chance, and it had been wasted.

Meanwhile Daddy's head appeared over the banisters. "Leave that clock alone, Tom. How often have I told you not to touch it!"

"I just wound it up," Tom explained guiltily, "just to save you the trouble."

But he sighed directly afterwards. There must be a doom upon this house. He had only been back about five minutes, and already he had told a lie and begun thinking in the old way. "Where's Henry?" he asked William gloomily.

"I've hardly set eyes on him, Master Tom; not since yous all left. He's taken to running wild, though he comes home for his food and it's always gone in the morning. Once or twice I got him sleeping up in the loft when I'd left some boards that he could climb up by, and one evening, after dayligh'gone, I see him along the loanin' that takes you up by the old churchyard. There's a wheen o' rabbits there and he'd likely be hunting them."

"I just thought he wasn't here," Tom answered, frowning. "I knew it the minute we arrived."

William reassured him. "Oh, he'll be back, Master Tom; you needn't fear that. He'll know when the family gets home: cats always knows."

"If he knew, he should have been here to meet us," Tom said.

"Give him time, give him time," William muttered. Then with a renewed sense of social requirements: "Did you enjoy your holidays, Master Tom? I suppose you'd be bathing three and four times a day."

Tom gave him a quick look. "I bathed once a day," he replied suspiciously, for William before now had been known to attempt a joke.

And even that, he reflected, as he accompanied William out on to the lawn, was an exaggeration; there had been coldish days when he hadn't bathed at all.

He did not stay with William, but began a tour of inspection

182

which brought him to the yard, and eventually up to his play-loft. Everything seemed undisturbed, from the cobwebs to the mice—for a tell-tale rustle reached his ears. His paper man was still there, lying on the floor. But he was no longer spotless, he was marked all over with Henry's footprints. Tom stood looking down at him, and then, moved by a superstitious impulse, lifted the paper and tore it into fragments. He was about to throw these fragments away when a second thought occurred to him. He climbed down the ladder, made a little heap of paper on the cobblestones, and lit the heap with one of Pascoe's matches. "Why had he done this?" he asked himself, as he watched the paper burning. . . . All the same, he knew the answer.

He returned to the house, for it must be nearly tea time, and went on up to his own room. Mother and Daddy were still in *their* room, and through the not-quite-closed door he could hear them talking. Tom sat down on the side of the bed.

He was perfectly *certain* that Henry had been in his room. All was as he had left it, except that his suitcase was on the floor and the windows were as wide open as they would go. Also there were clean sheets on the bed, clean pillow-cases, clean pyjamas, clean towels—everything was spotless, and yet he knew Henry had been here—and not once only, but repeatedly, perhaps every day.

Suddenly Mother appeared in the doorway. "Where have you been, and why aren't you getting ready for tea? Mary says she found your room in an awful state. Birds must have got into the chimney. The grate was full of soot, and there was even soot on the carpet and on the bed, though how it can have got *there* is a mystery. Anyway, the chimney will have to be swept. I told Mary to telephone about it, so if you hear unusual sounds in the morning, you'll know what they are."

"It wasn't birds, it was Henry," answered Tom, with complete conviction.

Mother laughed; she even called out the joke to Daddy.

But Tom could see nothing to laugh at. "Birds don't build nests at this time of year," he told her; "and a bird wouldn't get on to the bed even if it did come down the chimney. Besides, it would have been there for Mary to see, it isn't very likely to have found its way *up* again!"

"It may have been an old nest," Mother answered rather wildly. Then, noting his expression: "At all events there's no need to look so worried about it. What's the matter? Why are you looking so glum? Surely it's not because we're home again. You didn't expect to stay on at the Fort for ever!"

"No," said Tom, "of course not."

"And if Pascoe got staying longer, he didn't *come* till after you did."

"It's not that," cried Tom, repudiating indignantly such a suggestion. "As if I cared how long Pascoe stayed! It's nothing to do with Pascoe."

"What has it to do with then? Why won't you tell me—instead of scolding me?"

Tom smiled. "Well, I will tell you. . . . Whisper."

Mother bent down her head, and he first kissed her cheek, and next put his mouth to her ear. Then he blew.

"Don't!" cried Mother, who particularly disliked this trick and had told him so before. She gave him a push, half annoyed and half relieved. "You're a little humbug," she said. But her voice sounded reassured, and Tom himself, a minute or two later, was whistling and singing while he washed his face and hands.

CHAPTER XIX

Though he could only extract a sort of half-promise from Mother that she *might* play tennis later on if she didn't feel too tired, Tom put up the net, cleaned the balls by rubbing them on the back of the doormat, and begged Phemie to be punctual with dinner because the evenings were getting so short. Then he changed into his white flannels, hoping that this would make it more difficult for Mother to refuse.

She didn't refuse, in spite of Daddy, who seemed to want her to, and asked in the most dubious tone: "*Are* you going to play? I should have thought you'd done enough!"

"So I have," Mother replied, "but I don't expect it will kill me."

Tom was pleased—though not with Daddy naturally. As for Mother, he couldn't see what she had done except sit in the car and afterwards unpack, both of which he had done himself. He hustled her out as fast as he could. "Rough or smooth?" he called.

"Rough," Mother said, "and don't be knocking the balls over the wire netting or else I'll stop."

"I must play my ordinary game," Tom replied; and Mother said: "That's not anybody's ordinary game, and it's when you're fielding the balls that you usually do it. So remember I've warned you!"

Tom promised to be careful.

They played two sets, Mother winning the first easily, because Tom found that he was off his game. While announcing this he couldn't help wondering what one's game was? *His* appeared to be something that happened about twice a season. He won the second set however—not without suspicions. He didn't often win —except against Pascoe, who was putrid—and in spite of the bad light, which certainly was in his favour, he didn't feel that his performance had been brilliant. "Of course I was trying," Mother assured him, but he didn't believe she'd been trying very hard. She could be quite good when she liked, and used to play in tournaments before she was married. He balanced his racquet on the end of one finger—a sign that the tennis was over. "Why are people who are rotten at games called rabbits?" he asked her; but she didn't know why.

There must be a reason, all the same: or at least there must have been a reason the first time the term was used. Tom began to let down the net, his mind still running on the question of rabbits, and how they could have earned their unathletic reputation. Why rabbits any more than hedgehogs? Rabbits were rather lively as a matter of fact; he'd watched them himself, in the evenings, from the battlements of the Fort. Besides, the only game *any* animals played was tig, which required no skill. Except cats, perhaps, who played a sort of one-sided socker if they could get a ball, and were obviously good at it—quick as lightning. . . .

He imagined a very small tennis court, with a low net, and four rabbits contesting a final. All round were the spectators—a motley gathering—not only rabbits, but ducks, squirrels, seagulls, several fox-terriers, a bulldog, and a polecat. The babel of encouragement was amazing. . . .

Mother, who was watching him and waiting patiently, at this point asked: "What is the problem?"

Tom finished his task and straightened himself. "Nothing. Only a tournament," he explained. "The bulldog was the umpire and they didn't dare to dispute any of his decisions. When he thought a rally had gone on long enough he just said 'Out!' and they had to stop."

"Well, come along," Mother murmured, without seeking further enlightenment.

But at supper, and apropos of nothing, she suddenly declared: "I've been thinking it over, and I've made up my mind that it would be the greatest mistake possible to send Tom as a boarder. It wouldn't do at all."

Daddy was so taken by surprise that he nearly spilled his tea. "But, my dear!" he expostulated, "it's all settled. And he's only to go as a weekly boarder, which means that you'll have him at home on Saturdays and Sundays. Mr. Rouse was particularly urgent about it. Actually, what he would like is to do away with day-boys altogether: he told me so. Besides, it's not as if Tom would be going to a school where he knew nobody. Pascoe will be in the same House with him."

"Pascoe isn't Tom," Mother answered briefly.

Daddy couldn't deny this, so he put the matter from a different angle. "There's the distance to be considered," he pointed out, "and the time it would take. Going to and from school, Tom would have to travel twelve miles every day—and right through the centre of town."

"Of course he'll have his dinner at school," Mother said, "and most of the way he'll be in the tram. . . . I don't pretend it's ideally convenient," she added, yielding the point, "but the only alternative would be for us to move."

"Or for Tom to go as a weekly boarder," Daddy repeated. "It's really a concession on Mr. Rouse's part to allow him to come home for the week-ends; the other boys only get the half-term holiday, and that's all Pascoe will be getting. . . . Also," he went on, "Tom would have to catch two trams, which means an extra delay, and there's the walk from our house to the terminus."

"I know," Mother admitted. "As I say, it's not ideal. We'll have to wait and see how it turns out. But he needn't always go in the tram. On fine days he could ride to school on a bicycle, and in that case he needn't go near town. If he went by the road under the Castlereagh Hills it would be just as short—probably shorter. I suppose you'll have to speak to Mr. Rouse about it at once, but I shouldn't think he'd raise any difficulties. . . . At all events," she added firmly, "even if he *is* silly about it, it can't be helped. We're certainly not going to send Tom as a boarder simply because Mr. Rouse wants to do away with day-boys. For one thing the idea's absurd. As if the people living round about the school—some of them within a stone's throw of it—are going to send their sons as boarders because of Mr. Rouse's fads!"

Daddy sighed. "I've spoken to him already, as you know; and it's a little late in the day to go back on arrangements that have actually been made."

"Made by you and Mr. Rouse," Mother reminded him. "*I* never approved of the plan."

"You agreed to it at the time, when we first talked it over."

"You mean I was bullied into it," Mother corrected.

"Bullied!" poor Daddy exclaimed.

"Well, argued—it comes to the same thing: I never liked the idea or no arguments would have been necessary. And as for being too late to change—that's nonsense. People must have time to think things over. If Mr. Rouse doesn't want to take Tom as a day-boy he needn't, but I suppose I know more about my own

187

son than he does. . . . However, if you like I'll speak to him myself: it might be better if I did."

"Why?" Daddy inquired, raising his eyebrows.

"Well, I only mean if you don't care to do it."

"If anybody is to speak to him," Daddy said in an offended voice, "I should think I'm the proper person."

"I think so, too," Mother at once agreed. "I merely suggested doing it myself because I'm not in the least in awe of Mr. Rouse."

"Neither am I," Daddy replied.

"I should hope not!" said Mother.

This left Daddy silent, but he looked neither convinced nor pleased. "He'll think it most peculiar," he presently began again, evidently thinking so himself—"as if we didn't know our own minds."

"Perhaps," Mother murmured. "But I don't see really that it matters very much *what* he thinks. He'll have nothing to do with Tom after their first interview."

"I don't mind trying it," Tom at this juncture put in obligingly.

It was a pretty safe speech, of course, and he knew this or perhaps he wouldn't have made it. Mother took no notice of it whatever, but Daddy immediately chirped up. "You see!" he said.

"Yes, I see," Mother answered dryly. And there, for the time, discussion ended.

Tom really was extremely pleased—especially about the bicycle. The only drawback to the plan was in relation to Pascoe. It was a bit rough on Pascoe undoubtedly, and he'd have to write and tell him at once. Most of Tom's own nervousness about going as a boarder had been removed by the knowledge that Pascoe would be going too, and Pascoe might have had similar feelings. On the other hand he mightn't; certainly he'd never expressed them. Pascoe was about the least nervous person Tom knew. In his own way he was just as tough as Brown—tougher in fact, for Brown, Tom suspected, would cut a much less dashing and self-confident figure if he happened to get among boys different from

188

himself, whereas nothing could alter Pascoe. The lucky thing for Brown was that there always *were* boys like himself, and always a majority of them.

Mother's sudden decision, none the less, puzzled him. He knew she would get her own way in the end, but, like Daddy, he felt that Mr. Rouse might be annoyed. And he couldn't imagine what had made her change. It couldn't be because of anything he had said to her, for he had accepted the fact that he was to go as a boarder without protest, and had even, in more optimistic moments, thought he might like it. At any rate the prospect hadn't troubled him much. Not really—not deeply. He had always known that if he *dis*liked it—that is to say, if he was actually unhappy—neither Daddy nor Mother would force him to stay on.

The mystery behind Mother's change of plan, however, was a good deal less important than the change of plan itself, and it was in a very contented frame of mind that Tom went up to bed. Soon Daddy and Mother came up also, but he did not hear them, for by that time he was sleeping peacefully.

Another hour or two passed, and perhaps now the sleep was not so peaceful. A watcher—a guardian angel—Gamelyn—might have noted that every now and again he stirred uneasily—might have heard something broken and uneasy in his breathing. Presently his face began to twitch, and then his hands. Something louder than a sigh, yet not loud enough to be a moan, coming from his own throat, almost awakened him, but apparently did not change the nature of his dream. Then a sudden noise that was neither sigh nor moan, and quite outside the dream, did awaken him—and with a start.

He sat up and switched on the light, while the noise continued —a violent scuffling in the chimney. That was no bird; that was Henry—Henry surprised and very angry, because he had fallen into the trap Tom had set for him. Henry seemed to think it a trap anyhow, though all Tom had done was to pull down the iron flap and thus close the opening over the grate. Henry had come down, had found the way unexpectedly barred, and was now swearing at this and at the difficulty of getting up again. Not that

189

Tom could hear him swearing; but the row he was making showed that he was far from accepting the situation calmly.

Defeat it certainly was, and presently the sounds of scuffling grew fainter, and at last they ceased. About thirty seconds afterwards a wild caterwauling burst out from all directions—from the window-sill, from the garden below, and from the roof above. "Gracious!" Tom cried, springing out of bed and running to the window. Two grey shapes that were actually looking in at once vanished, but down on the lawn there was light enough for him to distinguish other shapes—at least a dozen of them. And he wasn't the only one to be awakened either, for he heard a window going up and Daddy's voice "shooing" at the invaders. There was an immediate stillness, as of silent parley, but no retreat; the invaders remained obstinately at their posts—a whole line of them. This was more than Tom could stand. A martial spirit flamed up in him; he rushed from his room and down the stairs; grabbed a walking-stick of Daddy's, and hurriedly unbarred the door. Out into the garden he ran, while the enemy fled before him. In a trice there was not a cat visible; but Tom continued the pursuit—shouting and flourishing his stick—beating the shrubs with it, but without raising a single opponent. Next he heard Daddy's voice calling to him from the porch. Daddy too had come down, though he had waited to put on slippers and a dressing-gown.

Tom in a fever of excitement returned to the house. Daddy himself seemed astonished at what had happened, and together they went upstairs. The light was on in Mother's and Daddy's room, so Tom popped in his head. "Did you ever hear anything like it?" he spluttered. "And it *was* Henry who came down my chimney. He came down again to-night; only I shut it before I went to bed, so he got caught!"

Mother was now sitting up. "Do you mean to say he's still in the chimney?" she asked. "You must let him out at once. If he's been struggling there all this time, goodness knows what he'll be like!"

"Oh, he's *out*!" cried Tom. "He's away over the roof; but he had to *climb* up!"

"Are you sure he's out?" Mother questioned unbelievingly. "You'd better open the chimney and see."

"Quite sure. I heard him. But it was he who brought the others. Just imagine it! That's what the place has been like the whole time we were away!"

Tom's eyes were round and shining. Mother had begun to laugh, however. "Yes, dear; don't get so excited about it! I suppose now you'll lie awake for the rest of the night. Dry your feet, at all events, before you get back into bed."

He left them, but he could hear her and Daddy still talking as he returned to his own room. He *was* excited, but he also felt justified, and on the whole triumphant. Perhaps *this* would give them an inkling of the truth! At any rate, if they didn't now see what Henry was really like, they never would!

CHAPTER XX

Having given himself away so completely—for this was no mere outburst of ill-temper such as had led to the scratching of Phemie—Henry, for all Tom could see, might now do the most reckless things. He had shown his hand, or perhaps it would be more accurate to say that an accident had shown it. Henry's cards had all tumbled on the floor face upwards, with a startling display of trumps and aces; and though he might try to gather them up again, in the hope that they'd be forgotten, this hope was a pretty poor one. Or at least it ought to have been poor; only with players so guileless and inexperienced as Daddy and Mother nobody could tell what would happen. They seemed incapable of grasping anything beyond the fact that Henry had made a few friends, and Mother still clung to the idea of birds in the chimney—in pursuit of whom, apparently, Henry had made his descent. That is to say, if he ever *had* made one;

191

for, to Tom's astonishment, next morning saw her provokingly sceptical on the point.

Daddy, it is true, didn't think much of the "birds in the chimney" theory; but Daddy's own theory, that Henry simply had found a way of getting in and out of the house during their absence, though obviously the right one, didn't lead him to the right conclusions. It led him instead to several anecdotes in which cats who had been removed to new homes performed extraordinary feats of pedestrianism in order to get back to their old ones. This was to prove to Tom that Henry in coming down the chimney had merely acted after his kind; the attachment cats conceived for places being notorious. And when Tom reminded him of the army Henry had recruited, he got out of that difficulty too. Such feline gatherings were also in character. Daddy remembered how, when he was a boy, the lawn of an empty house next door to theirs was the recognized meeting-place of every cat in the neighbourhood; so that frequently he had been sent out by his mother to disperse them, just as Tom had done last night. Henry's food and milk, too, left in the porch for him every day by William, might well have proved an additional attraction.

These and similar remarks, made while he and Tom were working in the garden next morning, showed that Daddy misunderstood the entire situation. Tom did not express *his* view, but he did admit that he wasn't particularly fond of Henry, which Daddy thought strange, seeing that he had always shown so marked a sympathy with animals. Daddy mentioned several early examples of this which Tom himself had forgotten. They were childish certainly—things one would conceal from Pascoe, for instance—but Tom found them amusing. On the whole he and Daddy passed a very pleasant morning.

It was a queer kind of day—warm, even close, yet much more like autumn than summer. Daddy said it *was* autumn, and indeed it had autumn's yellow misty look, even while the sun was shining. Some of the leaves were beginning to change colour—especially the chestnut leaves, which were already falling. The creeper above the porch was crimson, the dahlias were in full bloom, and the sweet-pea was over. It was among the pea-rows and bean-rows that Tom and Daddy were at work, cutting down and tidying up. The withered plants Tom wheeled away in a barrow, dumping them down on a bare patch of soil beyond the strawberry bed; and as the heap grew it reminded him of the evening at Aunt Rhoda's—the Yorkshire terriers, Pascoe in Etons, the bonfire. . . .

In the afternoon he was left to his own devices, because Mother and Daddy went out in the car. Nothing further about school had been mentioned in his presence, and he had asked no questions, nevertheless he had a strong suspicion that they had gone to interview Mr. Rouse. Again he thought of a bonfire. William was against it—as usual. William was still collecting rubbish—damp heavy stuff that would not burn easily—and he objected to Tom's using up the more inflammable material, which he said he needed for a foundation. It was William's invariable policy to object. *His* kind of bonfire was one which merely smoked and smouldered for a couple of days. But he was obstinate as a mule, and far more disobliging, so Tom in the end left him, and left the garden, and set out with a vague idea of looking for mushrooms.

He wandered across the dreaming fields, but only found some puff-balls. A few of the blackberries were black, but they were hard and sour, and when he spat them out he discovered that they had mysteriously turned red again in his mouth. Presently, and quite by accident, he came to the lane leading to the old graveyard. He had not been in the graveyard for ages, so he determined to visit it now, and see if there were as many rabbits as William said. He scrambled through the hedge and dropped down into the narrow grassy track.

Mushrooms grew in the graveyard, Tom remembered; but Mother wouldn't touch any that were gathered there, though Daddy said this was mere prejudice, because all the bodies must have crumbled into dust long ago. And in fact, at first sight, it would have been hard to recognize it as a graveyard at all. Not a headstone was left standing in its original position. Some still survived, indeed, but they were propped up against the broken wall that surrounded the whole enclosure, and their inscriptions, as Tom knew, were for the most part indecipherable.

When he entered, through a gap on the north side, the place looked for all the world like some ancient earthworks, except that the surface was everywhere uneven—all heights and hollows, hummocks and tussocks—with a sprinkling of bushes, of whin and bramble. It was impossible to tell where the paths had once been, where individual graves had been; and when you crossed the long tangled grass your feet unexpectedly sank into holes, or sometimes struck against a hidden fragment of stone. Walking over it gave Tom a queer feeling, not altogether pleasant, though this was entirely due to the suggestions of a too active imagination. He trod gingerly, his eyes lowered to watch carefully each footstep, as if he feared he might tread on something he did not wish to tread on. A movement in the grass of frog or rabbit, a flutter of a bird in the brambles, would have made him jump. But there was no movement; the afternoon, which had clouded over, was profoundly still; the air stagnant and heavy. Tom had been gazing at the ground immediately before him, but as he approached the side wall he looked up, and then, and not till then, became aware of something extraordinary. Ranged along what was left of the wall were perhaps a score of tombstones— broken oblong slabs, chipped and stained and lichened—and on each of these stones, seated motionless and upright, was a cat. Tom stood stock still: it was like a scene one might come on in a dream, but hardly in waking life. Not a movement, as Tom stood there in astonishment. The cats might have been asleep, had it not been for their wide-open watching eyes—green eyes, yellow eyes—bright, steadfast, and beautiful. It was the strangest sight he had ever beheld. Each cat had his own stone, and took not the slightest notice of any other cat. There was something weird in their stillness, in their presence in this spot, in the fixity of their gaze. They might have been entranced, or simply lost in meditation.

Tom drew nearer still. "Puss, puss," he whispered, but received no response: the eyes watching him never even blinked. He had a sense of unreality, a feeling that he had strayed inadvertently into an unknown and fantastic world—a world not human, but feline and necromantic. He wasn't alarmed, wasn't even momentarily startled. He realized this and was pleased, though directly afterwards felt a little ashamed of his pleasure, for what was there to be alarmed at? The hint of sorcery in the air was not malevolent, only strange, dreamy, and rather lovely. He passed along the line of cats—cats of all sizes and ages—grey cats, striped cats, orange cats, and black cats—pausing a minute or two in front of each, until he reached the seventh. . . . The seventh cat was Henry.

And Henry knew him; Henry's mouth opened to emit the faintest sound of recognition. And then a stranger thing than any yet happened. For it seemed to Tom that a struggle was taking place in Henry, that he was on the point of jumping down, that he wanted to be stroked and petted, but something was preventing him, an alien influence which had at that very moment entered into him and was fighting for possession. The battle was soon over. There was no palpable difference in Henry; the only difference was in the light shining in his eyes. Tom had seen precisely that light in them when they had been watching a bird.

Presently, while he stood there looking into Henry's eyes, he felt a drop of rain splash on to his hand, and then another and another. Glancing up, he saw that the clouds had gathered threateningly overhead; and there was no shelter here unless he crept in between those furze-bushes and the broken, overhanging wall. After a brief hesitation he did so, and snuggling well in, curled himself up in the hollow beneath the wall, where he could wait till the rain was over. Henry and the other cats would soon go too, he thought, for they disliked getting wet much more than he did. . . .

The rain was taking a long while to pass—or had it already passed?—for he must have been thinking of other things. At the same time it struck him that it had grown very dark, which possibly was why, when he stood up to look, everything appeared strange, and vaguely different. It must be the effect of this mist, which had floated up and now hung in a thickening veil over the fields. At any rate he had better go back, for after all he was not much more than a mile from home, and he set off at a trot in the direction he had come from. The rain grew no heavier, it was the mist which had this curious effect on the aspect of things. But it was thinning a little; and soon through it, and down below him, he caught a glimpse of the river. He ran on and on, while all the time it was growing lighter.

Only where exactly was he? He was standing on an upland; beside him was a long narrow ravine, thickly wooded; before him was the river valley. All this he recognized, yet with a swiftly increasing uneasiness. For the scene was not quite as he knew it, and that grey stone house, bare and gaunt, was certainly not his home. The garden, too, was gone. He felt a strange drumming in his ears, and a dizziness. The memory of the garden, the memory of his own house, began to wink and flicker. Instinctively he clung to it, feeling that if his mind relaxed ever so little the memory would go out. And it seemed even now to be very faint, and difficult to keep before him. He bent his whole mind, with a painful concentration, on that wavering vision. The struggle was acute, and it was like the struggle against a powerful anæsthetic. A rapid succession of waves of light and darkness swam before his eyes, through which, very shadowy and dim, the phantom of a garden hovered. Only the great stone house before him was solid and real, and drew him with a fascination that was stronger than his will. Then the struggle was forgotten. . . .

It was winter, and the fallen leaves lay soaked and sodden on the grass. The house showed no sign of being inhabited, except that a dense coil of smoke curled up from one chimney and spread sluggishly against a leaden sky. Tom drew nearer still; he passed round the side of the house. He saw a heavy door, studded with iron nails and ornamented with a design in beaten ironwork. And though the door was shut he felt quite sure that it was not locked, that he had only to push it and it would open. He did not do so; he peered through a window, but could see nothing except a dirty empty vault-like room. Ten yards from the front of the house rose a tree, with black leafless twisted boughs that were patterned against the cold grey sky. By jumping he might just reach the lowest branch, and he did so. Pulling himself up, he clambered astride this branch, and once there, the tree was easy to climb. He climbed till he was on a level with the upper windows, and then, hugging the trunk tightly, he stood gazing into a familiar room. On the bare floor were traced the magic symbols; a fire burned on the hearth; an old man was sitting in a chair, absorbed in a big book which lay open on a table before him— and staring straight out of the window, with fierce hungry eyes, was a huge black cat. . . .

The cat saw him, the cat's tail began to twitch, his mouth opened, and, though no sound reached Tom, the wizard raised his head. Simultaneously Tom half slid, half tumbled down the tree. For a moment he lay sprawling on the cold wet grass; then he was up and running as hard as he could. He ran and ran and ran, till he could run no longer. He staggered a few steps further, but presently, tripping over a hidden ivy root, he tumbled down —lost, breathless, and exhausted.

CHAPTER XXI

It had begun to rain again. Tom wriggled in between two whin-bushes growing under a tumbled-down wall. . . .

A wall! And the ground was rough and broken into mounds and hollows: he was back once more in the graveyard.

He had neither looked nor cared whither he was running, yet it seemed an evil omen. A yellow twilight swam between earth and sky, and beneath it the landscape had taken on a livid unnatural hue. A black motionless figure crouched at a little distance.

He was trapped. To try to go home would only be to return to the house he had run away from—the house of his dream, the house the serpent had shown him: how could he ever go home again if his true home was not there?

But if it was not there, where was it? And instantly the answer came to him that it *was* there, only not there for him. Something had happened to him which shut him out. It was there, but *he* was not there. And if he could not get back to it, get back to Daddy and Mother, then neither would they be able to get to him. They might be looking for him even now, but their "now" was not his "now". He could do nothing: he was lost. . . .

For a while sheer helplessness produced a kind of mental inertia; and then, without seeking for it, he saw the flaw in his reasoning, and hope revived. He *must* have escaped—escaped at least from *that*, which was the worst. The proof was staring him in the face: the proof lay just in this ruined graveyard, for *it* could not be in the same "present" as the house he dreaded. Centuries stretched between them. Moreover he remembered the drifts of fallen leaves, the black naked tree, the winter sky— and this was not winter. It might seem to him a long long time since he had set out to wander over the fields, but the season was the same, it must be the same afternoon; he would go back, he must try it again at whatever risk, and this time perhaps all would be well.

Then his eyes fell on the crouching beast, which at the first movement he made had raised its head. Half hidden in the long grass it lay—sleek, with pointed ears—a cat, but not Henry, much larger than Henry, as large nearly as a lynx—as large as the cat in that house. And with this last recognition Tom cowered back again.

He shut his eyes. Some minutes seemed to pass—how many he did not know—perhaps only one or two, perhaps none, merely an infinitesimal interval of silence, not ordinary silence, but a total absence of sound, such as must exist in the unimaginable void of outer and empty space. It was simply there, and then it was gone, though it had been broken only by a ripple of light. But Tom was breathing again, the earth was breathing, and very far and faint, he now heard a positive sound, hardly audible indeed, and yet surely a sound of barking. Again came the drifting wave of light, and this time through the heavy canopy of cloud a thin lance of

198

sunshine pierced—stretched across the graveyard and vanished. Tom lifted his head. The clouds were splitting into two solid masses, were drawing back like dark immense gates between which a hot gush of sunlight swept, spreading over the fields and flooding them. In another second it had reached the graveyard, and the big cat rose to its feet, angry and threatening, but not threatening Tom, for its back was turned to him, and it was watching a young man who had just then come into sight at the edge of the adjoining field. Tom stood up to watch him too. He was still some distance off, but he was moving swiftly, and a few yards in front of him ran a white woolly dog about the size of a sheepdog.

Tom's heart leapt; he dared not shout; but he saw the dog raising his head as if to catch a scent, and directly afterwards he sprang forward at full gallop.

What happened next happened quickly—so quickly that Tom had no distinct view of it. There was a leap, a furious snarling, but there was no battle—the black cat was gone.

And while Tom still stood staring at the spot where it had been, the young man reached the graveyard. Tom heard him and turned round. He had seen him twice before—once as a boy, once as a youth. Then, without quite knowing why, but to hide a deeper feeling that he could not express, he stooped and began to stroke and make friends with the dog.

There were no greetings; the young man simply sat down on the broken wall and Tom sat beside him. The white dog stretched himself at their feet.

It was enough; there seemed to be no need for speech; at any rate Tom felt none. The young man understood; Tom too understood. And merely to sit like this was in itself a happiness, which no words could deepen.

"All the same," Tom thought, "I very nearly forgot to call him." And after a while he asked, remembering the vanished beast: "Where did it come from?"

"From you," the young man said, and so quietly that Tom glanced at him in doubt.

"From me?"

The strangely bright eyes were fixed on his; the young man spoke again. But his voice had not the tone Tom wanted, nor were his words the words he wanted. "In itself it was nothing," he said; "only the image of your fear, which you brought to life."

Tom hung his head; he had perhaps deserved some such answer, but that was not what troubled him. He knew the answer to his next question also, though he could not keep it back. "And when you go away from me again—will that too be all?" Suddenly he felt that it would be very easy to cry, though quite useless—useless unless he could be given the comfort, find the comforter, he longed for.

But the angel did not comfort him, nor did he seem to notice the hand that Tom instinctively half held out and then quickly withdrew. Did not take it at all events, but only counselled gravely: "Do not think about it; it will do no good; because at present you cannot understand. . . . I *am* you; the beast that is gone was you; do not think about it, but go to sleep."

"I don't——" Tom was beginning sadly, when a sudden drowsiness covered up his thought. For a moment, as he tried to grasp it, the thought flickered back into consciousness, or something like it. What he wanted to say was: "Can't you——"

Only somehow he was listening to the waves, and watching them, and lying on the sand at Glenagivney, and Pascoe, not the angel, was beside him. . . .

CHAPTER XXII

A grasshopper was singing near the furze-brake. "Tom!" it sang in a shrill thin voice. "Tom—wake up now—Tom!" The voice grew louder and more insistent; it no longer sang, it spoke—and a little anxiously, for it had become Miss

Jimpson's voice. "It seems very strange, Geoffrey! Do you think there can be anything the matter?"

The "Geoffrey" was interesting, therefore Tom hung on a little longer to a now pretended slumber. He didn't even peep, though sorely tempted to, for he was both curious and faintly amused; but he kept his eyes fast shut. Then, like the turtle's, the voice of Geoffrey was heard in reply. "No, Anna, I don't. His eyes are tighter shut than they were a minute ago. He's shamming."

Tom smiled and looked up at them. "I was really asleep at first," he protested, scrambling to his feet. "Honestly."

"But wasn't that very foolish of you!" Miss Jimpson exclaimed. "I'm sure the ground must be damp."

Tom, after the least hesitation, remembered that it *had* been raining, though nothing to speak of. That was why he had got in under the whin-bushes, he told her, and added: "I'm really looking for mushrooms."

Miss Jimpson laughed. But presently she asked: "How long have you been tucked in there?"

Tom hesitated again. He knew he had come out soon after lunch, but how long ago was that? "I'm afraid I've been here most of the afternoon," he was obliged to confess. "What time is it now?"

"It's nearly half-past five," Miss Jimpson answered. "We were on our way home when we saw you, or rather saw the dog."

"The dog!" cried Tom quickly, turning abruptly round. But no dog was visible.

There was a brief pause. "A big white woolly thing," Miss Jimpson then went on in a tone of faint surprise. "He seems to have disappeared. . . . It was he, anyway, who attracted our attention. He looked exactly as if he were mounting guard over something—as apparently he was—so we came to have a closer inspection. . . . Oh!—here he comes."

But Tom had already seen him, and also seen that Mr. Holbrook's face wore a curiously speculative expression. The white dog came trotting up.

"He must be a stray dog," Tom began. "I mean—he's not mine."

Mr. Holbrook was still watching him, and now he spoke. "He doesn't seem to be aware of that," Mr. Holbrook observed quietly, and there could be no denying that this was so. The white dog had suddenly planted his two fore-paws on Tom's shoulders and was licking his cheek. Tom's arms clasped him tightly. "I wish he *was* mine," he said.

"Can do, I should think," Mr. Holbrook murmured, while Miss Jimpson looked at them both, frankly mystified.

"There were only cats here when I came," Tom continued, with a glance round at the now abandoned tombstones. "A whole lot of them—sitting like a row of images—but they all seem to have gone."

"And we ought to be going," Miss Jimpson declared. Then she said to Tom: "I shouldn't pet him too much or you'll have him following you the whole way home."

"Yes," Tom answered gravely, "I'm going to take him home. He's a stray dog."

Miss Jimpson was quite sure he was nothing of the sort. "Nonsense!" she said. "No stray dog ever had a coat like that. He looks to me as if he had been washed and combed within the last hour."

"He hasn't a collar," Tom maintained with a hint of stubbornness.

"No," replied Miss Jimpson, "which is a further proof that he's been washed quite recently."

Tom said nothing, but his silence was not submissive, and Mr. Holbrook intervened. "Oh, I shouldn't worry," he told Miss Jimpson. "The dog can look after himself, I expect. He's by no means a pup, and if he wants to see Tom home why prevent him?"

"I'm not preventing him," Miss Jimpson answered. "Only it would be easier to get rid of him now than it will be then, and less disappointing to the dog."

"I don't intend to get rid of him," Tom muttered under his breath.

But Miss Jimpson heard him; she had very sharp ears. "Now, Tom," she said firmly, "you know very well that you can't take possession of other people's dogs."

"Not this one—with any safety," Mr. Holbrook agreed tactfully. At the same time he laid a friendly hand on Tom's shoulder. "He's pretty conspicuous, isn't he?"

The white dog appeared to be following the discussion, though not as if it mattered much.

"Dogs are such queer things!" Miss Jimpson unexpectedly murmured. "You can *see* he's taken some notion into his head. . . . About Tom, I mean."

"Well, he *found* Tom," said Mr. Holbrook. "Found him when he was asleep—like Moses in the bulrushes—and 'finds' are 'keeps', I suppose."

Miss Jimpson supposed so also, and her manner, Tom was quick to perceive, had lost its slightly dictatorial tone. "What sort of dog is he?" she mused. "Not a sheepdog and not a poodle. . . . I've never seen a dog like him before."

"Oh yes you have," Mr. Holbrook contradicted.

"Where?" asked Miss Jimpson, still pondering. "And when?"

"Last Easter," said Mr. Holbrook. "And in Italy."

Miss Jimpson gave a little shrug. "For that matter, I don't remember seeing any dogs in Italy—which, judging from the way they treat their horses, is just as well."

"All the same, it was there you saw him," Mr. Holbrook persisted. "A smaller version of him, I admit, and in a picture—several pictures. My dear Anna, look at his colour; look at those little curls! He's the dog who invariably accompanies Tobias and his Angel in old Florentine pictures. He's a Botticini."

Miss Jimpson gazed in silence.

"There's no deception," Mr. Holbrook laughed, "it's him."

"He," Miss Jimpson corrected abstractedly. Then suddenly she smiled and looked at Tom very much as she had looked at him across the table in the teashop. She had liked him then, he knew, and he was pretty certain that she liked him now; yet behind this she remained puzzled. "It's a very queer thing to me," she murmured, "that if anything extraordinary happens, it always seems to happen either to Tom or when Tom is present."

"That's the magic in him," replied Mr. Holbrook gaily.

Miss Jimpson smiled at Tom again, but thoughtfully. She sighed, shook her head, and, as if finding reverie to no purpose, abruptly emerged to the practical affairs of life. "Well, magic or no magic," she announced, "I must return to my home. . . . Come along," she added to Tom. "Perhaps he won't follow us after all."

In this conjecture at least she proved correct, for the white dog trotted on ahead.

"He's a white Chrysanthemum," Tom whispered to himself, "and I'm going to call him Caleb."

But he had now time to think of other things, and among them of all the "Geoffreys" and "Annas" he had heard. It was clear that in his absence the "romance" had not stood still. Mother had been quite right when she had said that Miss Jimpson would be able to manage her own affairs; and she must have managed them jolly cleverly, he reflected—innocently giving her all the credit both for the original idea and for the efficient way in which it had been carried out. It wasn't a matter, however, that one could very well allude to, so he refrained from comment. "How did you get here?" he inquired instead, knowing that neither Mr. Holbrook nor Miss Jimpson lived near.

"We came in a tram," Mr. Holbrook told him. "After that we walked. This old graveyard of yours wasn't in the programme at all. Like yourself, it was an accidental discovery; we didn't even know that it existed."

But Miss Jimpson—who was obviously in a most unstable mood—had again begun to look thoughtful. There seemed to be something on her mind which she could not quite bring herself to say; though she *would* say it soon, Tom was sure, because it was very evident that she wanted to. He smiled at her encouragingly, and once or twice she nearly spoke, and then at the last minute didn't.

"Why not trust us?" suggested Mr. Holbrook, who also must

have noticed the preoccupation. "You're making *me*, at least, extremely nervous."

Mr. Holbrook spoke lightly, but Tom could see that Miss Jimpson was serious. It was queer that they should be lovers, he thought, because really they were very different, and you saw this even more when they were together than when you met them apart.

Miss Jimpson coloured, and next moment Tom found himself blushing in sympathy, which was idiotic, and annoyed him. Then suddenly she said: "It's only that Tom somehow—— I don't know—— But in a way I can't help feeling that he's been connected from the beginning with——" She broke off, and finished almost crossly: "Oh, what I mean is that I don't see why we shouldn't tell him."

Tom looked at Mr. Holbrook, but Mr. Holbrook only laughed and said: "Well, tell him then."

"I should like him to be the first to congratulate us," Miss Jimpson went on. "It's just a—superstition."

"I do congratulate you—very much," Tom hastened to assure her, and Mr. Holbrook laughed once more, and slapped him on the shoulder.

"You're a particular friend of ours," he said. "I imagine that's what we're trying to convey. . . . For that matter, always were of mine," he added half to himself.

Tom felt pleased, though his pleasure was mitigated by an alarming impression that Miss Jimpson wanted to kiss him. Hang it all, she couldn't! Fortunately she herself appeared to be doubtful about it, and had less time to make up her mind than she knew. "This is my turning," he was able to tell them half a minute later, when they had reached the main road. "I mean, I go to the right here, and the way to the tram is on the left."

So they stopped, and shook hands, and the dangerous moment went by. Miss Jimpson didn't kiss him—though he still believed she wanted to, and indeed he might have let her if Mr. Holbrook hadn't been there. He suddenly found himself feeling a little sorry for Miss Jimpson—and understanding her—understanding her better than Mr. Holbrook did perhaps.

Miss Jimpson told him that he would be the first person they'd invite to their new house when they'd found one, and that anyway she hoped she'd be seeing him before that.

"Of course," Tom replied, and thanked her. After which he and Caleb took the road to the right, but they hadn't gone far before it occurred to him that it would have been nicer if he had asked Miss Jimpson and Mr. Holbrook to dinner. He half thought of running back to do so, only when he looked round they were already hidden by a bend in the road. So he scudded on, with the white dog galloping beside him.

When he reached home he found Daddy pottering about the garden as usual, but abruptly he stopped pottering to stare at Tom's companion. Luckily Daddy was not an excitable person and was always willing to listen to explanations. He listened to one now, without comment or interruption, though at the end of it he announced: "We must ring up the police."

"Yes, I know," Tom hastened to agree. "But if he *isn't* claimed mayn't I keep him?"

Daddy looked dubious, pulled up a weed or two without speaking, and finally said that they'd first have to see what Mother thought about it. "You needn't keep on thanking me," he added after a minute or two, rather dryly. "I haven't given you a present and I haven't said 'yes'. You're a great deal too impulsive, and in this case it's only going to lead to disappointment: the dog's certain to be claimed within twenty-four hours."

Tom did not argue the point, but he mentioned what a good dog Caleb was, winding up hopefully with: "Mother will like having him—I mean of course if we *don't* find his owner." After which he sat down on a stone and watched Daddy's slow and deliberate movements, wondering what he would think were he to be told of all that had happened that afternoon. He knew of course that he never *would* tell him, because Daddy, he had long ago found, neither welcomed nor cared for such confidences. But he might tell Mother—particularly now that the whole adventure was over. And somehow he felt that it *was* over—felt this very strongly—so strongly that he didn't believe it would make

206

the least difference whether Henry came back or not. He had even the feeling that it had all been in some way explained, so that it could never trouble him again. It had lost its power to trouble him; it was like an imaginary phantom, which you suddenly discover to be only an effect of light and mist. And with this he remembered that he had not written to Pascoe.

He had intended to write; he must write this evening; though Pascoe himself, he was sure, would be returning home at least a day or two before the holidays ended.

How quickly things ended! Tom thought. Nothing lasted very long, and nothing seemed the same when it was gone as it had seemed while it was there. Summer was gone, or nearly gone, and it would be a year very likely before he visited the sea again. Pascoe was luckier; Pascoe had Aunt Rhoda's house always there for him to go to, and Aunt Rhoda herself always dying to have him at any time and to keep him as long as possible. Tom hadn't an aunt even of the most ordinary kind, let alone one who lived in a lovely place like Greencastle. But he had an uncle—Uncle Stephen. What would it be like, he wondered, if he were to go to stay with Uncle Stephen the way Pascoe did with Aunt Rhoda? True, Uncle Stephen didn't live beside the sea; but he lived in the country, which was the next best thing. Supposing he *did* get an invitation from him then, would he be allowed to accept it? And immediately this question became so urgent and fraught with possibilities that he was obliged to put it to Daddy.

Daddy seemed to be more amused than interested. He merely laughed, said that it wasn't in the least likely to happen, and began to tie up one of the rambler roses. Tom felt secretly irritated. How could Daddy *tell* what would happen! For all he knew, Uncle Stephen might at this very moment be writing a letter of invitation. Mother would at least have admitted the possibility and been ready to discuss it, but Daddy's next remark was: "Aren't you satisfied with your mother and me?"

As if that had anything to do with it! Tom felt inclined to say "No". It was meant as a joke, doubtless; yet none the less it closed up the entire subject, so that he couldn't go on without seeming childish and silly. You can't go on talking when the other person is like that. And Pascoe was like that too, though he didn't make jokes.

Daddy must have noticed the silence, and perhaps been surprised by it, for presently he glanced round and observed: "Your Uncle Stephen's a rather strange person from all accounts."

But it was now too late; Tom's desire to talk about Uncle Stephen had subsided; and he only replied, while he stooped down and pressed his mouth against the top of Caleb's head: "Mother likes him." Then he remembered that Daddy had been very decent about Caleb, and that he was very decent in lots of ways, though he was so against what he called "flights of imagination".

"All the same," Tom thought, "it's just because Uncle Stephen doesn't happen to be his kind of person that he says he's strange. . . . Like the Blakes—and like me. . . . But he's Mother's kind of person."

With which he was content until he added: "And so am I."

January 1934
  October 1935

also by **Forrest Reid***:*

UNCLE STEPHEN
With a new introduction by John McRae

Although this was the first of Forrest Reid's Tom Barber trilogy to be published, in 1931, in narrative terms it is the last of the series: a trilogy where the novels are the "reverse of a sequence", as Reid himself described it. Here Tom is fifteen, the oldest we are to meet him, undergoing the pangs of adolescence under the tutelage of his mysterious uncle.

"By far the best book he has written. It may be that we all have our Uncle Stephens, and not only in boyhood; it is certainly true that we all have our secret worlds, even though we may rarely trouble to explore them. And here is one of those worlds explored for us. Mr Reid has written a sin-gularly beautiful book" – *Sunday Times*.

"An exquisite book and a tender one, it is often subtle, often naif, and like all Mr Reid's art, it is intensely personal and stands apart from contemporary movements in literature. This gives it its unanalysable strength" – E. M. Forster.

FICTION
ISBN 0 85449 083 3
UK £ 4.95
US $ 9.95

YOUNG TOM
With a new introduction by John McRae

"His three books about the childhood of Tom will probably remain as one of the most original and most perfect works of imagination of his time' – Edwin Muir.

The third volume of the trilogy, in which we meet Tom at his youngest, in a tender and understanding study of a sensitive but resolute eleven-year-old boy.

"So lucid, so limpid, so totally without affectation" – Francis King.

"There is no living writer in English who can describe growing boyhood as well as Forrest Reid can" – *New Statesman*.

"His illumination of boyhood, with all its sharpness and freshness, is as fragrant as a water-colour" – *Daily Telegraph*.

FICTION
ISBN 0 85449 055 8
UK £3.95
US $7.95

GMP books can be ordered from any bookshop in the UK, and from specialised bookshops overseas. If you prefer to order by mail, please send full retail price plus £1.00 for postage and packing to: GMP Publishers Ltd (M.O.), PO Box 247, London N17 9QR. (For Access/Eurocard/Mastercharge/Visa/American Express, give number and signature.) Comprehensive mail-order catalogue also available.

In North America order from Alyson Publications Inc.
40 Plympton St, Boston MA 02118, USA.

NAME AND ADDRESS
IN BLOCK LETTERS PLEASE:

NAME _____

ADDRESS _____

_____

_____